# A Girl of White Winter

# A Girl of White Winter

# Barb Hendee

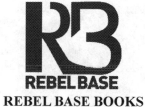

**REBEL BASE BOOKS**
Kensington Publishing Corp.
www.kensingtonbooks.com

# Prologue

*Long ago, a vain lord enslaved a young witch so that he might force her to use her powers to keep him handsome and young. His most valued possession was an ornate three-paneled mirror in which he could see himself from several angles. Looking into its panels, he loved to admire his own beauty.*

*Seeking revenge on him, the young witch began secretly imbuing the mirror with power, planning to trap him in the reflection of the three panels where he might view different outcomes of his useless life over and over, and he'd suffer to see himself growing old and unwanted. But unknown to her, as she continued to cast power into the mirror, it came to gain a will and awareness of its own.*

*One night, the lord caught her as she worked her magic, and he realized she was attempting to enchant his beloved mirror. In a rage, he drew a dagger and killed her. But her spirit fled into the mirror. Though she had been seeking escape, she was once again enslaved...this time by the mirror itself. It whispered to her that it would protect her and use the power she'd given it for tasks more important than punishing a vain lord. Together they would seek out those facing difficult decisions and show them outcomes to their choices.*

*"Wait!" she cried, inside the mirror. "What does that mean?"*

*The mirror vanished from the lord's room, taking her with it.*

*And no one knew where it might appear again.*

# Chapter One

While growing up, I never realized how carefully the Lady Giselle hid me from the eyes of men. She did not do this from jealousy or selfishness, but to protect me...as my position in the household was not easy to define.

On an evening in early autumn, as she sat in a chair before me, I piled her dark hair atop her head and fastened it with silver clips. In her late forties, she was still lovely.

Tonight, she wore a green velvet gown with a full skirt and long sleeves. "Would you like your diamond pendant?" I asked.

Her mind was elsewhere. "Mmmmmm?"

She'd seemed unsettled since mid-afternoon, and I knew she was worried about the outcome of tonight's dinner gathering.

"Your diamond pendant?" I asked again.

This evening was important, and she would wish to look her best.

Nodding, she said, "Yes, my dear."

But as I went to fetch it, she reached out and stopped me. "Kara...his lordship has requested that you join us for dinner. The Capellos did not bring their wives or sisters, as this is a business gathering, and his lordship fears the numbers will appear too skewed at the table." She paused. "Once you finish dressing me, we'll need to find you a gown. He wants you to be decorative."

I tensed. "Must I?"

She nodded again, this time more tightly. "Yes. It is his lordship's wish."

Though it was common for me to join the family for dinner, over the past summer I had turned eighteen, and I'd not been invited to join a formal dinner with guests in nearly three years. Lady Giselle kept me hidden, even from most of the manor guards.

"Which gown?" I asked, nervous at the thought of dining with strangers. "One of your white silks, I think."

* * * *

That night, as Giselle and I walked into the dining hall, my stomach tightened when I saw what appeared to be a sea of men milling around before dinner. In truth, only five of the men would be joining us at the table. The rest were merely guards of either our house or the Capellos'.

The group of five had gathered near the hearth.

The lord of our house, Jean de Marco, stood with his and Lady Giselle's two sons: Geoffrey and Lucas, who were both older than me by a few years. Lord Jean was a large man, and only recently had some of his muscle begun to sag a little. Glancing in our direction, he offered his wife a nod, but did not acknowledge my presence.

He had no love for me.

The other two men were strangers. One appeared to be late middle-aged and the other was in his early thirties.

A table stretched out in the center of the hall, laden with goblets, fine pewter plates, and a centerpiece of the last of our autumn roses.

Beside me, Lady Giselle drew a long breath as her face transformed into a welcoming smile. She took my arm, and we swept into the vast room.

"Gentlemen," she said, approaching the group of five. "Forgive our tardy arrival."

This was a polite but expected comment. Women of her station never arrived at a formal dinner before her guests. It was the lord's duty to meet them.

Both strangers turned to offer a greeting, but at the sight of me, the words froze on their lips.

I was not taken aback, as this was a normal response from anyone seeing me for the first time. My lady assured me that it was due to my unusual coloring. I was small, slender, and pale-skinned, but my hair was so blond that she called it "silver" and my eyes so crystalline blue that they seemed to glow against the pale background. Once, Lord Jean had shivered as he studied me and said, "She looks like a winter morning."

I had long wished for dark hair and brown eyes.

Lady Giselle was accustomed to men going speechless at the sight of me, and she pretended not to notice their half-opened mouths. "May I present our ward, Kara."

Lord Jean flinched slightly at the term "ward," but I was the only one who noticed.

Turning to me, Giselle motioned to the men with a graceful hand. "Kara, this is Lord Trey Capello and his son, Lord Royce."

Lord Trey must have been past fifty, but he was slender and striking, with light brown hair and a close-trimmed beard. He recovered himself quickly, kissing first her hand and then mine.

"My ladies," he said. "We'll be blessed with your company at dinner."

Somehow, he sounded sincere, and I began to relax a little. Perhaps I would be required to only nod and smile and not answer any difficult questions about my identity.

But Royce did not recover so quickly and continued to stare, running his eyes over my face and silver-blond hair. He bore little resemblance to his father, taller and more muscular with sandy blond hair and a clean-shaven face.

I hoped he would not try to engage me in conversation, as I was not nearly so skilled as my lady and had little experience in talking to men.

"Shall I ring for dinner so that we might sit?" Giselle asked.

Lord Jean nodded to her, and we gathered at the table. To my relief, I was seated between Geoffrey and Lucas. I didn't know them well, but they had long grown accustomed to my appearance, and neither would expect me to talk.

Unfortunately, Royce was seated directly across the table and although he'd stopped staring, he continued glancing in my direction.

A number of servants entered the hall carrying trays of food and decanters of wine.

Wine was poured, and the fish course was served. I was not fond of wine but tried to sip politely.

"You understand I wish to buy the entire two hundred acres?" Lord Jean asked after swallowing a bite of trout.

This was the reason for the Capellos' visit. For nearly three centuries, the noble de Marco family had boasted one of the most renowned vineyards in the nation of Samourè. They grew mainly white grapes, but of late, demand for white wine had been waning, and Lord Jean had long coveted a large piece of undeveloped land just off our southern border—and on the Capellos' northern border. Both its soil and its positioning were perfect for growing the purple grapes of dark red wine.

I'd learned all this information from my lady. To date, the Capellos had never responded to any of Lord Jean's offers, but…it appeared the land somehow belonged to Royce and not to his father, and now, Royce might be willing to sell. They'd been traveling, visiting other nobles, and we were their last stop on the way home.

Lady Giselle had impressed upon me the importance of this meeting.

Lord Jean could not accept failure in these negotiations.

His question about the two hundred acres hung in the air. Royce didn't answer, but he was again staring at me.

"My son?" Lord Trey asked.

Royce turned his head to look down the table at Lord Jean. "Let us talk of business over breakfast. The ride was long today, and for tonight, I'd rather dine and speak of less weighty matters."

His voice was deep and possessed a serious quality that suggested he rarely made jokes. I knew that he and his father would be spending at least one night with us, as their own manor was a full day's ride south.

Lord Jean's jaw twitched, but he nodded. "As you wish." Then he looked to Lady Giselle. "Time for the next course, I think."

* * * *

Somehow, I made it through dinner and dessert without being required to enter the conversation. I made certain to pay polite attention to all that was said in regards to crops and taxes and other matters men tended to discuss over dinner, and I smiled whenever Lucas or Lord Trey said something amusing—for they were the only men in the group disposed toward humor.

Finally, at the end, I breathed in quiet relief that the women would be excused so the men might switch to a stronger port wine and play cards.

Lady Giselle was a woman of flawless timing, and at the precise moment, she rose. I stood quickly.

"Gentlemen," she said, "it has been a pleasure. Kara and I will leave you to your amusements, and I shall see you at breakfast."

All the men stood in respect, and the two of us turned to leave, heading for the archway. I looked forward to a quiet night of either reading to her aloud or perhaps telling her a story from memory (which she loved) or playing at chess or working on our embroidery or hearing her thoughts on how Lord Jean might approach Royce in this land deal.

"My lady?" Mistress Duval, our housekeeper, came to the archway just as we reached it. "Forgive me, but the cook fears we don't have enough eggs for the breakfast that was planned. Could you come and approve a new menu?"

"Of course."

Lady Giselle was a woman who oversaw every detail of the running of her household. Normally, breakfast menus did not require approval, but we all knew the importance of this meeting. Everything from the guest rooms to the food had to be perfect.

Turning to me, Giselle said, "My dear. You go up, and I'll come soon."

"Yes, my lady."

She turned and swept down the east corridor for the kitchens. I headed for the west stairwell, so that I might ascend to her private apartments where she would meet me.

I'd walked only about six steps when a voice sounded from behind.

"Wait."

The voice was deep and possessed of a serious quality.

As I turned, my stomach again tightened at the sight of Royce walking toward me. Desperately, I looked down the east corridor, but my lady was gone, and I was alone with Royce. He strode to me with purpose. Facing him, my eyes were level with his collarbones, which were visible through the V-neck of his tunic. I did not look up at his face.

"Who are you?" he asked bluntly.

Despair washed through me. I would not escape the evening without answering questions.

"Lady Giselle's ward," I whispered.

"That's not an answer. If she had a ward from one of the noble families, it would be common knowledge. You'd have been seen at court." He paused and, if possible, his tone hardened. "Who was your father?"

I could not raise my eyes from his collarbones any more than I could answer his question, because the truth was a family secret.

I knew the story well.

Nineteen years ago, Lady Giselle's brother, Jacques, had visited these vineyards. Giselle adored her handsome brother, who was charming and reckless—or so she described him to me. At the same time, she had a beautiful lady's maid named Coraline, of whom she had grown fond.

Upon his visit, Jacques seduced Coraline, and as soon as he learned she was with child, he fled. For a marriage to a wealthy wool merchant's daughter had already been arranged for him.

When Lord Jean learned of Coraline's condition, he ordered that she be dismissed, but for the first time, Giselle went against him, begging that Coraline be allowed to remain. Such a state of affairs was unheard of... to keep a pregnant woman as a lady's maid.

In the end, Giselle won, for she seldom asked him for anything, and though Lord Jean did not spend much time with her, in his heart, he liked to please her.

I was born.

At first, out of guilt, my father sent Coraline some money, but he never visited or took any action to see me and remained at his home with his new wife. When I was two years old, he drank too much wine and took up a challenge to ride one of his horses in a race.

In his drunken state, he fell off over a jump and was killed.

When I was five, a fever passed through our lands, and some of our household, including my mother, died.

I had no parents, and I was alone.

Lord Jean might not have noticed my existence had I been given to the kitchen women and raised as a servant. But Lady Giselle had only given birth to sons, and she had come to love me. She insisted I be raised as her ward, calling me her niece in private.

Again, Lord Jean protested, seeing me as the bastard child of a lady's maid, certainly not worthy of the title of ward in the house of de Marco. But again, Giselle prevailed. I grew up as her companion; not exactly a niece, but neither was I a servant. I had duties for her, but I ate with the family and wore the fine clothing of a noble.

All was well until I turned fifteen and the house guards began watching me enter a room. Of course they did not dare speak to me, but this was a forerunning of things to come. At that time, I was allowed to join dinners when we had guests, but then, during a visit from the Larues, the second son of Lord Alan Larue stared at me over the table. A week later, he asked Lord Jean for my hand in marriage—with no questions regarding my birth. Lord Jean thought it an astonishing offer and wanted to accept, but Lady Giselle pleaded that at fifteen, I was too young.

After that, she stopped including me at dinner when we had guests. She kept me to herself, and I loved our quiet time together. For she often fell into sadness, and I knew how to distract her, how to make her smile. She promised she would keep me safe.

And now…three years later, I was in a corridor, alone with a strange nobleman who continued demanding answers.

"Who was your father?" Royce repeated.

No matter that Giselle called me her niece in private, I would never expose her beloved brother as a seducer of women or a man who abandoned unwanted children.

So I whispered, "I do not know."

Before I knew what was happening, he grasped my chin and forced me to look up at him. Though his grip did not hurt, he allowed me to feel some of the strength in his hand. His eyes were a shade of light brown. "What do you mean you don't know? If you're the de Marcos' ward, how is that possible?" He didn't sound angry, only confused. "Who was your mother?"

Wanting him to let me go, I tried to meet his gaze and answered, "Lady Giselle's maid."

He let go and stepped back.

I hadn't told him the whole truth, but enough to give him an understanding. No matter what Giselle called me, I was the illegitimate child of a servant. I was no one, not worth his attention.

Whirling, I hurried for the west stairwell.

\* \* \* \*

The next morning, Lady Giselle sent word to my room, informing me I would be expected at breakfast, but I was not concerned. By now, Royce would have told his father of my low status, and they would not notice me. Besides, the men would be focused on the land deal, not upon any women at the table.

I wore my hair down and donned a muslin dress of a shade my lady called ice blue, the same color as my eyes. All of the day dresses or evening gowns she had made for me were either white or this same shade of light blue. She said the colors suited me, and she sometimes enjoyed dressing me and trying different styles with my hair.

My own private room was near to Lady Giselle's apartments, and as I reached her door, I found it open, suggesting she had already gone down.

"My lady?" I asked from the doorway.

Silence told me she was not there.

Quickly, I made my way to the stairwell and descended to the main floor. Upon arriving at the dining hall, I found everyone from last night had already gathered—with the exception of Lucas and Geoffrey. Would they not be attending? Perhaps they were not necessary for the business dealings this morning.

Then why had I been asked?

Royce stood apart with his arms crossed, and he appeared to be watching the archway as I entered. At the sight of me, he went still and gave me the same fixed attention from last night, taking in my long silver-blond hair and light blue gown. But this morning, I was beginning to recognize the expression on his face; it looked like hunger.

"She's here," he said. "We can begin."

Two things about these statements puzzled me. First, was he the one who'd requested my presence this morning? Why? And second...breakfast had not even been served yet. Did he wish to conduct the business dealing before eating?

Lord Jean seemed equally nonplussed, but he gestured to the table. "By all means."

I could see that he didn't care when or how these dealings took place, so long as he acquired the land.

Walking over, I greeted my lady and sat beside her. Lord Trey and Royce sat across from us, and Lord Jean took his place at the head.

As of yet, we'd not even been served tea.

Lord Jean began immediately. "I'll pay two thousand in silver for the land. That's more than what it's worth and a fair offer."

Royce studied him. "I'm willing to take fifteen hundred." Then he motioned to me with his head. "But I want the girl."

I went cold.

Lord Trey turned to his son in open surprise.

Lord Jean frowned.

Lady Giselle stiffened, and she spoke first. "My lord," she said to Royce. "I don't understand. You cannot be asking for Kara's hand as you already have a wife. You were married eight years ago, and to the best of my knowledge, the lady Loraine still lives."

Royce turned his cold gaze upon her. "You need not remind me of my marital status."

Lord Jean's frown deepened. "Then what are you asking?"

Royce leaned back in his chair. "I want the girl."

At this, all polite pretense vanished from my lady's voice. "As what? Your mistress? You'll set her up in some cottage near your manor until you grow tired of her? I think not!"

They spoke as if I weren't there.

Lord Trey raised one hand to her and addressed his son. "This girl? You're certain?"

Royce nodded, but the brief exchange only increased the confusion in Lord Jean's expression.

Lord Trey sighed. "What my son suggests is not so shocking as it first sounds. We are more...modern at the Capello estate. Your ward would hold a position of honor, and she would reside with us, in her own rooms, at the manor. She would have a place in the family."

"As his mistress?" my lady demanded. "No."

"Giselle!" Lord Jean barked, perhaps trying to take control of the conversation.

Royce shrugged. "The girl is of no birth. She cannot remain your ward forever, and this is a good offer."

I remained frozen, but beside me, I could hear my lady's quick breaths. "Kara is the daughter of my brother," she said. "She is my blood."

All three men were taken aback, but I knew Lord Jean's response was one of embarrassment. This truth had never been spoken outside her rooms.

For just an instant, Royce's face flickered, and then he shook his head. "It is of no matter. She's of no name and no house."

My lady's hand clenched into a fist, but Lord Jean broke in, this time speaking directly to Lord Trey. "My lord, you can see the attachment my wife has for the girl. Surely, some other arrangement can be made in exchange for the land. I would offer twenty-five hundred pieces of silver."

Royce leaned forward in his chair, addressing Lord Jean. "There will be no further bargaining here. I'll take fifteen hundred in silver for the land. But if you don't agree to my terms, I won't sell to you. And since I find myself in need of funds, I'll sell the land to someone else." He paused to let the effect of his threat sink in. Then he repeated slowly, "I want the girl."

A long moment of silence followed, and then Lord Jean looked to Lady Giselle. "Get her packed."

My lady shot to her feet. "No!" Reaching out, she took my hand and pulled me up. "We will be in my apartments until these gentlemen leave."

Needing no urging from her, I gripped her hand and we fled from the hall.

\* \* \* \*

Once she and I were alone in her apartments, her anger began to fade and I could see fear in her eyes. The sight of this was more terrifying than anything that had transpired downstairs.

"Don't let them take me," I said.

But before she could answer, the door to her apartments opened, and Lord Jean stood on the other side with two of our house guards behind him. Upon seeing the guards, Giselle went pale.

As Lord Jean stepped inside the room, she shouted at him. "This is your fault! You were the one who insisted she be at the table last night to create a distraction and put them off their game."

His expression was difficult to read. I'd never once heard her speak to him in any other tone than polite deference. He appeared both angry and uncomfortable.

"They've promised me she'll be treated well," he said.

"Promised?" she cried. "And what good is that? You know nothing of Royce Capello. For all you know, he keeps a riding crop under his bed."

Lord Jean took a step back. "Don't be vulgar."

"Vulgar? Me? You stand there and say that when you are giving our girl away to be some nobleman's whore!"

His discomfort increased, but so did his anger. "She is not our girl."

I stood pressed against a wall, and she suddenly went slack in despair. "Please, my lord. Don't do this. Don't take her from me. I could not bear it."

He appeared to waver, and hope rose inside me. In his own way, he loved her. He cared for her feelings.

But then, his expression hardened again. "I have no choice. I've paid the fifteen hundred, and the deed will be sent. A maid is packing Kara's things now, and the Capellos are making ready to leave." Striding over, he gripped my upper arm but spoke only to her. "You will remain here until they are gone. I'll leave men to watch over you."

With that, he dragged me forward. I struggled to pull away, but I don't think he noticed.

When we reached the door, my lady spoke from behind us.

"I'll never forgive you for this, Jean. Do you understand what that means? I won't forgive you."

Again, he wavered.

Then he dragged me out the door.

* * * *

Down in the courtyard, I saw my trunk being lifted into the back of a wagon, which was already half-filled with the Capellos' trunks and supplies. A maid from the house came to me and wrapped a cloak around my shoulders, but I was too numb to respond or thank her.

I could not believe what was happening.

Lord Trey and Royce's horses were saddled, and their six guards were making ready to leave. One of our own guards led a white mare from the stables…with a sidesaddle.

The sight of this made me fear I would faint.

At the look on my face, Royce frowned. "What's wrong?"

Lord Jean's brows knitted and then smoothed. "Oh, Kara has never been on...She's never ridden a horse."

"How is that possible?"

Shifting his weight between his feet, Lord Jean answered. "Because she's never been off the manor grounds. She's rarely been outside the house. You must understand that my lady has kept her...sheltered."

Silence followed, and even in my frightened state, I sensed there was a good deal taking place beneath this conversation. I simply did not know what.

"You could have her ride in the wagon beside your driver?" Lord Jean suggested.

"No," Royce answered. "I'll lead her horse."

Turning, he gripped my waist and lifted me as if I weighed nothing, setting me into the saddle. Then he mounted his own horse and drew up beside me, lifting the reins over my mount's head and gripping them in his left hand.

As opposed to reassuring me, this act only made me feel more trapped.

Five of their guards sat on horses. The sixth drove the wagon. The guards wore sheathed swords, but Trey and Royce did not.

I cast a pleading look at Lord Jean, but he turned away. My horse lurched forward, and I gripped her mane. Within moments, I found myself outside the gates of our manor for the first time in my life, in the company of strangers.

I was not even allowed to tell Lady Giselle good-bye.

# Chapter Two

My fear of Royce—combined with having been forced onto the back of a horse—was soon overridden by a fear of the open sky and the vineyards stretching all around us. Everything seemed to go on forever. The sights made me dizzy and sick to my stomach, and I gripped the horse's mane tighter.

Where were we going? Could I find my way back?

Although Royce rode slightly ahead of me, gripping the reins of my horse, he did not speak and glanced back at me only occasionally. His expression was impassive, as if he felt nothing.

The six guards ignored me.

Lord Trey was the only man to appear visibly unsettled, and when he looked at me, his expression conveyed a mix of concern, alarm, and pity. Through his eyes, the reality of my situation began to sink in. Lord Jean had traded me for a piece of land. I had been taken from my home and now *belonged* to Royce Capello. Lady Giselle had promised to keep me safe, but she had been unable to stop this. I'd always viewed her as my protector, someone with power in a world where I possessed none.

Had my vision of her been an illusion?

Though I couldn't gauge how much time had passed, at what I guessed to be mid-day, we left the seemingly endless vineyards behind and traveled down a narrow road lined on both sides by a forest of trees covered in yellow and red leaves. Long branches reached over the road and intertwined with branches of trees from the other side, creating a kind of tunnel. For some reason, this helped me to feel calmer, not so exposed.

"We should pause for a short rest," said Lord Trey.

The guards pulled in their horses. Royce dismounted and reached up, gripping my waist and lifting me down. The physical relief was immediate, as my right hip had begun to hurt from the sidesaddle.

"Wait here," he said. "I'll bring food and water."

In autumn, the day was cold, and I stood shivering inside my cloak as he walked toward the wagon bearing luggage and supplies. Quickly, his father moved to join him, and when they both reached the wagon, Lord Trey reached out and grasped Royce's arm.

"Stop."

They were a good twenty paces away, and Trey's voice was low, but I could still hear him.

"What?" Royce asked, his tone not inviting an answer.

"There's still time to turn around. This is madness. Take her back."

"No."

"You can't possibly mean to bring her into our household?" Trey's tone was incredulous now.

"You're the one who's been after me to choose a companion."

"A skilled courtesan! Someone who could be of assistance. That girl has no education, no conversation, no experiences outside of Lady's Giselle's apartments, and in case you hadn't noticed, she's terrified of you."

Royce turned to face him. "After eight years with Loraine, does it surprise you that I'd choose someone more biddable?"

Trey's voice rose. "You know how isolated the de Marcos live. You've seen how Jean keeps Giselle away from society and neglects her at the same time. From what I could see last night and this morning, that girl is her only companion, and you...you, who could have any woman, would make claim on Giselle's one comfort?" He paused. "This is an impulse on your part, and you'll regret it. Take the girl back."

His words brought me hope.

Without responding, Royce dug through a burlap sack, removed a few objects, and turned away from his father, walking toward me. My flicker of hope died. Royce was not going to take me home.

Approaching, he carried an apple and a biscuit—with a canteen on a cord draped over his wrist.

"Here," he said, handing me the apple. "It's not much and we have a good distance to go, but there will be a decent supper waiting for us at home."

*Home.*

My home was falling farther and farther behind. But he was trying to be kind, and I was hungry, having eaten no breakfast. So, I took the apple.

"Thank you."

My voice sounded small, and his gaze passed over my face. Then he uncorked the canteen and held it out. I took a long drink, grateful for the water.

"Can we eat while we ride, my lord?" the eldest of the guards asked. "As it is, we're not going to make the manor before dark."

Trey came walking back, carrying an apple of his own. He offered Royce a questioning look. "Forward or backward."

Royce gripped my waist and lifted me onto the mare. "Forward."

Lord Trey sighed.

We rode on. I tried to eat my apple with one hand while gripping my mount's mane with the other, but I managed only a few bites.

The tunnel of yellow and orange trees gave way to a dense forest of evergreens. Their branches did not reach across the road, and once more, this gave me a view of the open sky. Again…I felt exposed. The same inexplicable fear began rising. I understood why I feared both Royce and the horse, but I didn't understand why I feared the open sky. Forcing myself to focus, I noted the sun sinking in the sky to my left. Though I'd never had an opportunity to practice navigating the four directions, I made note that we were traveling south. This knowledge spurred me to pay attention. Should any opportunity arise, I must to be able to find my way home.

We stopped once at a stream to water the horses, but Royce did not dismount—and so neither did I. We pressed on.

Hours passed.

The discomfort in my right hip grew into pain. I tried shifting in the saddle several times, but nothing helped. The sun dipped low, and dusk approached.

"Another stop," Lord Trey called.

He was riding behind us, and Royce turned with an annoyed expression, as if to argue, but his father cut him off.

"Look at the girl. She's nearly done in."

Royce looked at me. I must have made a pitiful sight because he pulled up his horse and swung his leg over before hopping to the ground. Then he lifted me from the saddle to stand beside him. This time, he had to hold me up for a few moments before I could stand on my own.

Trey and the guards all dismounted as well, walking around to stretch their legs. No one complained at Lord Trey having forced a halt. I was grateful for the respite and accepted the canteen from Royce when he offered it. The water was stale, but it quenched my thirst.

"Not far now," he said.

His words brought no comfort. What was waiting for me ahead? I would be alone, without my lady, in an unfamiliar place with unfamiliar people—and no one who loved me. I was in no hurry to be lifted back into the saddle.

After far too short a break, the same guard who'd spoken at our lunch stop began heading for his horse. Looking over his shoulder, he spoke to Lord Trey. "We should get moving, my lord. I don't like the idea of passing through this forest at night."

Trey nodded and said. "Royce, perhaps the girl could ride straddle behind you for the remainder of the way? At least she could lean on you to rest."

*My name is Kara.*

None of them ever used my name.

"Yes," Royce answered him, turning to lift me once again.

His hands never reached my waist.

In that same instant, something whizzed through the air and struck the shoulder of a guard standing near us.

An arrow.

The man dropped, and Royce whirled.

More arrows flew from several directions, striking the guards' shoulders and thighs. Most men were hit multiple times. The man up on the wagon grabbed a sword from beside him on the bench and jumped down, as if looking for someone to fight.

An arrow struck his right shoulder and then another protruded from his left arm. With a cry, he dropped the sword. An arrow hit his thigh, and his leg gave way.

This all happened so fast that I was unable to take much in. One instant, Royce had been reaching for my waist, and the next instant, our guards were all on the ground, too wounded to fight—but none were dead. Only Trey, Royce, and I remained untouched.

"Don't move!" commanded a voice from the trees.

Four men rushed in from different directions to surround us. They had dusky skin and black hair, with long bows and quivers slung over their backs and carrying short swords. Scraps of cloth, tied around their heads, covered the lower parts of their faces.

At the sight of the masked men coming toward us, the eldest guard somehow pulled his sword and tried to stand, but the tallest of our assailants put a sword to his throat.

"Drop it," he ordered.

Another wave of fear rose up, and I was not sure how much more I could bear.

Royce's head moved back and forth, taking in the sight of all four of our attackers, but Lord Trey stepped forward.

"Take whatever you want," he said.

My breaths came in short gasps as the leader strode toward us. He was even taller than Royce. His hair was cut very short, and his eyes were black. Like the rest of his men, even in the cool evening, he wore an open, sleeveless vest with no shirt beneath, exposing long, defined muscles in his arms. Looking to Trey, he began to say something and then saw me.

The words never left his mouth. He stared, and I drew back against the side of my horse. He looked at me with the same startled quality of most men, but then his expression shifted to something else. Even amid my fear, I could see it: a searching recognition.

I did not know him.

Royce stepped in front of me.

Another of the masked men came striding toward us. This one was of average height for a man, perhaps a head taller than me. His build was solid, and his hair hung halfway down his back.

He gripped the hilt of his sword. "Everyone stay where you are," he called to our guards. "We won't be long. I'd rather not kill anyone, but I will if I must." Turning his head, he said to the other two men who'd attacked us. "Get the wagon and horses."

As of yet, Royce hadn't said a word. His body was rigid. The man with the long hair moved to one side to take a quick of view of me, but he merely nodded to me once, and I swear I saw humor in his eyes.

"My lady," he said lightly.

"Just take the horses and wagon and go," said Lord Trey.

"We intend to," the man answered. "Along with that silver ring you're wearing."

At first, I'd thought the tall man was the leader, but now I wondered. The longhaired man appeared to be giving the orders.

Without hesitation, Lord Trey removed his ring and handed it over.

The tall man moved to the left to continue studying me.

"Do you know who we are?" Royce asked quietly, and the rage in his voice made me shiver. I hoped he would not take some foolish action. "I am Lord Royce Capello, and this is my father."

"I don't care who you are," answered the longhaired man. "Just another rich noble." He watched his other two comrades as one gathered our horses and the other climbed up in the wagon to take the reins. Then he turned back to us.

"Any other jewels or metal trinkets?" he asked as if we were conducting a business transaction.

But when he took a step closer to inspect my neck and ears, Royce moved between us. "Keep away from her!"

"The girl has no jewelry," Trey said, his voice calm.

The longhaired man gripped his sword tighter and studied Royce but then stepped back. Though I couldn't see his mouth, I sensed he was smiling. "All right, then," he said. "It's been a pleasure." He turned away, walking toward our gathered horses. "We're done here."

Although I was still frightened, I was beginning to understand these men were thieves—who'd taken pains not to kill our guards. They would take anything of value and leave.

After a brief hesitation, the tall man began to walk away as well, but suddenly, his head swiveled back toward me.

"We take the girl," he said.

His companion spun around, and all traces of joviality vanished. "What?"

"Lay a hand on her, and I'll have the king's army hunt you down," Royce said.

Pointing his sword at Royce's chest, the tall man ordered, "Step away."

My fear turned to terror as a roaring began in my ears, and I heard an echo of Royce's voice back at the manor.

*I want the girl.*

Again, the man motioned with his sword, but instead of stepping aside, Royce rushed inside his guard, shoving him with one hand and grabbing his sword arm with the other.

I had never seen men fighting, and I could not seem to breathe.

But the struggle didn't last long. The tall man used one foot to sweep Royce's leg, and Royce went down. The man kicked him in the head twice. Both times, as his foot connected, I heard a thud.

"What are you doing?" his longhaired companion nearly shouted.

"Get back," the tall man ordered Trey.

Royce's eyes were closed, and for the first time, Lord Trey looked alarmed as he stepped away. His alarm grew when the man reached out and grasped my wrist.

"No!" I cried.

His longhaired companion stood in shock. But I was dragged forward, and the roaring in my ears grew louder. Before I understood what was happening, my wrist was free and two strong hands grasped my waist, lifting me onto a horse. Then the tall man was up behind, reaching around and taking the reins with one hand. His other arm encircled me.

"Go!" he called.

A clatter of hooves and the rolling of wheels sounded. Darkness was falling, and I was aware of nothing but the movement of the horse, the arm around my waist, and the roaring in my ears.

Then I lost awareness of anything at all.

* * * *

I remember hearing the sound of an angry voice.

"Stop."

I could still feel the arm encircling my waist. Our horse slowed. Full darkness had fallen, but I had no idea how much time had passed as I tried to take in my surroundings. The longhaired man was on Royce's horse. He nudged the animal so that it blocked ours from moving forward.

"Caine, what are you doing?" he demanded.

*Caine.*

That was my captor's name.

"Raven, we don't have time for this," Caine answered.

"No one can follow us…yet. Get down. Right now."

The arm around my waist tightened as Caine swung his leg over, and a moment later, I was on the ground. We were in the forest, but the moon shone through the trees, and I had my first clear look at both men, as their cloth wraps were gone. They appeared in their late twenties or early thirties. Caine's features were narrow and his cheekbones were high.

Raven—as Caine had called him—had a broader face with a solid jaw.

The other two men in the group were now off their horses and came to join us. These men appeared in their late thirties with weatherworn skin. Their black hair hung to their shoulders.

"What are you doing?" Raven asked again.

"She's coming with us," Caine answered.

"Do you want the king's army hunting us down?" When no answer came, Raven pointed at me. "Look at her! Have you ever seen anything like that?"

*Anything.*

They spoke as if I were not a person.

"No," Caine answered slowly. "I have not."

Raven turned to me. "Who are you?"

I dropped my eyes to the ground, not knowing how to answer. Who was I?

Reaching out, he lifted my chin with his finger. "Look at me. Who are you to those two nobles back there? A wife? Sister?"

This was an easier question, and I shook my head.

"Then who?" he demanded.

"I...belong to Royce," I whispered.

"Belong?"

"My own lord traded me for a piece of land."

He breathed out through his teeth.

But Caine nodded to him. "You see? She's property. I could have told you that without asking her. No one is coming after us."

"Logan won't like it. Neither will Grandfather."

Caine gave him a level stare. "She comes with us."

Sighing, Raven looked back to me. "What's your name?"

My throat felt as if it was closing, but I managed to answer. "Kara."

He motioned to the two older men. "This is Tannen, and that's Badger. You're safe with us." His following glance at Caine made me wonder about this assurance.

Then, I was forgotten.

"We need to get back to our own horses before making camp," the man called Badger said. "And tomorrow, we'll need to get to a road or this wagon isn't going much farther."

Casting around, I saw that we were deep in the forest, and these men had been driving the wagon around the trees and through the brush. Though their swords had long been sheathed, all the men but Badger still wore bows and quivers slung over their backs. Now, they took these off and tied them to their saddles.

I dreaded the thought of getting back on a horse.

Thankfully, instead of lifting me, Caine laced his hands.

"Up," he said.

I'd never mounted a horse on my own, but I knew what he wanted. Stepping into his hand, I swung my over leg over and settled my skirt to ride astride. He came up behind me again, reached around, and took the reins.

There were eight saddled horses plus two harnessed to the wagon. Caine and I rode one horse. Raven rode another, and Tannen rode a third, but he had the other five connected on a long lead. Badger drove the wagon. Raven led the way, and within moments, I could hear Badger swearing as he tried to maneuver through the dense brush.

I felt numb and lost. I kept thinking of my lady and how alone she must be feeling.

Perhaps an hour later, we rode into a clearing where four other saddled horses walked about, eating grass and brush. They were on long ropes tied to stakes in the ground. But our arrival caused some excitement as the new horses entered. An abundance of sniffing and snorting sounded, and the space felt smaller with so many horses gathered inside.

Badger drove the wagon into the clearing, and it moved more easily over the open ground.

"Thank the gods," he said in relief. "Raven, you'd better get us to a road tomorrow."

Caine hopped down and lifted me off the horse, allowing me to become steady on my feet. Then all four men set to work tying off the horses to settle them for the night.

A few moments later, Raven walked to the wagon and jumped up into the back, opening trunks and rifling through burlap sacks. "There's a pouch of silver," he called. "But the rest is mainly men's clothing. The tunics are silk, and there are a few cloaks worth selling."

He hadn't opened my trunk yet.

"Those trunks are worth keeping," Tannen said.

Raven hopped back to the ground, holding up a burlap sack. "You hungry?" he asked me.

It was still hard for me to speak, but of the four men, he frightened me the least.

"Thirsty," I whispered.

At my single word, his expression turned abashed, and he strode over to a saddle lying on the ground. After unlashing a canteen, he walked back, holding it out.

"Here."

I drank the water gratefully as the four of them passed around apples and biscuits from the Capellos' food stores. Caine offered me a biscuit, but I shook my head. I didn't think I could swallow more than water.

Still eating an apple, Raven jumped back up onto the wagon's bed. I wasn't paying attention, but I could hear him moving things around.

"Kara," he called. "Come up here."

He'd used my name.

Without thinking, I crawled up onto the wagon's bed and saw that he'd arranged several trunks with a space in the middle, where he'd laid down a cloak.

"We can't risk a fire," he said. "But this should shield you from the wind. It's the best I can do tonight." He paused and added, "The rest of us are fine on the ground."

He'd gone to the trouble to make me a bed up here, and then he'd assured me it was a private space. His kindness left me undone, and everything that had happened to me from that morning to this moment came crashing down. I could feel my exhausted body begin to shake and unwanted tears sprang to my eyes.

This reaction was not lost on him. Startled, he reached out and drew me over. "Lie down and use your own cloak as a blanket."

Like a child, I obeyed him and even let him arrange my cloak to cover me. "Go to sleep," he said.

My body and mind were so weary that I closed my eyes.

# Chapter Three

The next morning, I woke up to male voices, but couldn't remember where I was.

"That sounds like a waste to me," someone said.

Sitting up, I realized I was in the back of a wagon, covered by my own cloak.

Four men stood nearby, on the ground. Everything from the day before came rushing back: that I'd been a captive of Royce Capello, and now I was a captive of these strangers. I hadn't eaten more than a few bites of an apple since the day before that, and I was cold. All four of the men were dressed differently this morning, wearing thick, woolen shirts and canvas jackets more suited to the weather.

"We can put anything of value into sacks and tie them to the spare horses," Raven said.

"And just abandon the wagon and those trunks?" Tannen asked.

"We'll never get that wagon through these trees, and after...taking the girl, I don't think we should risk traveling by road. Besides, if we ride straight east through the forest, we'll make it home by nightfall."

Tannen grimaced. "Still sounds like a waste."

But Caine had already reached the wagon, motioning to me. "Come down."

I climbed down quickly, and he began pulling trunks toward himself.

It was odd to stand there watching them go through Lord Trey and Royce's possessions. They stuffed everything they could into burlap sacks until Raven opened the last trunk. This one was small, more of a chest than a trunk.

It was mine.

He didn't touch anything inside.

After looking at the gowns of white and ice blue, he glanced to me first and then to Badger.

"This one's not large," he said. "Could we tie it to the back of a horse?"

"Shouldn't be much trouble," Badger answered.

In surprising short time, they had everything they wanted secured for a journey, with extra horses tied on long lines. The wagon and the trunks on the ground would remain behind.

"Do you want to ride on your own today?" Raven asked me.

I dropped my eyes. "I don't know how."

"What do you mean?"

"She can ride with me," Caine said. But this time, he mounted first and reached down. "Swing up behind."

Grasping his hand, I let him pull me up. Sitting behind him, the arrangement was more comfortable. But…where were we going? I didn't want to go with these men. I didn't want to go farther away from my lady.

I wanted to go home.

Clucking to the horse, he started forward, and I gripped his waist.

* * * *

We rode all day.

At one brief stop, I managed to eat part of a biscuit, but found myself growing more and more frightened by the fact that I couldn't keep track of the path of our progress. We were in a forest, and Raven was leading. He appeared to know exactly where he was going, but the trees all looked the same to me.

I remembered that he'd mentioned heading east and tried to keep my bearings.

But by late afternoon, I was so weary from having spent nearly two days on the back of the horse that I found myself leaning forward into Caine's back. Though I would rather not have touched him, I had little choice and kept my arms around his stomach.

At some point, my eyes closed. I didn't exactly sleep while needing to hang on, but I began to drift.

"There it is," Raven said.

I opened my eyes. Darkness had fallen.

Half turning his head, Caine said to me, "Hold on tight. The climb gets steep."

What did he mean?

I couldn't see much, but just ahead, Raven appeared to vanish into a line of tall brush, and Caine nudged our horse forward to follow. We passed through the brush as well, emerging into a natural chute with rock walls on each side of us. Suddenly, I felt myself sliding backward and gripped Caine's waist tighter. Tannen and Badger followed us through, leading the extra horses.

Without hesitation, Caine pressed onward, leaning down slightly, as we were on a sharp incline. When we reached a curved corner of the chute, Raven stopped ahead of us and held up his right hand. Caine halted our horse. Putting two fingers in his mouth, Raven let out three long whistles.

Four whistles sounded in return, and we pressed onward—upward. The climb was so steep that our horse began to sweat in the cold night air. A flickering from above caused me to look up. Far above us, standing on the edge of the cliffs, I made out the shapes of men holding torches out over the edge.

"Don't be afraid," Caine said. "Those are our own people, giving us light." After a moment, he added, "But if Raven hadn't signaled, we'd be dead by now."

At first, his meaning was lost on me, but then I reasoned we were exposed here in the chute. Anyone up above with a bow and arrow could have easily killed us.

Though the chute was wide enough for two horses to walk side-by-side, we continued in single file to travel up…and up. The torches grew closer, and a new fear washed through me—that I no idea of where I had arrived.

Finally, with our horses soaked in sweat and breathing hard, we emerged at the top and rode out onto a plateau. Up here, it was almost as heavily forested as down below, but a wide stretch had been cleared for a settlement—or that was the word that came to mind. I'd read of such places in books. From my vantage point, I could see about twenty wooden buildings or dwellings stretching out before me. There were also several wagons with what appeared to be small homes set on top. The place might have been much larger, but in the darkness, by a combination of the moon overhead and the torches coming toward us, this was all I could see.

As the torches—and people—drew closer, I had my arms still around Caine's stomach and did not let go. Raven jumped to the ground, quickly surrounded by men, women, and children offering greetings and asking questions.

"Oh, Raven, such fine horses!" someone exclaimed.

"Did you take any sugar?" a woman asked. "We're nearly out."

"Anyone hurt?" another woman asked.

Two men came walking up from the darkness. One was aging, with long, gray hair. He walked with a slight limp. The other was about thirty and as tall as Caine.

"Where have you been?" the younger man asked Raven. "We expected you days ago."

Raven shrugged. "Pickings were poor until last night. Then we spotted some traveling noblemen."

"Noblemen?" the old man repeated. "Did you kill anyone?"

"No."

Tannen and Badger were already on the ground as people hurried to them, inspecting the new horses when a stocky woman with a thick braid spotted me sitting on the horse behind Caine.

She froze.

She was silent for a moment and then looked backward.

"Logan…"

Beneath my hands, I felt Caine go stiff as the tall man who'd been speaking to Raven came striding over.

"What is it, Brida? Is Caine injured?"

At the sight of me, he stopped. "What in the…?"

Swinging his leg over the horse's neck, Caine jumped down and reached up for me. Exhausted and sore, I said nothing as he lifted me down and held me on my feet.

"She's with me, Logan," he said.

Others began to notice my presence and fell silent, staring at my hair. The people here were of the same coloring as Caine and Raven, with dusky skin, dark hair, and black eyes. I stepped halfway behind Caine, pressed against the back of his right arm.

The aging man with gray hair came limping up, favoring his right leg.

"What do you mean, she's with you?" he asked.

To my surprise, Caine bowed his head in a sign of respect. "She came with me."

The woman called Brida stepped closer, looking curiously at my eyes. "Was she lost somewhere? Did you find her, and she asked to stay with you?"

When Caine didn't answer, Logan turned his head and barked, "Raven!"

Raven came quickly through the crowd, but his expression showed clear discomfort.

"What is this?" Logan demanded. "You brought an outsider into the settlement? Where did you find her?"

Raven drew in a long breath. "Caine took her from the noblemen, from the House of Capello."

"Took her?" Logan's tone was incredulous.

Apparently, Caine was finished with this conversation. Grasping my wrist, he walked forward, through the people, but called back over his shoulder. "She was property, not family. I claimed her as property."

Gasps and surprised voices sounded from behind us, but he kept walking, dragging me with him. On instinct, I tried to pull away, but he didn't even slow down. We passed several dwellings, and he cut between two of them, pulling me toward the tree line. Out at the back of these dwellings, I saw a small clapboard shack with no door. He dragged me around to the back of the shack, nearer to the tree line, and there was the door. Opening it, he drew me inside.

The interior consisted of a single room with no furniture and no windows, but a stone fireplace graced a side wall to my right. The hearth was dead, and though it was difficult to see in the dark, by the moonlight coming in the door, I saw a few musty blankets piled on the floor. When Caine let go of my arm, I hurried away from him, pressing up against the faded front wall.

Why had he brought me in here?

The sound of his voice referring to me as property rang in my ears. Is that how he viewed me, as his own? Like one of the horses he'd stolen?

At my fear, his expression flickered, but then it hardened again. "I need to go speak with my grandfather. I'll send someone with a warm meal and firewood soon." He pointed to the door. "This locks from the outside, but you won't be here long, just tonight."

Although I had feared the open lands and open skies, the thought of being locked in this windowless shack brought panic. What if I was forgotten?

"Don't," I begged. "Please. I promise I'll stay here if you don't lock the door."

Again, his expression flickered, but he turned and walked out, closing the door behind himself. With no moonlight, the room went black. Upon hearing something like the sound of a bolt sliding, I ran across the room, trying the door.

It wouldn't open.

* * * *

Crouched in a corner, in the darkness, I sat with my arms wrapped around my knees, longing for someone to come and fearing someone would come. The night was cold, and even in my cloak, I'd begun to shiver when a familiar voice sounded out back. "Put down the tray and unbolt the door. I'll take it in myself."

Raven.

Relief flooded through me. I didn't know him any more than I knew Caine, but he had talked to me more, and last night, he'd made me a private bed up on the wagon.

The door opened, and moonlight filtered in. Raven stood there with an armload of firewood. I never saw who was with him because he turned his head and said, "Go home. I can manage from here."

Striding in, he glanced at me once before walking to the hearth and arranging the logs. A flint appeared in his hand, and he used it to build a fire. I was even more grateful for the light than the heat.

Once the flames had taken, he went back to the door and returned with a wooden tray. A savory scent wafted upward as he knelt in front of me. The tray contained a bowl, a spoon, and a tin cup.

"Vegetable stew with gravy," he said. "Go ahead and eat. I know you're hungry."

I was famished, but Lady Giselle had always impressed the importance not showing any rush when eating. It was the height of poor manners.

"Thank you," I whispered, reaching slowly and picking up the bowl, taking a small bite of potato. Then I took a sip of water from the cup.

He watched me.

"I'm sorry," he said.

His unexpected apology made me brave. "What does Caine want with me?"

"I don't know. I've asked him, but he won't tell me. He's speaking to our grandfather now."

I'd heard the word "grandfather" from one or both of them before. "Is Caine your brother?"

Raven nodded. "So is Logan. He's the eldest. I'm the youngest."

Absorbing this news, I took another small bite and swallowed it. "Caine called me his property."

"I know he did. I heard him." He studied my face. "But you don't need to worry. He won't sell you, and he won't hurt you. I promise."

"Why did he bring me here?"

Raven hesitated. "I told you I don't know...but Caine is a man who believes in fate and in prophecies."

"And you don't?"

"I believe in choices." He stood up. "And I don't like this. I don't like you being locked in here, and I don't like you losing control over your own decisions."

His words washed over me. I'd never heard anyone talk like this before. I'd never thought about having choices.

He crouched again. "My people all used to be travelers. We traveled the kingdoms as we pleased, never settling anywhere, but that life grew hard for some of us, and my grandfather founded this place. The location makes it safe, and some of us, like Logan and Caine, prefer to grow food and live here year round." Tilting his head, he added, "But some of us don't."

"What do you mean?"

"I have a troupe who travels with me from village to town, putting on shows to earn money, living as we please. We come back here in autumn so I can help with some of the raiding parties. Then we leave for a few months and come here again for the hard part of winter."

I wanted to ask more about the term "raiding parties" but had a feeling he was trying to convey something more important.

"My troupe leaves in the morning," he said.

For some reason, this news brought a fresh wave of fear. He was the only one who really talked to me. And he was leaving in the morning?

Standing up again, he walked to the door.

"But for now, I'm going to head back to the common house and see how Grandfather is faring with Caine." He paused. "I'm not going to lock the door."

Setting down the bowl, I stood as well. Firelight reflected off the side of his face.

"The way I see it," he went on, "you have three options. While everyone is distracted, you could slip out of here tonight. No one guards the mouth of the chute. On foot, in the dark, you could press close to the near wall of the chute and make your way down with no one up above on watch seeing you."

My breaths quickened in fear at the thought of trying to flee this place and make it back to de Marco lands, to my lady, on my own.

"Or," he said. "You can stay here and take your chances and find out what Caine wants."

"Or?" I whispered.

"Or…you could come on the road with me." He amended quickly. "I mean with us, with my troupe. You'd belong to yourself, but you could travel with us."

A wild rush of hope rose up. "Could you take me home, to the de Marco manor?"

"No. Only small raiding groups of men ever go north into those estate lands. I won't risk any of my people. We're heading east. If you want to go back, you're on your own."

Despair replaced hope. His refusal had been swift and final.

But another thought occurred. "I couldn't go with you if I wished to. Caine would never allow it."

"He would if I asked him. He owes me...or thinks he does. I've never asked him for anything, but I'd ask him for this, and he wouldn't refuse."

I was moved that Raven would use up a favor to help me, but I also feared the prospect of joining a troupe of strangers traveling east, farther from my home.

He watched me a few moments longer.

"Choices are all that matter in this life," he said. "And we have to be free to make our own. You think on this, and I'll be back before dawn. If you're gone, I'll know you chose to run. If you're here, you can tell me what you've decided." He walked out. "I won't lock the door."

But he closed it.

I was alone again.

The fire crackled in the hearth, and I looked at the door. Slowly, I walked over and reached down for the latch.

It opened.

Peering outside, I saw only the moon and the tree line, not a soul in sight. Stepping out, I looked around. From back here, behind the settlement, there was a good chance I could reach the chute without being seen, and Raven would not have misled me. If he said I could press against the near wall in the darkness and make my way down without being spotted from above, I believed him.

But then what?

I'd be alone, in a forest, with little idea how to get home besides to head west until I found the main road and then to head north...alone and under the open sky.

Perhaps I could go with Raven, at least to gain my freedom in some semblance of safety and try to find a way to send my lady a message? But I would be exposed to one new sight after the next, traveling in the company of strangers.

Or...I could wait here. Raven had promised Caine wouldn't harm me. What if I simply bided my time? Could I find a way to send my lady a message from here? If she learned what had happened to me, she would bribe men to find me. Or perhaps I could learn the name of the nearest village or town. I could send a message with the location and then escape this place?

But what if I could not find a way to send a message from this place?

Raven said he believed in choices and yet how could I possibly make this one?

Turning, I went back inside the small dwelling, moving to the hearth. What should I do?

Suddenly, the air to my left began waver. Alarmed, I whirled and stepped backward, but the motion of the wavering air grew more rapid, and then... something solid began taking shape.

I went still.

There, right in front me, a great three-paneled mirror now stood where there had been only empty air an instant before. The thick frames around each panel were of solid pewter, engraved in the image of climbing ivy vines. The glass of the panels was smooth and perfect, but I didn't see myself looking back.

Instead, I found myself looking into the eyes of a dark-haired woman in a black dress. Her face was pale, and she bore no expression at all.

There she was, *inside* the right panel gazing out me.

Was I going mad? Had events from the past two days driven me mad?

"Don't fear," the woman said. "There is nothing to fear."

I couldn't help my rising fear, but I also could not seem to speak.

"You are at a crossroad," she continued, "with three paths." As she raised her arms, the material from her long black sleeves hung down. "I am bidden to give you a gift."

Could this be real? Was it happening?

"You will live out three outcomes...to three different choices," she said. "Three paths await you. Three actions...or inactions you might decide upon. Then you will have the knowledge to choose."

I shook my head, finding my voice. "Wait! What are you saying?"

Lowering both hands to her sides, she said, "The first choice."

My thoughts went blank, and the shabby room around me vanished.

# The First Choice
# The Road

# Chapter Four

I was standing in the darkness just outside the door of the shack, feeling dizzy and disoriented, as if I'd forgotten something and needed to remember. What was I doing out here?

Then I remembered. I had to make a decision.

Looking to the left, I saw the long tree line stretching along the backs of several dwellings. I could make my way along these trees far enough to slip down into the chute and escape.

But instead, I just stood there, knowing I could not force myself to take such an act.

Ashamed, I went back inside and crouched down by the fire, still feeling disoriented. What was it that I had forgotten?

I stayed like that all night, even after the logs had burned to ashes.

Outside, once the sky had begun turning gray, I heard footsteps approaching, and I watched the door. Caine entered first, with Raven behind him. Both men appeared tense, but Raven's eyes flickered in surprise at the sight of me. Had he expected me to run? Perhaps I should have.

Caine wasted no time. "Raven's just asked me that you be given a choice to go on the road with his troupe. I'm asking you to stay."

His voice was tight, but before he'd finished speaking, I'd made up my mind. I didn't know either one of them. And yet, I knew Raven a bit… more, and leaving with his people would give me the best chance to send my lady a message.

"I'll go with Raven's troupe," I said quietly.

Caine's expression grew desperate as he stepped toward me. "Don't. Stay here."

Quickly, Raven moved in front of him, cutting him off. "You told me you'd let her choose. It's just for the autumn. We'll be back in winter, and she might want to stay then."

Caine ran a hand over his face. "Don't take her with you. Please."

I had a feeling he rarely said please to anyone, but Raven was unmoved. "I'm not *taking* her anywhere. She's choosing to travel with us. And you gave me your word you wouldn't stop her."

After drawing in a harsh breath, Caine walked toward the door. "You'd better bring her back this winter."

Then he was gone, and I was alone with Raven, two strangers thrown together.

"Come on," he said. "My people are packing up."

* * * *

Walking through the settlement in daylight, I could see it was indeed larger than my initial view in the night. At least forty dwellings were scattered about in no apparent pattern. Several constructions were larger then others, such as the stable and barn and what appeared to be a smithy.

Beyond the farthest dwelling, I could see more cleared land now growing apple trees. Each dwelling we passed sported its own kitchen garden, but at this time of the year, only potatoes, carrots, turnips, and onions remained in the ground. Chickens pecked in the dirt, and goats wandered loose, eating grass and weeds. There were pigs inside of fenced areas. Even at the crack of dawn, a number of people were up and about, feeding chickens, gathering eggs, and milking goats.

As Raven and I continued on, people nodded to him and cast surprised glances at me.

"It's just your coloring," Raven said. "They've never seen anyone like you."

Lady Giselle had often told me the same thing.

Finally, he rounded a large dwelling, and we came upon a gathering of six wagons. I remembered some of these from last night. Houses had been built atop them, some with rounded roofs and others with square ones, but they all had windows and back doors. Most were painted in bright colors of yellow or blue or red. The lead wagon was by far the smallest, with a flat roof. It was faded white with blue shutters.

But I didn't study the wagons for long, as my attention was drawn to the people working busily to load food or supplies or harness horses or catch chickens for cages. There were nearly twenty people—men, women, and children—bustling about at these tasks.

"Tannen," a woman on the ground called up to the top of a roof. "That crate on the end won't hold. You'll need to tie it down more securely."

She wore a purple wool dress with long sleeves.

Up on top of a wagon, Tannen was helping to arrange crates. "I heard you the first time," he called back.

"Then listen to me!" she answered.

In her late twenties, she was tall for a woman, about the height of Raven. Her skin was flawless. As opposed to black, her hair was a rich shade of chocolate brown—and so were her eyes. Though her waist was small, her body showed more curves than mine.

She was lovely.

With her hands on her hips, she scolded Raven. "It's about time. Where have you...?" The words died on her lips when she spotted me partially behind him. As opposed to staring in shock, she assessed me from toe to head.

"Is that Caine's girl? The one he took? Everyone was talking about her last night. Logan nearly had an apoplexy."

Holding in a sigh, I readied myself for another conversation as if I weren't there.

"She's coming with us," Raven answered.

"With us?"

"Look at her. We'll use her in the show."

"What does Caine have to say?"

"Jade..." he said slowly as if to cut off further questions. "She's coming with us."

With a slight frown, she said. "I don't know where she'll sleep. We might be able to fit her in with Lizbeth and Ash, but that would make five in one wagon."

Raven shifted weight between his feet. "She can stay with me."

In an instant, Jade's expression went dark. "With you?"

The tension was strong between them, but I didn't understand it.

He shrugged. "I can sleep on top of the wagon."

Her eyes narrowed, and she stepped closer. "Up top? If you say so. But if you get too cold up there one night and decide to go scratching on another door, it may not open."

With that, she whirled and began walking down the line of wagons, calling orders to the people settling crates.

Beside me, Raven let out a sigh. "That went well." Then he motioned me forward. "This way."

I followed him to the smallest wagon, the one in the lead. Two horses had already been harnessed to the front, but he took me to the back door and opened it. The bottom of the door was the height of my waist.

"Normally, I have a set of portable stairs positioned here," he said, "but we're getting ready to leave."

Peering inside, I saw how a table and bench had been built into a side wall. A set of cupboards had been built into the wall directly across, and a bed had been built into the front wall. My own chest was sitting up against the bed. I could hardly believe it.

Raven must have read my face because he said, "You're one of us now, and those things belong to you. We don't steal from each other."

In truth, I had no idea what the housemaids had packed for me, but I was relieved to anticipate a change of clothing…and at the thought that I was not traveling into the world with nothing but the dress on my back.

"Does anyone besides you live here?" I asked, for it had sounded like numerous people lived in each wagon.

"No. I don't take many privileges, but I need my own wagon."

And yet, he was allowing me to stay here.

Looking down the line of wagons, he said, "I need to go and help. But we'll be off soon. You can ride inside the wagon or up on the bench with me."

"Inside," I answered instantly. I'd not known this would be an option, but at least I would not be under the open sky after all.

With a nod, he laced his hands together and leaned down. "Up you go."

Placing my foot in his hands and one of my hands on his shoulder, I let him toss me up into the back of the wagon.

"Secure the door so it doesn't fly open," he said. Then he was gone.

I looked around the narrow interior. His clothes, mugs, and other possessions were scattered all about. The table was dusty, and the bed was unmade.

Still, for now…I was home.

At least until I could get a message to Lady Giselle.

* * * *

Not long after we rolled out of the settlement, I began to wonder about my decision to remain inside. I should have given thought to the steep downward incline of the chute, and I found myself nearly hurled forward, taking refuge on the bed.

The window shutters were open, and outside, I could see the rock walls only a few hands' length from the wagon. There was enough room for the wagons to pass downward, but barely. We rolled down and down, and I began to feel queasy.

Just when I thought we'd never level out, we did. Then I remembered all the fuss over Badger driving the Capello wagon through the forest, and I wondered what would happen next, as these wagons were much larger and less wieldy. But Raven turned us east onto a dirt path, and the wagon rolled easily. Not long after, we reached a road.

Though I'd hoped my feeling of queasiness would pass, it continued growing worse, and even though we'd eaten no breakfast, I soon feared that I might start to dry heave. The sensation was miserable.

Not an auspicious beginning to this journey.

Hours passed.

I sat on the bed, suffering in nausea until I began to wish I had run off in the middle of the night to try and find my way back alone. Then finally, I heard Raven call a halt from up above, and the wagon lurched to a stop.

Within moments, the back door opened, and he peered inside.

"Are you faring all...?" Taking in the sight of me, he motioned with his hand. "Out. Now."

Standing on wobbly legs, I managed to reach him, and he lifted me down.

"Lean over and put your hands on your knees," he said.

Jade, Tannen, and Badger came around from the wagon behind us. A boy about nine years old walked beside Jade. His hair was chocolate brown.

"How's the princess?" Jade asked, and when she saw me with my hands on my knees, she appeared both amused and pleased. "Doing well, I see. What a good idea it was to bring her along."

Tannen cast her a sideways glance and held a canteen out to me. "Water?"

"Thank you. In a moment," I answered.

Jade carried a light tray in one hand, and with the other, she handed Raven a slice of ham. The smell of it caused my stomach to lurch, and I had little interest in eating lunch. But outside of the rolling contraption, I was beginning to recover and stepped out to look down the line of wagons. There were other people on the ground, sharing food and water, and I wanted to begin taking some stock of my traveling companions. From where I stood, I saw an elderly couple, a middle-aged couple, and two small children—both girls.

At the sound of barking, I looked left to see three small dogs dashing about, chasing each other as if celebrating a few moments to run. All three were white with brown patches.

No one spoke to me, but numerous curious glances were cast in my direction.

After far too short a break, Raven called out, "Time to go! We need to make it halfway to Fayette before dark."

Instantly, everyone began climbing up the sides of wagons or on to the benches to drive.

Though I dreaded the thought of getting back into Raven's wagon, I grew more alarmed when he walked up and said, "You're riding on the bench with me. It's not good for you in the back."

Drawing away from him, I begged, "No. Raven, please."

He frowned. "You can't still be afraid of me?"

How could I explain? But I didn't want him to think that I feared him, not after his kindness. "No, it's not you. It's the sky."

"The sky? What do you mean?"

"I've never seen it like this...so open."

"But you were riding with the Capellos. You told us you were Royce's property."

"For a day. Before that, I'd hardly left the manor, and then only to sometimes walk in the garden just behind the house with my lady. From there, I could not see how big, how open everything is."

He stepped close, speaking quietly. "Wait. Are you telling me the Capellos only bought you that same day we found you? And before that, you lived in a manor?"

I nodded. "With my lady."

"What did you do there at the manor?"

"I was companion to my lady. When she grew lonely, I found ways amuse her or make her glad. She was so kind to me." Speaking of these things broke my heart. "She fought to keep me, but Lord Jean wanted the land, and Royce wanted me."

"And Royce took you away that same day we took you?"

Again, I nodded.

For a long moment, Raven said nothing. Then he grasped my hand and led me to the step up to the wagon's bench. "You'll get used to the sky, but you can't ride in the back if it's making you sick. Climb up onto the bench."

I obeyed him.

* * * *

In truth, sitting on the bench beside Raven as he drove our team of horses proved a great relief. Out in the fresh air, I was not queasy. Thick trees lined the road we traveled. I kept my eyes on the tail of one horse, and this kept me from panicking at the open sky.

Raven had a water bottle, several apples, and salted crackers on the other side of him, and after a while, at his prompting, I was able to eat lunch.

At first we did not speak much, but it was a comfortable silence. Every now and then, he'd point out something like wild roses growing beside the road or a rabbit hopping across our path. So long as I did not look up, I was all right.

Then suddenly, he asked, "Where are your parents?"

"Dead. My lady took me in as her ward."

He didn't press me, but his question made me wonder about him. He had two brothers and a grandfather.

"Where are your parents?" I asked.

"They're dead too. My mother died when I was thirteen." He paused. "One summer, she lost her appetite, and my father couldn't get her to eat. She grew so tired and weak she could barely stand. We couldn't seem to heal or help her. She died before autumn."

From his voice, I could tell this memory was painful. I'd never known my father, and I barely remembered my mother. But for a boy to lose his mother at the age of thirteen must have been tragic. My lady possessed some knowledge and skill in the healing arts, and I had seen the ailment that Raven described before—with one of the manor servants. My lady had called it *consumption*.

"I'm so sorry."

"We lost my father four years ago in a raid gone wrong," he went on. "I wasn't there, but some of our men attacked a large caravan…too large, and they couldn't contain all the guards. We lost three men that night."

How awful. But this was different. Why did these people insist on conducting raids at all? They seemed to have most of what they needed. Still, I didn't press the point. I was more interested in hearing of his family. His life to date had been so different from mine.

"Is your grandfather the leader of the settlement?" I asked, for although I was uncertain, it had seemed so during my short stay.

"Yes." The word was clipped, as if the question was awkward. "Our word for leader is *tórnya*. My father was intended to succeed him, but now it's down to Logan or Caine."

"Not you?"

"I don't want it. That's why Caine thinks he owes me. I asked Grandfather to take me out of the running and give more consideration to Caine. But the truth is that I don't choose to be trapped at the settlement year-round."

His hands gripped the reins tighter. "Caine would make a better tórnya than Logan. He knows how to listen. But Grandfather wants someone who's married, with a family of his own. So far, Caine's shown no interest in marriage."

"And Logan is married?"

"Yes, to Brida. I think you saw her? She wears her hair in a thick braid?"

I did remember her. She was the first one to see me last night.

"Logan and Brida have two sons," Raven said. "So unless Caine marries and starts a family, I think Logan will be Grandfather's choice."

"And you don't like the idea of Logan in charge of the settlement?"

"No, I do not."

"Why?"

He never answered me. Glancing at his face, I could see he wished to end this line of discussion, so, I pointed ahead. "Look, another rabbit."

Beside me, his body relaxed. "A big one too. I wish I had my bow handy. He'd make a fine stew for supper."

We fell back into comfortable silence, and the wagon rolled on.

* * * *

We stopped for the night well before dusk had set in. Raven had clearly made this journey before, because he appeared to know where he was going and pulled off the road into a clearing large enough for all six wagons.

"There's a stream down below for fresh water," he said.

I followed him off the bench as everyone around us scrambled off wagons and set to work. The men began unharnessing horses and fetching water in buckets. Several of the women built a fire, and Jade carried over a metal tripod with a hook in the center. As she arranged this over a fire, an older woman hung a pot on the hook, and a young woman poured in half a bucket of water.

I stood to one side at a loss. Then I took off my cloak, hoping to help. "Is there anything I can do?"

Jade stood and put her hands on her hips. "I don't know. *Is* there anything you can do?"

As I felt my face turning pink, the young woman laughed. She wasn't much older than me.

"Oh, leave off, Jade." But she took in the sight of me with some trepidation. "You don't look strong enough to haul a bucket, and you'll ruin that gown if it drags in the mud."

"My gown?"

Embarrassed, I noticed they all wore dark wool dresses in shades of brown, purple, or burgundy. I was still in my ice blue muslin. The color was so light it showed every mark or stain.

"I'm Jemma," the young woman said. "And this is Lizbeth." She motioned to the older woman.

Jemma was not so lovely as Jade, with a wiry build and pointed chin, but she was pretty and blessed with silky black hair. Lizbeth looked to be perhaps sixty with ample breasts and hips. She moved quickly for someone of her age.

"I'm Kara," I answered.

"Well, you must know how to do *something*, Kara," Jemma said, laughing again. "Or Raven wouldn't have you living in his wagon. That's a first for him."

Lizbeth laughed too, but Jade didn't. I had no idea what Jemma meant and was beginning to grow uncomfortable.

Then Jade's eyes softened as she looked beyond me, and I saw the boy coming toward us, carrying a load of twigs and branches. "Sorry it took me so long, Mama," he said. "I had trouble finding anything dry."

"It's all right, Sean," Jade answered. "We've got a fire going with wood I brought."

This news surprised me. He was her son? Who was her husband? Even with my lack of knowledge of the world, I'd sensed there was something between her and Raven.

"Here, Kara," Jemma said. "Come and help me chop these vegetables."

Looking down, I saw she was on the ground with a knife, a cutting board, and a pile of potatoes, carrots, and onions. Grateful for something to do, I hurried to join her.

"Is there an extra knife?" I asked.

"Yes, right beside that sack."

The middle-aged woman I'd seen earlier came to join us, introducing herself as Teresa. The two small girls appeared to be hers. Then two other young women, about Jemma's age, arrived. They offered their names, Emlee and Deidra, but I was beginning to feel overwhelmed and barely heard them, trying to focus on my work.

The large pot was boiling by now. We added potatoes, onions, and carrots. Jade dropped in bits of some type of dried meat.

"All right," Lizbeth said. "We should go see if the men need help with the horses. Jade, you watch the stew."

Before I knew what was happening, everyone walked away from the campfire—except for Jade and myself.

She stirred the pot and studied me. "You're something to see. I'll give Raven credit for that. He knows an attraction for the show when he sees one."

I had no response, but she didn't seem to notice.

"Just be careful around him," she went on. "He doesn't mean any harm, but his head is more swelled than most men, and he's got a wandering eye. Any girl back in the settlement would have him in a heartbeat. For all Logan's strength and Caine's handsome face, it's always been Raven the girls chase after."

Her voice had an edge to it. She did not appear to have a husband here, and again I wondered if there was something between her and Raven. I wished that I could assure her I was no threat and that I would only be with them until I could get a message to my lady.

But of course I couldn't tell her this. I didn't want any of them knowing my plan.

"He can make you feel the sun rises and sets around your head," Jade said. "But then he spots another pretty face, and the sun rises around her head."

"He sounds inconstant," I said.

Her brow lifted. "Inconstant?"

"Fickle."

She nodded. "That he is. So long as you know."

Voices carried on the air as everyone began gathering around the campfire. We passed around mugs of water, and then Jade announced the potatoes were soft enough to eat. She dished bowls, and I helped to serve. Tannen and Badger both nodded politely to me, and I was glad for their presence. But this also gave me the opportunity to take account of the entire group, which consisted of six women, three children, and ten men—counting Raven. I knew some of the men and women were couples, but as of yet, I hadn't quite entirely placed who went with whom.

It did seem strange that they all appeared to live practically on top of each other, and in a moment when everyone was otherwise engaged, I asked Jemma to help me make a few connections. She told me that Badger and Tannen were Jade's older brothers, neither were married, and they shared a wagon with Jade and Sean.

When the meal was nearly over, Raven left for a few moments and returned carrying a small cask and a wheel of yellow cheese. This met with delight from the group.

"Cheese!" Jemma exclaimed. "Did you bring that back from the raids?"

The cask contained ale, which I declined, but I did accept a slice of cheese—and wondered if he'd taken this from the Capellos' stores.

Before long, several of the men took out violins and began to play. I sat near Jemma to listen. The first song was lively, but the second was possessed of a sad sound, with haunting strains. It made me think of my lady and how lonely she must be. But then I looked across the camp and saw Jade with her son, Sean. He was holding his stomach in pain. Quickly, I rose and went to them.

"What is it?" I asked.

She was so concerned that her previous dislike of me had vanished. "I don't know. It's happened before, but only a few times."

Kneeling, I asked Sean. "Show me where it hurts."

Nearly gasping from pain, he put his hands to his lower abdomen. I had seen this before and suspected what might be wrong. Though I'd noticed many goats around the settlement, I'd not seen a single cow.

"I believe the cheese he ate tonight was made from cow's milk," I said. "Has he ever had this happen to him after drinking milk from a cow or eating butter?"

She blinked, as if thinking, and then nodded. "Yes...yes every time." Her expression shifted back to concern. "But it lasts for hours, and this time seems worse."

Lord Jean had suffered from this same affliction. It could be managed by simply having him avoid any foods containing milk from cows, but occasionally, he would take a foolish risk and eat something such as a dessert with cream in it. When this happened, my lady needed to help him.

"There's a tea made from herbs that will ease the pain," I told Jade.

The boy groaned as stomach cramped, and Jade asked, "Which herbs?"

"Fennel and thornapple."

Several of the women had gathered around us.

"Oh," Jemma said. "Poor Sean. Is it his stomach again?"

"Can you find some fennel and thornapple?" Jade asked her. "Quickly."

Jemma and Lizbeth both hurried into the trees and thankfully, they were not gone long. When they returned, I was relieved to see they'd brought the herbs I recognized—the ones my lady had used for Lord Jean.

I ground up the herbs in a bowl. After this, I boiled water over the fire and ladled it over the mixture. Then I used a cloth to strain the liquid into a mug. By now, Sean was in so much pain, he didn't object as I drew him against me. Everyone was watching, but I shut them from my mind.

"Sip a small mouthful of this," I told him, holding the mug of warm liquid to his mouth. "It's bitter, but I promise it will help. Take small sips only when I tell you."

He took a sip and made a face. A moment later, I had him take another sip. This was a slow process, and he needed a distraction, something to keep his mind occupied. Whenever my lady was sad or needed distraction, I told her a story.

"There was once a village beset by wolves," I said in Sean's ear. "Not ordinary wolves, but large, great wolves the size of ponies. They killed sheep and carried off children, and the women of the village begged their men to hunt the beasts down, but the men were afraid." Sean was listening to me, and I paused in the tale, "Take another sip."

He sipped and swallowed.

"There was a boy, just about your age, who was not afraid. And in the night, he slipped from the village to hunt down the wolves."

"By himself?" Sean asked.

"Yes, all by himself. Take another sip."

I went on to describe the hunt and how the boy once barely escaped the wolves with his life, but in the end, he played a trick and set up heavily-leaved bushes at the edge of a cliff and lured the wolves to chase him, and then he dove under the brush at the last moment, and as they jumped it, seeking to find him on the other side, they all went over the cliff, falling hundreds of feet below to their deaths.

In between parts of the story, I had Sean sip more of the herb tea until it was gone and the story ended.

When I looked up, Jade was watching me.

"How do you feel?" she asked her son.

Sean touched his stomach. "It's getting better."

Then I realized everyone, including Raven, was watching me. I had more information for Jade, but it was indelicate, and I wasn't sure how to word it.

"In the night...at some point, he will probably need to relieve his bowels," I said quietly.

"Relieve his bowels?" she repeated.

"I think she means he'll need to shit," Jemma offered.

With a jolt at her crude use of words, I dropped my eyes to the ground, but the group laughed, and their mood seemed improved after the worry over Sean.

"It's time for sleep," Raven said. "We have an early start."

Jade drew in a sharp breath as she looked at him. "Sleep well on top of the roof."

He ignored her and walked away.

She came over to take Sean from me. "Thank you," she said stiffly, and then she shook her head once and touched my hand. "I mean it. Thank you."

I did not understand her well, but she loved her son. That much was clear. With a nod, I rose and followed Raven to our wagon. He opened the back door for me.

"There are plenty of blankets in there," he said. "But you'll need to get a few for me."

The night was cold now that we'd left the campfire.

"Are you really going to sleep on the roof?" I asked. Surely, some other arrangement could be made.

He flashed a grin. "Unless you're inviting me to sleep inside?"

Startled, I stepped away, and his expression changed to alarm. "Oh, Kara, I was joking," he rushed to say. "Don't mind me. I just need to watch myself when I'm talking to you."

Leaning down, he laced his hands. I stepped into his hands and then stepped up into the back. After retrieving two blankets, I handed them down to him.

"Good night, Raven," I said.

His dark eyes scanned my face. "Good night."

Closing the door, I was relieved to be alone.

In spite of the fact that the wagon contained no source of heat, I couldn't resist slipping out of my dress—as I had been wearing it for three days—and crawling between the blankets in nothing but my shift.

Raven's blankets were warm, and the bed was surprisingly soft. I gave one more thought to his lack of comfort up on the roof, and then I fell asleep.

# Chapter Five

The next morning, I was awakened by the sounds of voices outside. Light came in through the windows, and I remembered that I had yet to go through the belongings in my small trunk.

Kneeling on the floor, I opened it.

Inside, I found a white silk gown, an ice blue silk gown, and two muslin day-dresses…one white and one of ice blue. None of them would offer much warmth, and the colors would show every speck of dirt or mud. I also found clean slippers, stockings, undergarments, and a fresh shift. My silver hairbrush and mirror lay at the bottom, along with a few silver hair clips that had been gifts from my lady.

With so few choices, I decided upon the blue muslin dress, very similar to the one I'd taken off last night, except this one was clean. I brushed out my hair until it hung in silver-blond waves. The impractical slippers I'd been wearing were soiled, but they were still wearable, so I decided not to change them out yet.

I'd never purchased clothing for myself and wondered how one might go about buying a wool gown and pair of boots. Then again…where would I obtain any money?

Someone banged on the door.

"You up?" Raven called. "Come get breakfast. We need to get on the road."

Quickly, I went over and opened the door.

He took in the sight of me and then turned away. "Get something to eat, and meet me on the bench. Don't forget your cloak." His tone was tense, and I wondered why.

I climbed down from the back of the wagon on my own.

Jemma and Jade were crouched near a morning campfire. Today, they had set up small benches, one on each side of the fire, and laid a sheet of metal on top of them—across the fire. They were frying up what appeared to be oatcakes. The scent made my mouth water, but I felt guilty for not having helped with breakfast.

Jemma didn't seem to notice my lack of help and smiled at me. "Come have a cake. I made tea as well."

*Tea.*

I hadn't had tea since leaving the de Marco manor. Forgetting everything but my own comfort, I accepted a mug of tea and a warm oatcake.

Jade glanced at my clean dress. "Do you have anything sensible to wear?" The words came out sounding like a growl.

"No," I answered honestly.

Shaking her head, she walked away. I wanted to sigh but finished my breakfast in a few bites. "I'll help clean up," I told Jemma.

She nodded. "I think everyone's eaten. Grab that bucket, and we'll put out the fire."

Soon, everything was packed and stowed and the horses were harnessed. After fetching my cloak, I climbed up onto the bench beside Raven. Without a word to me, he clucked to our horses and led the way back onto the road. Unlike yesterday, the silence that followed was not comfortable.

Finally, I couldn't help asking, "What's wrong?"

"Mmmmmm?" he turned his head toward me. "Oh, nothing. Jade's in a mood this morning, and she has a sharp tongue."

"Was she unkind to you?"

To my surprise, he laughed. "Unkind? You have the strangest way of speaking. Yes, she was...*unkind*." Then he shrugged. "But that's just her way. She has a good heart."

After this, he seemed to feel better and pointed out a doe with a fawn hiding in the brush as we passed them.

We traveled all day, stopping only briefly for a light lunch. While on the road, Raven and I didn't speak much, but we didn't need to. I was comfortable beside him, and he seemed happy enough to drive along, look at the sights flowing past us, and occasionally speak of small things. My fear of the open sky did not trouble me so much today.

In the late afternoon, he said, "We'll be staying two nights in Fayette and putting on two shows tomorrow, one in the late morning and one in the late afternoon."

"What do you mean by 'shows'?" I asked. "You keep using that word, but I'm not sure what you mean."

He'd ceased to find my ignorance about nearly everything in his world as a curiosity—and he'd begun to accept it.

"You'll see soon enough," he said, "but setting up camp tonight will take longer, as we'll need to get costumes and the curtain and parts of the stage down from atop the wagons."

Helplessly, I nodded, not understanding anything to which he referred. We arrived at our destination before dusk.

"Pull up the hood of your cloak," Raven said. "Cover your hair and as much of your face as you can."

I did as he asked as we rolled into a town that spread out as far as I could see, with hundreds of dwellings and shops and cross streets. There were people and horses everywhere. As I'd never even visited a village, the sheer size of the place and number of people was daunting.

"It's so big," I whispered.

"Fayette? This is nothing. We're only staying a day. Wait until we get to Narbonnè. That's a city. We'll stay two weeks."

"A city?"

But he must not have heard me as we rolled through a crowded open-air market and a number of townspeople waved a greeting. It seemed our small caravan was expected. Raven waved back.

As always, he appeared to know exactly where he was going and turned us left down a side street until we came to a stable with a large cleared area on its west side—with enough room for all the wagons.

"We're always allowed to set up camp here," he offered. "I have an arrangement with the town constable. We don't go anywhere we aren't welcome."

"Why would you not be welcome?"

He didn't answer.

Instead, he pulled in first, closest to the stable, and Jade—who was driving a wagon—pulled up beside him. One after another, all six wagons lined up neatly with enough room to walk in between.

After that, everyone burst into a flurry of activity.

Raven had not been wrong about the evening's setup.

First, the horses were unharnessed, fed, and watered. Then small sets of steps were brought down from the tops of the wagons and attached to the backs, making entries and exits between the ground and the doors much easier. Chests were passed down and carried inside various wagons.

With no idea of what to do, I sought out Jemma.

"Can I help with dinner?" I asked.

"Of course. I stowed some spare branches in our wagon for firewood. Come help me carry it."

I appreciated her easy manner and was relieved for something to do. She led me to a bright red wagon on the end.

"I travel with Ash and Lizbeth," she said. "So does Marcel. Ash is my uncle, and Marcel is my man. Our wagon's large, and we've managed to curtain spaces off for some privacy. It works."

I hadn't known Marcel's name, but I'd seen her with a young man and had wondered if he was her husband—though that was still unclear. At least I was picking up more names.

Climbing up into the wagon, Jemma began handing down narrow branches.

"My parents prefer to stay at the settlement," she went on, "but I like to be part of the show."

The show.

My ignorance of exactly what this group did for a living was beginning to concern me, but now that I had Jemma to myself, I wanted to ask a more pressing question.

"Jemma, who is Sean's father?"

She paused in her work. "Oh, that was big Sean. We lost him four years ago in a raid gone wrong."

Raven's words echoed.

*We lost three men that night.*

"Big Sean was her husband?" I asked.

"Yes." Her eyes drifted. "My mother says that when Jade and Raven were younger, everyone thought they would marry, but Raven just…he's not the marrying kind. And then one summer, Jade married Big Sean. After he was killed, she and Raven took up again, but you see how he is."

I did not. Not really. I understood only snippets of what she was telling me.

"Lately, though," she went on, "he's stopped taking up with tavern girls, and he's only been with Jade. And he's good with young Sean. We were all starting to think this autumn he might finally ask her to hand-fast with him. Jade was beginning to think so too."

"Hand-fast means marriage?"

She nodded again, and her full attention returned to me. "But I'm not surprised you've caught his eye."

My body stiffened. "I assure you I have *not* caught his eye."

"Haven't you?"

Turning, I walked away, carrying my armload of firewood.

* * * *

Once the camp was set up for a slightly longer stay, the evening followed a similar pattern to the night before, and I was already beginning to understand some of the rhythms these people followed.

Tonight, I didn't need to ask what I could do and helped Lizbeth and Teresa with dinner, chopping vegetables. Raven killed one of the chickens, and Jade plucked it. We boiled it until the meat fell from the bone, and then used it to make a chicken stew.

It was good, but I thought it would have been better with some oregano and parsley.

Jade did not speak to me once.

After dinner, I helped to clean up and then retired to the wagon for solitude.

My mind kept turning over the things Jemma had told me about Jade and Raven in their youth…and then Jade marrying someone else…and then him being killed and the connection between her and Raven renewing itself.

I wished I could assure her that he had no interest in me and was only helping me out of pity. But I sensed her emotions in this matter were strong and complicated, and acknowledging the situation might only make things worse. Besides, I had other worries. I needed to find a way to send a message to my lady, and that was going to take money.

How would I be able to earn money?

As I fell asleep that night, I thought on "the show" that would take place tomorrow and wondered what this meant.

* * * *

The next morning, the entire camp again burst into activity.

While I helped clean up from breakfast, Raven was in and out of his own wagon several times, but I didn't pay attention to what he was doing. I understood that we shared the space, and so far, he'd left it mainly to me.

But all around me, trunks and chests were dragged out into the open, and brightly colored clothing with sashes and polished boots emerged. I did notice a few of the chests were in poor condition and remembered Tannen's regret at leaving the Capellos' fine trunks behind.

Jade walked from wagon to wagon, checking on everyone and helping with costumes.

"Am I going on first or second?" Jemma called from the back of her wagon.

"First, I think," Jade called back. "Raven's got Badger and Tannen up second."

"I can't find my silk scarves."

"What?" Jade asked, aghast as she hurried up the stairs into the wagon. "We have to find them."

With no idea what any of this meant, I stood back, trying to keep out of the way.

Near mid-morning, Raven went into our wagon and closed the door. Not long after, he emerged again wearing no shirt, a black vest, black pants, and high polished boots. The autumn air was rather cool to be walking around without sleeves, but he seemed immune to the cold.

"Cover yourself with a cloak," he said, "especially your hair."

Then he took me, along with a number of the men, through the town to the open-air market. We traveled on foot, and I carried two folded but heavy curtains. Raven carried a rope and stout wooden pegs. Tannen, Badger, and two other men carried a thick board about the width and length of twelve doors. Teresa's husband, Michel, carried long poles. Like Raven, Tannen and Badger were dressed in black pants and vests—without shirts beneath—and high polished boots.

On one edge of the market, the men went to work pounding in pegs and then setting up a platform about a foot off the ground. The platform had a hole on each side, near the back, and Michel set in the long poles. Raven fastened one end of the rope to the top of a pole and then called me over. Together, we strung the curtains, and he tied off the other end of the rope to the second pole.

"The stage," Raven said.

Some of the people at the market watched us work until he pulled me behind the curtains. Almost as if summoned, the others from our group came walking toward us from behind, shielded from the crowd by the stage and curtains. I nearly gasped at the sight of their transformation. The women were dressed in gowns of vivid blues, greens, reds, and pinks. Jemma wore a red silk dress with a royal blue sash. Jade was resplendent in emerald green. I could see the fabrics were a bit worn and of the cheapest quality, but it didn't matter. The mix of colors alone was so festive that the sight would bring cheer to anyone with eyes. The men were dressed like Tannen, Badger, and Raven, and two of them carried violins. While the three children were not in costume, each of them had one of the caravan's small dogs on a leash trotting alongside.

A few of the men who'd come with us to set up the stage now broke off to set up a tent to one side.

As I watched this, Raven explained. "Once we start, you'll see how this works, but Lizbeth works on her own. She'll read fortunes in private. Ash reads them on stage to entertain the crowd."

Without true understanding, I nodded, assuming he would soon tell me how I might be able to help from back here, but he just rushed onward.

"Right now, we're running six acts, and it's best to alternate a musical act followed by a non-musical act."

Again, I nodded but felt forced to ask, "What would you like me to do?"

"Do? Nothing yet. This morning, you just watch the performances and then you can tell me what you might do and where you might fit in. I'm thinking with the dancers at first. We could work out a new act with you in the middle as the visual center point."

I stared at him, uncertain I'd heard correctly. "You want me to dance?"

"Well, you don't have to choose dancing. Can you play an instrument?"

He wanted me to take part in the show?

I shook my head. "Oh, no…Raven, I can't go out on that stage in front of people. I thought you wanted me to *help* with the show."

"Yes, I want to you help. Your hair and eyes alone will have everyone's attention." He peered through the crack in the curtain. "I need to start calling the crowd. You just watch this morning and decide what you might want to do."

Then he was gone, through the curtain and out onto the stage with his arms in the air.

Jade was behind the curtain with the rest of us, doing a final check of Jemma's dress.

"Marcel and Bonham, get ready," Jade ordered.

Jemma's husband—or "man" as she'd called him—and another of the younger men stood near the curtain with their violins.

Bonham.

Now I could place another name with a face.

"Welcome my friends!" Raven called from the stage. "To the finest show in all of Samourè!"

Moving to one end of the platform, I peered through a crack between the pole and the curtain. People were beginning to gather in a crowd. Teresa and Michel stood at the edges of the crowd, and they each held an upside down hat in their hands.

"You'll not see more beautiful dancers anywhere!" Raven called. "You'll be amazed by feats of acrobatics and strength. Learn your fortune from a true seer. Come and be dazzled!"

The quality of his voice carried, and he made quite a sight out there with his muscular arms and the way his long, black hair swung when he moved. The crowd continued to grow.

Motioning to the curtain with one hand, Raven called, "The dance of the sprite!"

Then he came back through the curtain as Marcel and Bonham dashed out holding their violins and bows up over their heads. They each ran to one side of the stage.

"Now!" Jade whispered.

Jemma ran out, silken skirts flying, holding three sheer scarves in her hands.

Marcel hit the first note.

Then he hit a long second note, and Bonham joined in. The violins made music in perfect sync...and Jemma began to move, swirling the sheer cloths around herself.

People in the crowd fell silent, watching her.

I'd never seen anything like this, and Jemma was mesmerizing when she danced. Marcel and Bonham began playing faster, simultaneously moving around Jemma as she danced. The music kept growing faster, and Jemma danced faster...and people watched.

She swirled so fast her body became nothing but a flow of color and motion.

When the song ended, it finished on one sharp dramatic note, and Jemma dropped to her knees.

The gathered audience burst into shouts and applause.

It was then that Teresa and Michel began moving through the crowd, holding out their hats, smiling in encouragement, and people began tossing coins into the hats. My mouth fell partway open as I realized how this worked. I'd never possessed my own money, as my needs had always been provided. But when Raven had used the words, "earn money," he'd meant that people would give it voluntarily if they were entertained enough. I could barely get my head around this. Still, I didn't have long to ponder as Raven was back out on the stage.

"And now feats of strength and skill to astound you!" he called. "The great Tannen and Badger!"

As he came back through the curtain, Tannen and Badger moved out, both holding their arms in the air as they jogged back and forth several times across the stage. People cheered them.

Then, suddenly, Badger dropped to his knees and put his hands on his shoulders, palms up. Tannen climbed up to stand on his hands, and Badger slowly rose. Tannen never lost balance and I was astonished to see him standing on Badger's shoulders. The crowd gasped.

Then even more slowly, Badger began to move his hands upward, holding Tannen's feet, until his arms were straight and Tannen was high over his head.

Again, Tannen never lost balance.

The crowd cheered more loudly, but I stepped away from the curtain, unable to watch anymore. I could not play an instrument. I certainly could not dance like Jemma. Tannen and Badger could perform feats I could hardly believe…and Raven wanted me to watch these acts and then tell him what I might be able to do?

I couldn't do any of this. Even the thought of stepping out in front of all those people made my stomach turn. The crowd gasped and applauded, and I wondered what Tannen and Badger were doing now, but couldn't bring myself to look.

When their act ended, I saw Jade and Bonham at the curtain, ready to step out.

As Tannen and Badger came back, Raven again walked through the curtain, smiling broadly. Forcing myself to peek out, I saw people dropping coins into the hats as Teresa and Michel passed through the crowd.

"Have you ever seen such strength?" Raven called, as if encouraging the crowd to give more. Then Raven stepped to one side and called, "The beautiful songbird, Jade."

As Jade and Bonham came out, Raven vanished behind the curtain.

Bonham played a long, sad note that hung in the air, but I noticed he was playing much more softly than when Jemma had danced.

Jade began to sing as Bonham played.

Her voice was clear, and she could carry a tune. The song was about a girl who fell in love with a soldier and gave herself to him the night before he left for war.

The chorus repeated stanzas of her waiting for him to return.

The verses told her story of sorrow and fear once she learned she was with child.

The solider did not return.

I thought Jade had chosen a good song, with a story for the crowd to hear, but I noticed she stood near the back of the stage and did not make eye contact with anyone in the crowd. I don't know how I knew that was a mistake—only that it was.

As opposed to hanging on her voice and words, the crowd appeared to be listening politely.

In the final chorus, she repeated the strain of the girl waiting endlessly.

She and Bonham finished on a long note, and the crowd applauded, but few coins were tossed into the hats. As Jade and Bonham stepped off, Raven took their place with his hands in the air.

"And now…" he said slowly, "The next act needs no introduction, as many of you have seen him before, the Amazing Ash."

I'd never paid much attention to Lizbeth's husband Ash, but as he took the stage, I watched him. He was slender, with gray hair hanging to his shoulders, and a somewhat pinched face. Moving to the front edge of the stage, he stood close enough to touch people, and everyone fell silent.

"Who among you has a question?" he posed. "Ask and let me answer, for the spirits speak to me, and I will share their secrets."

His voice was low, but it carried, and at first, the crowd appeared so daunted by him that no one spoke. Looking down, he made eye contact with a girl of about sixteen.

"You have sorrow," he said.

She blinked.

"You've lost someone dear to you," he went on.

Tears sprang to her eyes.

"A father," he said. "No…a mother."

The girl choked back a sob, and I wondered how he was doing this. Did the spirits really speak to him?

"You have a question for her?" he asked.

Pushing forward to the front of the crowd, she looked up at him. "She was so afraid of being alone. Can you tell me if she found her sister, my Aunt Marta, on the other side? Are they together?"

Ash closed his eyes and opened them again. His voice softened. "Yes, she tells you not to worry, not to fear. She has found her sister on the spirit plane, and they are together."

The girl sobbed again and put one hand to her mouth. "Thank you… thank you."

The crowd all seemed to breathe at once, as if pleased and moved by Ash's announcement.

I couldn't move. He had them in his hand.

Then a man from the crowd called out playfully. "Is my wife unfaithful?"

People laughed, but Ash focused sharply on the man, and the man flinched ever so slightly. I didn't think many people noticed, but I did. His question was more serious than he pretended.

Ash had seen this too.

"What makes you think she might be unfaithful?" he asked. "Have you not been a loving husband? Not shown her your love?"

The man's left eye twitched.

"And because of this," Ash went on, "she's ceased showing her love for you?"

The man went still, but the crowd was still too, hanging on this exchange.

As I waited to hear what happened next, I realized Raven was standing right beside me, leaning down to speak quietly.

"Can you see what he's doing?"

I hesitated and then decided to say what I thought. "He's reading faces. He's reading reactions."

Raven nodded. "Yes."

"And he tells them what they need to hear."

At this, Raven started in surprise, but answered, "That's exactly what he's doing, and he's better than anyone I've ever seen."

With that, Raven took his place at the center break in the curtain again.

Turning back to the events playing out on the stage, I heard Ash tell the man, "Your wife is not unfaithful. But unless you change, she might be. Go home and show her love, show her your value of her. Then you never need worry."

Many people in the crowd were nodding.

I stood frozen as this type of exchange played out five more times. Someone would ask a question, and Ash would return with questions of his own, and then he would dispense wisdom or provide an answer.

The crowd loved him, and when he finished many coins went into the hats, but my own despair only grew. What Ash was doing out there required incredible confidence—which I lacked. I could never do what he was doing.

After his act, a more involved dance number followed in which Marcel and Bonham played wildly, and Jemma, Emilee, and Deidra danced in a circle, often running past each other and then reforming the circle. This took perfect timing as their legs and arms moved in unison.

It was both beautiful and exciting to watch.

But again...I could never do it.

When this dance finished, Raven introduced the final act, and Marcel ran back out onto the stage, without his violin, but holding three long handkerchiefs. To my astonishment, the three small dogs—now off their leashes—ran out after him, barking and yipping.

A comic display followed, in which the dogs would leap up and bite on the handkerchiefs, and Marcel would pretend to be jerked and pulled about. Every few moments, he fell down and the dogs took turns jumping over the top of him as he dramatically begged them to stop.

Then he would get up, and the whole process began again.

The crowd roared at their antics, and then he fell to the stage, as one dog jumped over the top of him, the second dog simultaneously jumped higher over the first dog, and the third dog jumped over the top of the second dog.

It was something to see.

This act was clearly a favorite, and I could understand why Raven saved it for last.

When the comedy ended, all of the players ran out onto the stage to hold hands and bow, and Raven thanked the audience for their kindness. But I barely saw or heard this last part as the unwanted roaring in my ears was beginning to shut out other sounds. I was terrified.

Everyone came back behind the curtain, chattering excitedly, and moments later, Teresa and Michel appeared with the hats.

"A good take for such a small town," Teresa said, handing her hat to Raven. "Look."

He glanced at the hat and kissed the side of her face, and then took the hat from Michel and poured them together. A few moments later, he began handing out coins, giving some to everyone who had performed, and then giving some to the three men who had not performed, but who had helped set up the stage and Lizbeth's tent.

From what I could see, he gave away about half and then poured the rest into a brown canvas pouch. When this was over, he looked to me.

Of course I received nothing, as I had been only a spectator.

"What did you think?" he asked, his voice still filled with excitement.

I was speechless.

"What do you think you might do?" he pressed.

Jade heard this and looked at him. "What do you mean? You told me you brought her along to use her in the show. You must have a plan."

"I…I…" My stammering sounded weak, but I had no idea what to say. "Could I not work behind the curtain?"

"Behind the curtain?" Jade stepped closer to us both, and her eyes were blazing.

But Raven held up one hand to stop her from speaking, and he looked to me. "Kara, you'll need to take part in the show. Surely you can dance?"

When would I have ever have learned to dance?

"No," I answered. "I cannot dance…I cannot sing…I cannot do any of the things you do. Please let me be of use in other ways."

Jade hissed through her teeth and glared at Raven. "You liar."

Whirling, she stormed off, heading in the direction of the camp. Raven stood stunned for a few seconds and then ran after her. "Jade!"

The others glanced at me askance, but no one said anything.

\* \* \* \*

Although the last thing I wanted was a confrontation with Jade, I knew I had to fix this. There must be *something* I could do for the group besides perform.

Only moments after Raven left, I started back for the camp myself, hoping I could catch the two of them alone, and they might find some duties to assign me. My only concern would be payment. Earning money would be necessary if I was to send a message to my lady.

Remembering the way back easily, I entered the camp determined to find a resolution to this problem. But the sound of raised voices reached me, coming from inside the wagon parked beside ours: Jade's wagon.

The shutters were open, and Raven and Jade were shouting at each other.

"Don't ever call me a liar in front of the troupe!" he yelled. "Not ever."

"Why not? You are a liar. You told me the girl was coming with us because you wanted to use her in the show. I believed you! I can see she'd draw a crowd. I even kept quiet when you moved her into your wagon!"

"You've hardly kept quiet."

"Don't play the fool with me. It doesn't work. Now, I find out she has no skill in performing at all? You never had any idea what she'd do. Why did you bring her along then, Raven? Why?"

Silence followed. Then Raven said, "She'll be in the show. I'm just not sure what I'll have her do yet."

"Well, you'd better figure it out! She's not strong enough to build up or take down the stage, and we don't need anyone else passing hats, and I'm not feeding dead weight. None of us will." Another silence followed, and she said more quietly. "You'd better figure it out."

As I absorbed her words, one thing became clear to me. Of the men, only three did not partake in some way in the show itself. Even Michel worked the crowds passing a hat. But of those three men who did not partake, they'd done most of the heavy work setting up the stage and Lizbeth's tent. All six of the women in the group took some part in the show, with Lizbeth reading fortunes and Teresa working the crowd with a hat.

Footsteps sounded, and the door to the wagon slammed open. Raven came down taking the stairs two at a time. When he saw me on the ground, he stopped.

For the first time, when he looked at me, his eyes held neither amusement nor protection nor pity. Instead, they held…regret. I couldn't draw a breath. He regretted bringing me along. What would happen if he and Jade decided I wasn't worth the trouble? Would I be cast out with no money and no way to send a message to my lady?

Without a word, he walked past me, heading back toward the market. I let him go. He was not the one who needed to figure this out.

I was.

# Chapter Six

Late that afternoon, everyone gathered once again behind the stage. I kept myself apart, determined to watch and think of something I might do to help—anything. I was frightened of being cast away, and I needed a share of the coins that were earned.

Raven still hadn't spoken to me, and it appeared he and Jade weren't speaking to each other more than was necessary. However, they were both determined the acts would be perfectly timed and flawless, and I suspected that in spite of their differences with each other, they shared a mutual love of running this show.

After a deep breath, Raven stepped out to begin calling the crowd. Hours had passed since the first show, and now different people, doing their shopping, occupied the market.

"Welcome my friends!" Raven called from the stage. "To the finest show in all of Samourè."

I took my same place downstage, peering out from between the curtain and the pole. The acts went on in the same order as this morning, and watching Jemma dance or Tannen and Badger's feats of strength did nothing to help me. It was only when Jade stepped out and began her song that something tickled the back of my neck. Again, I couldn't help noticing how far she stood back and that although her voice was lovely, she did nothing besides sing the words to tell the story of the poor girl who loses her love to war—and then pays the price. It was a fine story, but the audience was not engaged. They listened. They applauded. But few coins were thrown into the hats.

Then Ash went out and began his act, and I noticed how he moved, how close he was to the crowd, how he looked into their faces.

An idea hit me. The prospect was terrifying, but doing nothing was worse.

I went to Raven, who was watching the stage between the break in the curtains.

Touching his arm, I whispered. "I can tell stories."

He glanced down at me. "What?"

"I can tell stories," I rushed on. "My lady had many books with stories… adventures, comedies, ghost stories, romances, tragedies. I would read the stories to myself first, and to entertain her, I'd act them out. I can do voices, and I know when to pause and when to speak slowly and when to speak quickly."

I had his attention now, but he looked over the top of my head. "Jade, come here."

When he explained to her what I had in mind, to my relief, she appeared interested but said to me, "I don't know. You're just going to go out there and tell a story? You could lose the crowd, and if they wander off, we'll lose money on the remaining acts."

"I won't lose them," I said, trying for a confidence I did not feel.

She looked to Raven. "What do you think?"

He shrugged. "It's one show in a small town. I say we let her try."

Nodding, she said, "All right. Best send her out after the dance number but before Marcel and the dogs." Now that she was focused on the show, all personal hostilities appeared forgotten. "Kara, look at me. Let me get that cloak off you and do something with your hair."

Out on stage, Ash was wrapping up the last of his fortune telling, and Raven had Marcel, Bonham, and the girls ready to go out. I tried to ignore all the activity.

Jade removed my cloak and nodded at my ice blue dress. "It may not be sensible for travel, but it works well here." She brushed my hair and used her fingers to fluff it all around my shoulders so that it hung like a blanket of silver-blond. "Your slippers are dirty," she said. "That won't do."

"I don't have anything else with me. Might I borrow some?"

She thought for a few seconds and then said, "Just take then off and go barefoot. It will make you look even more otherworldly."

"Otherworldly?"

"That's a good thing here," she said. "Use it for all it's worth."

She had me ready by the time the second dance act was nearly finished. I stood nervous but determined.

Raven leaned down and asked, "What kind of story do you plan to tell?"

I already knew. "A romance."

"You'll have a few seconds' leeway while they get a first look at you. I've kept you covered since our arrival for a reason. Use those few seconds to gather yourself. Once you start, make sure your voice carries all the way to the back of the crowd. You don't have to be loud, just clear."

Swallowing hard, I nodded.

Marcel, Bonham, and the three dancers came in.

Raven stepped out. "My friends," he called. "We have a new performer for you today, someone special to tell you a tale that will tug your heart strings." Stepping back, he held open one side of the curtain. "May I present...the lady."

Drawing a breath, knowing there was no turning back, I walked out onto the stage as Raven vanished behind the curtain.

Gasps sounded as people took in the sight of my near-white hair, crystalline blue eyes, pale skin, ice blue gown, and bare feet. Remembering Raven's advice, I used the few seconds of shock to gather myself and then moved forward, all the way to the front edge of the stage, just as Ash had. The nearest people could have reached out and touched me.

As everyone stared, I looked one by one into the faces of several people who stood closest to me, letting them know that I *saw* them too, that we were connected. This was how I always told stories to Lady Giselle. The hearer needed to feel connected to the tale.

"There once was a soldier," I began, letting my voice carry to the back of the crowd, "who fell in love with the proud and beautiful daughter of a nobleman. She was tall and slender, with eyes of green and locks of waving red hair. She wore the finest gowns of satin and velvet. Though the girl was set above him, the soldier was of good name and family, and he found her alone in her family's garden. There, he fell to his knees, begging for her hand."

The crowd remained silent, and all eyes were upon me. Again, I looked out and down, gazing one at a time into several more faces.

"But she laughed at his pleas," I went on, "and spurned him, telling him he had nothing he might offer to her. In shame he fled the garden and had almost reached the gates of her family's manor when a voice came from behind, calling, 'Wait!' Turning, he saw a young woman running toward him. She was pretty, but small and simply dressed. Still burning in shame, he had no wish to speak to anyone, but the girl rushed to him, saying, 'Do not despair so easily. For I am the lady's maid, and I know her well. Go back to her and ask her to set you with three tasks. If you can fulfill three tasks for her, she will consider your proposal.'"

Here I paused for effect. Stretching out both my hands, I began to imagine that I was back at the manor, telling this tale to Lady Giselle. I went on to tell of the three tasks that were set for the solider by his haughty love.

First, she asked him to fetch a silver apple guarded by three great wolves. The soldier had little idea how to gain the apple, but the young maid went with him, and hid in the trees and howled like a wolf herself and distracted the wolves long enough for him to steal the apple. While telling this part of the story, I howled like a wolf and then acted out the soldier sneaking in to make his theft, fulfilling the first task.

He and the maid escaped to make their way back to the manor.

The haughty lady was not impressed, but she took the apple and then bade the soldier to steal a white stallion guarded by three giants. He had little idea how to gain the stallion, but again, the maid went with him, and dressed up like a fairy sprite and performed a dance to distract the giants just long enough for the soldier to steal the horse, fulfilling the second task.

He and the maid escaped together and rode the stallion back to the manor.

Again, the haughty lady merely sneered, accepted the stallion, and set him a third task of stealing a jeweled bracelet from a den of thieves. The young maid traveled with him, and when they reached the den of thieves, she told the soldier she would sing for the thieves and distract them.

"But in that moment," I said slowly to the crowd, "the soldier feared the thought of her placing herself in danger by letting the thieves even see her...and he realized that he no longer loved the haughty lady. Falling to his knees before the maid, he said, 'It is you who have helped me, you who have stood at my side, and it is you I love. I would ask for your hand'."

All around me in the crowd, I saw soft smiles on people's faces as the foolish soldier finally came to his senses.

"The maid fell to her knees as well and accepted his love, for she had long loved him. And he took her to his family home and married her, and neither of them ever saw the haughty lady again."

I dropped my arms to signal the tale was done.

At first, only silence followed, and then someone cheered, and the crowd burst into applause. On the outskirts, Teresa and Michel were both watching me in disbelief, but the sounds of clapping spurred them into action.

They wove through the crowd with their hats, and I heard many coins clinking.

Raven came back out onto the stage, and that was my cue to go behind the curtain so that he could announce Marcel and the dogs.

After bowing once, I walked past Raven off the stage.

Out back, all the members of the group, including Marcel, appeared speechless as I came through the curtain. Then Jade came back to herself.

"Marcel, go," she urged, and he ran onto the stage with his dogs barking and yipping at his heels.

Raven came back, but he wasn't looking at me. He looked to Jade. "She had them in her hand. Don't you think?"

As opposed to being angered by this praise of me, Jade nodded to him eagerly. "Yes. The way she does the voices and actions...It was like watching a play. Oh, and I liked that touch of you introducing her as 'the lady'. We can use that. Didn't you say she had some silk gowns in her trunk?"

"Yes, more than one."

"Good."

For once, I didn't mind them speaking of me as if I weren't there. They were both so pleased that all I could feel was relief.

Jade turned to me, "Kara, how many stories like that one do you know?"

"Dozens," I answered. "Dozens and dozens. I could tell two stories a day for weeks and never tell the same one twice."

To my shock, she grabbed my face, kissing the top of my head. Then she beamed at Raven. "We have a new act."

\* \* \* \*

Not long after this, the men began taking down the stage.

But as they worked, Raven passed out coins from the hats, again pouring about half the money into the brown canvas pouch.

He gave me five of the coins.

Though I was beyond relieved to have found some way to add to the show, I had no idea how much he'd given me or what the coins might be worth. Moreover, though I knew I should save them, I wanted to do something for the group to show my gratitude. They had fed and housed me when I had been no help to them at all.

Now, I had something to offer, at least while I was still with them, and I wanted to repay their kindness.

Going to Raven, I said quietly, "Would you do something for me?"

"Mmmmmmm?" he asked absently, still overseeing the last of the stage being taken down.

"I'd like to buy a few things at the market. Will you escort me?"

"The market?" He blinked and then appeared to actually hear what I'd said. "Oh...of course. I need a few things too." Turning, he called, "Tannen! Get everyone back and start getting the gear stowed. I'll be along soon."

With that, he offered me his arm and led me into the busy market. I was not wearing my cloak now, and people watched us walk past. A few stopped and told me they had enjoyed the story. I knew enough to simply smile and offer thanks. The cool autumn air smelled of bread, sausages, and perfumed candles. I'd never experienced anything like this.

In the heart of the market, Raven took out the brown canvas pouch. "I divide half the money between the group, and we save half for supplies, food, upkeep on the wagons, and grain for the horses."

Looking toward a stall selling beeswax candles, he said, "I'll be over there. What do you need to buy?"

The first thing I wanted was freshly baked bread to share at supper. "Over there," I said, pointing to a stall with a man selling bread and rolls.

With a nod, he walked off to purchase candles, and I headed toward the baker.

The man was about forty years old, with quick, light brown eyes and a beard. He smiled at me, "What can for you?"

Counting in my head, I pondered how much bread would be needed for everyone. "Five loaves please." As he readied the bread, I wondered how I might carry my purchases home, for I wanted to find some honey as well. "Do you have a burlap sack I might buy?"

"Yes, of course."

He placed all five loaves into the sack, looked at me expectantly, and I realized he wanted me to pay him. Embarrassment flooded through me. I had no idea what a loaf of bread cost or the value of the coins Raven had given me.

Holding the coins out to show him, I asked, "How much for the five loaves?"

He started in surprise, furthering my embarrassment, and then said, "Those coins will just about be enough."

This was disappointing. I wouldn't have enough to purchase honey after all.

"Torrence!" a voice barked from behind me.

The man's eyes widened, and I half-turned to see Raven striding toward us.

"What in the seven hells are you doing?" Raven demanded of the baker.

"I was just…just…"

"Just taking advantage."

I'd never seen Raven this angry.

He took a single coin from my hand and gave it to the baker, saying, "You try that again, and I'll complain to the merchants' guild and call you out for the cheat you are."

At this, the man grimaced and seemed about to spit a retort when Raven grabbed the bag of bread with one hand and put the other on my back, propelling me away from the booth. Only moments before, I'd been happy at the thought of shopping, of buying something with money I'd earned. Now I was humiliated.

Once we were several stalls away, Raven stopped. "How could you have held out your money like that, inviting him to take what he wanted?"

My humiliation grew, and I spoke barely loud enough to be heard. "I didn't know how much the bread might cost."

"What it costs? How can you not know the price of bread?"

All the fear and worry from the past few days rose up inside me. "Because I don't know the price of anything!" I cried loud enough to turn a few heads. "I don't even know how much money you've given me. How could I? These are first coins I've ever touched."

The remaining anger flooded from his face. "The first coins? Ever?"

Dropping my gaze, I nodded. "I told you I'd never been off the manor grounds. Where would I need money?"

For a moment, he didn't speak, and when I looked up, I saw the same flicker of regret in his eyes that I'd seen earlier.

"I'm sorry," he said.

"Are you sorry you brought me?"

"No. But come on, and I'll show you what things cost. What else do you need to buy?"

"Some honey. I wanted to share the bread tonight at supper. In truth, I was hoping that I had enough coins to buy supplies to cook a main dish for supper."

He offered his arm again. "If you're buying for the group, I'll pay for it. Just show me what you need."

Slowly, the afternoon began to brighten again as we walked through the market, choosing ingredients together. Raven took out the brown canvas pouch. He explained what things cost, and showed me coins of different values. Copper coins were worth less, and silver worth more. We bought an urn of honey. Then we bought red lentils, a ham hock, dried parsley, and oregano. The dish I had in mind required onions, but we had those back at camp.

"Do you think there's a chance of any late season tomatoes?" I asked.

"Vegetables are this way," he said, pointing, "But if we find tomatoes, they won't be cheap."

Each autumn, before the first frost, servants back at the manor had gathered up all the green tomatoes and brought them to the kitchen where they would still turn red over time. I knew this because I was sometimes allowed to help in the kitchen—as I enjoyed making a special breakfast or lunch for my lady.

Soon enough, Raven and I found a stall selling the last of the autumn tomatoes.

"Are they too expensive?" I asked. "They do add flavor to the dish."

He bought six of them, and I found myself feeling happy again.

It had been a good afternoon.

\* \* \* \*

The moment we arrived back at the camp, I began prepping dinner. First, I heated water in the large pot hanging over the fire, and I added lentils and the ham hock—knowing the lentils would take some time to soften.

Later, I added chopped onions, diced tomatoes, parsley, and oregano. When it was nearly ready, I began slicing bread and spreading honey. At dusk, the group gathered, bringing low stools and small benches, and Raven brought a cask of ale. The evening felt like a celebration, but more than that, there was a stark difference in how I was treated.

As I had performed today, I was part of the troupe.

As of yet, none of the men had said more than a few words to me, but now, Marcel offered me a stool, and he dropped down to sit on the ground beside me, chatting about how he might improve his act with the dogs.

Ash set a stool down beside me, and as he took a bite from his bowl of lentils, he made a sound of pleasure. "This is good, Kara. Thank you."

Young Sean sat near me, and I made sure he had a thick slice of the bread with honey.

Soon, everyone was eating and chatting, and for the first time, I felt at ease—even wanted—among them. Raven and Jade seemed to have forgotten their earlier argument, and they sat together.

"I shouldn't have been so harsh," Jade said to him. "You saw something in her that I didn't, and you did bring her along to put her in the show."

"I should have been more honest back at the settlement," he answered, "and let you know I wasn't even sure where to place her. I should have told you."

"With a little more work, she could have a fine act. I'll help her with a better costume once we reach Narbonnè."

"I'm wondering about the rotation. Maybe we should place her right in the middle of the show?"

"No, I think she works well in between the dance of the three girls and Marcel's dog act."

They chatted on, and again, I sensed that their mutual love of the show would keep them together above all other difficulties.

I had just begun enjoying my own lentils, when Jemma asked, "Kara, did you buy any butter?"

"No. Sean can't have butter, and I wanted to bring something he could have on his bread."

As I said this, Jade broke off her discussion with Raven. "You bought honey just so Sean could have some on his bread?"

Puzzled at her reaction, I nodded. "Yes. I knew butter would make him sick."

She glanced away, as if embarrassed. What did she have to be embarrassed about?

# Chapter Seven

The next morning, we rolled out of Fayette and traveled east for three days. By now, the rhythms of the day were becoming natural to me, and I required no instructions to help set up camp or start meals. I knelt on the ground to fry oatcakes on the metal sheet over the fire.

Raven told me we'd earn good money in Narbonnè and we'd be staying at least two weeks, perhaps longer. This was welcome news to me. If I could earn coins quickly enough, I could send a message to my lady, and she might have time to send a swift rider after me. It troubled me to think on how lonely she must be, or if she'd learned of my capture and spent her days worrying. I would set things right soon.

But for now, I was content to travel with this group and share a wagon with Raven. I'd managed to clean the interior, folding his spare clothing and stacking it in the cupboard. I'd swept and dusted. At first, this had annoyed him, but then he seemed to rather like the organized cupboard.

Though the nights were growing cold, he never complained about sleeping on the roof.

I sat beside him on the bench all day. Sometimes, he told me stories of his youth, traveling in these wagons with his father. He rarely spoke about his mother. But much of the time, we had no need to speak.

On the second night of our journey to Narbonnè, by the campfire, I overheard Jemma ask him, "Raven, would you like to send Kara to ride with us tomorrow? I know you prefer to drive alone, and she's been with you for days now."

"No," he answered. "She doesn't bother me. I like having her on the bench. She never argues or asks anything of me."

I couldn't help wondering what this meant.

The next morning, Sean asked if he could ride on the bench with me, and Raven did not object. Glad for Sean's company, I set him between us. He was clearly fond of Raven—and possibly seeking approval from the leader of the troupe.

But shortly into the day's journey, Sean leaned into me and asked quietly. "Will you tell me the story again? The one about the boy and wolves?"

I smiled and began, "There was once a village beset by wolves..."

After this story, he had me tell three more, and the time passed swiftly. I was both eager and nervous to reach the city, eager as it brought me closer to my goal, and nervous because I'd found the town of Fayette nearly overwhelming and feared the prospect of a larger place.

In the late afternoon, we came to a river, but instead of finding a way to cross, Raven turned us onto a road leading south along the shore, downstream.

"Not far now," he said.

"Tell me about Narbonnè," I said.

"It's the largest city in Samourè, but the oldest too, surrounded by a thick wall of mortared stone, and its position right on the river allows for trade and commerce. You'll see barges docked there, bringing goods all the way from Partheney."

In my mind, I couldn't visualize much of what he described, and his words brought me no ease or comfort.

"There's a castle on a hill at the center," he went on, "but King Amandine seldom lives there. As I said, the city is old, and the castle is said to be somewhat primitive. He prefers his newer dwelling in the west, in Lascaùx."

I knew where the king lived, as my lady had educated me, but Raven's explanations did not help clarify much, so I stopped asking questions. Before dusk, I caught my first glimpse of a great wall up ahead, and my stomach tightened.

But Sean leaned forward excitedly. "I can see it!"

As we approached, the wall loomed larger until the road gently curved, one side going around the city, and the other leading to the riverside docks. A short path led straight forward to the huge arch and rounded wooden gates of the Narbonnè north entrance. Guards in varied light armor manned the entrance, but they all wore bright red tabards with black trim.

"Colors of the city constabulary," Raven explained.

He drew in our horses, stood up on the bench, and looked backward. I assumed he was making sure we had everyone caught up and in the line before entering. Sitting back down, he said, "Kara, pull up the hood of your cloak."

Quickly, I did as he asked, and he gripped our reins to drive us forward.

The guards at the entrance didn't question us and waved us through. One of them even called a greeting to Raven.

"We've been coming at the same time for years," Raven explained.

Then...we rolled into the teeming city. As expected there were crowds of people walking or riding around us. Though my stomach was still tight, I felt safe enough up here on the bench with Raven and Sean. People made room for us, and Raven kept the horses at a steady walk. All five of the other wagons came behind us in a line.

Shops and taverns and eateries and dwellings passed by on both sides.

As always, Raven never hesitated and drove us on and on, turning left and right until I was completely lost, and then again, as in Fayette, we came to a large stable with open space on one side.

"It's best to set camp near a stable," he said, "with a ready supply of hay to buy for the horses. Plus, there's always a water pump."

"But as before..." I asked, "we are welcome here?"

"Absolutely. We put on a quality show. The city constable and I have an understanding."

He did not elaborate.

Though I'd expected to be terrified, as we lined up the wagons and began to set up camp, this seemed almost like any other night. We might be inside a vast city, but our group was set apart, in our camp, caring for our horses and building a fire. Along the road, we'd gathered a good supply of branches.

My blue dress was spotted with flecks of mud and trail dust, and the only other day dress in my trunk was white. I hoped we'd have an opportunity to wash clothing here.

As Jade and I got a fire going, Jemma said, "I've been saving eggs, and I think I have enough to make my egg drop soup for supper. Raven likes that."

"Oh, so do I," Jade answered.

"Don't bother on my account," Raven said, coming from our wagon and wearing a clean wool shirt. "I'm going out."

"Out?" Jade repeated, standing straight and putting her hands to her hips. "We haven't even unpacked the stairs yet."

He ignored her and continued walking out of the camp. Her cheeks flushed red with anger, but I was somewhat alarmed at the thought of him leaving us on our first night in this city.

"Where is he going?"

"To a tavern, I'll wager," Jade answered. "To drink and find himself some whore who doesn't cost much."

I flinched at both her words and tone, but Jemma shrugged as she poured water into the cooking pot. "It's Raven. He does as he likes."

Taking her hands from her hips, Jade's anger seemed to deflate. "Yes. He does."

* * * *

After dinner, Jade left the other women to handle the cleanup, and she called me over.

"I've had your trunk moved to my wagon for now."

"Why?"

"Come on, and you'll see."

I'd not been inside Jade's wagon before, but it was much larger than Raven's. Two bunks, one above the other, had been built into the back wall, with two more in a side wall. There was a secured table and bench, and a fine set of cupboards painted bright yellow.

"Tannen and Badger take the back bunks," she explained. "Sean sleeps in this lower side bunk, and I sleep in the one above him."

There was a time when I would have found such close quarters with other people unsettling, but now it seemed to offer a sense of comfort and safety. I'd come to feel safe with Raven sleeping right above me.

My trunk had been placed on the larger bed and a full-length mirror stood beside it. Going to my trunk, she opened it and breathed out through her mouth. "Oh, Kara."

I went to join her as she drew out my ice blue silk.

"Look at this fabric," she said. Then she saw my white silk. "Oh, that's the one. We'll have you all in white."

But beneath white silk, she saw my white muslin and frowned. "Why did you pack only gowns of white or light blue?"

"I didn't pack the trunk…and all of my gowns are white or light blue. My lady liked me only in those colors."

Slowly, Jade sank down onto the bed. "Your lady?"

"Did Raven tell you nothing?"

"I know Caine took you from some noblemen as property, but that's all I know." Her face softened. "Who is this lady?"

For the first time since being taken from my home, I felt a connection to another woman. Jade was asking about my life, and she was interested in hearing the answers. In a rush, I found myself telling her everything, from my birth, to being claimed as ward, to my life with Lady Giselle. How I always dressed her for dinner. How she sometimes enjoyed dressing me in these gowns and doing my hair. How I spent my days reading the emotions in her face and finding ways to amuse her or make her happy.

I thought Jade would understand my worry for Giselle, but after a while, she interrupted me.

"Kara, wait. Are you telling me that she's the one who ordered all your gowns in only these two shades, and until Caine took you, you'd spent your life inside a manor with a lonely, neglected wife...and your duty was to keep her from being bored? You served as an unpaid lady's maid. She kept you away from everyone else, and she liked to dress you up like a doll?"

"No! No, that's not what I'm telling you."

"That's exactly what you're telling me."

How could Jade have misunderstood?

"She was kind to me," I finished lamely.

"Maybe." She stood and reached into the trunk. "But I understand you better now, and I think you're better off with us." Holding up my white silk, she added. "Tomorrow, I'll be the one who'll dress you up like a doll, but for a good reason."

\* \* \* \*

I didn't know what time Raven got back that night, but I was awakened by the sound of him walking on the roof. Even under the blankets I was cold, and while drifting off to sleep again, I knew he'd not be able to continue sleeping outdoors much longer. Some other arrangements would need to be made.

When I awoke the next morning, the camp was already bustling, and as I looked out the door, Raven was up and about, seeming no worse for wear. Perhaps he'd not been drinking at a tavern the night before.

Upon spotting me in the wagon doorway, he strode over.

"As soon as I'm dressed, I'm going with some of the men to set up the stage. You stay here and let Jade get you ready. She mentioned washing all the girls' hair. What types of stories have you planned for today?"

"A comedy and an adventure."

He nodded. "Do the adventure this morning and save the comedy for afternoon."

Then he came up the short stairs, moving past me inside our wagon, and I went off to Jade's.

\* \* \* \*

By late morning, Jade had all the women—along with herself—dressed for the show. She covered me with a cloak and pulled up the hood.

"We need to leave now," she told everyone. "Raven will be waiting."

Ash, Marcel, and Bonham came from a wagon to join us, and soon, everyone who'd remained back here at camp was gathered.

I had no idea where to go, but Jade did, and I allowed myself to be swept along in the small sea of performers, children, and dogs. The walk was longer than I'd expected. With my hood up, I saw little of the city around me, but perhaps that was for the best.

Finally, I found myself behind the curtain at the back of the stage. Raven, Tannen, Badger, and Michel were already there.

Drawing me up into Raven's view, Jade asked him, "What do you think?"

Then she removed my cloak. Raven stood there taking in every detail of my appearance. After having washed my hair and let it dry, Jade had used a round metal rod to enhance the curl in the natural waves. I wore clean slippers, and the white silk of the gown made my hair and eyes glow.

Raven couldn't seem to speak.

Without noticing this, Jade was beyond pleased. "I can't wait to see how the crowd reacts. She looks like some winter fairy risen up from the snow."

"Yes," he managed to agree, his voice hoarse.

As Jade moved to fluff Jemma's hair, Raven's eyes were still on me. Then he turned away. "I need to start calling the crowd."

He vanished through the curtain, and I heard the now-familiar refrain.

"Welcome my friends! To the finest show in all of Samourè."

I didn't listen to the next part, as I was trying to drum up my courage, but then I heard him call out, "The dance of the sprite!"

Marcel and Bonham ran out with their violins. After giving them a few seconds, Jemma ran after.

Raven came back through.

I moved downstage so I could peer out the curtain. I hadn't even seen the size of the market, much less the size of the crowd. When I looked out at the seemingly endless rows of faces, I nearly felt ill.

Glancing at me from the center point, he mouthed, "You all right?"

I nodded.

Tannen and Badger went on next, performing feats of strength, then Jade, and then Ash. When Raven announced the dance of the three, I knew I was up next. Though the dance number was fairly long, it seemed to go by in an instant, and then Marcel, Bonham, and the three girls came dashing back through the curtain.

Raven took the stage again, and I took my place in the center, backstage.

"My friends!" he called. "We have a special performer with us today, someone to dazzle you with a tale of adventure and excitement." He held one side of the curtain open. "May I present, the lady in white."

As he stepped back, I stepped out and again walked all the way to the front edge of the stage. This time, there were no gasps. Instead, everyone, hundreds of people, fell completely silent, taking in my hair and the fine white silk of my gown.

Jade's words echoed.

*She looks like some winter fairy risen up from the snow.*

I knew I had to be otherworldly, and at the same time, I had to make a connection. Again, I said nothing at first and simply looked from face to face, making eye contact, connecting with people and allowing them to connect with me.

Then I thought of my lady and pretended I was acting out a story for her.

"There was once a young man who grew tired of his parents and his home and his life," I began, "He decided to become a sailor and run away to sea."

At the word "sea," I spread my arms wide to create an image of the ocean. Then I continued to tell of how the young man joined a crew, but he sailed only four days before pirates attacked the ship, and all the men aboard were killed and he was taken hostage as a slave to the pirate captain.

I acted out the pirates killing the crew and taking their hostage. I dropped my voice low whenever the pirate captain spoke.

The crowd remained silent, listening and watching.

In the story, the young man grew older and stronger and learned how to fight with a sword. Finally, the captain sailed the pirates to an island where they'd hidden a great treasure. But there, he planned to maroon most of his own crew, keep only a few to sail the ship, and keep the treasure for himself.

Since he considered the young man a weakling, he shared his secret and promised to spare the young man's life if he would help maroon most of the other pirates. But the young man played a trick, and that night he had the pirates hide all around a clearing, and inside the clearing, he got the captain to reveal his traitorous plan.

When the other pirates heard, they no longer trusted their captain, and the young man challenged him to a fight. The captain laughed and drew his sword, but in the end, the young man killed him, and then he became captain of the pirates.

Telling this story took some time.

I did not rush, but acted out each part of the tale for the crowd, and when I had reached the last word, I dropped my arms to my sides and bowed my head.

Silence hung in the air at first, and then thunderous applause broke out. People shouted for another tale. Teresa and Michel were ready this time and wove quickly through the crowd with their hats. I heard coins clinking as Raven stepped out, motioning to me with one hand.

"The lady in white!" he called again.

I bowed once and walked off the stage, not hearing anything that followed. Jade had to catch me as my legs almost gave way backstage, but then Marcel and the dogs went past, and suddenly Raven stood beside me.

His face was unusually pale, and he wouldn't meet my gaze. "That was...that was good."

Hearing his praise meant something to me, more than hearing praise from my lady, and I didn't know why.

"We need to get you out of that gown, so we can lay it on a bed and keep it clean until the next show," Jade said in my ear. "Can you come with me now?"

There was nothing I would have rather done than flee the stage with Jade, and I nodded, still clinging to her arm.

* * * *

Back inside the safe four walls of Jade's wagon, I finally felt able to breathe. She didn't appear to notice my state though, and could not contain her enthusiasm.

"You've a natural gift, Kara," she said. "Raven always describes us to town magistrates as 'a quality show', and you add something."

A thought nagged at me. "I'm not vain enough to think the crowd reacts only to my ability to tell a story. They're caught up in the illusion of how I look."

"They're caught up in everything! Yes, your unusual appearance matters, and so does that fine silk gown. It's the gown of a noblewoman. But...you can do more. You can do what Ash does. You hold their full attention. Few people can do that."

Her praise mattered to me, as did Raven's, and I tried not to think of my plans to earn money and then abandon them. But my lady certainly needed me more than they did.

Jade unlaced the back of my gown so I could step out. My dirt-specked ice blue muslin lay on a bunk, and I reached for it.

"Wait," she said. "I have a few things for you."

"Things?"

Going to the lower side bunk, she picked up a wool dress of deep red and a pair of small boots. "This dress was mine before I had Sean, and I've spent the past few nights hemming it. I think it will fit you. I know you need something warmer than what you have. The boots were Jemma's, but she bought a new pair last year. These are old but still usable."

As she spoke, I could hardly believe what she was saying. The women here had worried for me and found proper clothing for me. Jade had spent her nights hemming. Not trusting myself to speak, I put on the dress and the boots. They fit. I was warm and comfortable.

Then she wove my hair back into a single braid so the color was not quite so obvious.

"We'll take it down again before the afternoon show," she said, "but the braid will add even more waves."

Looking into the mirror, I couldn't help tears stinging my eyes.

"Oh, Jade."

She'd given me much more than a dress and boots. She'd made me look more like one of them. She'd helped me to blend. There was no way I could thank her enough.

Waving me off, she said, "Oh, it's nothing. No one was using those." Then she paused. "But…"

"But what?"

"Part of putting on a quality show means quality costumes, and Jemma's stage dress is worn thin and has been mended too many times. You don't have to say yes, but I was wondering if she might wear that blue silk in your trunk."

"Oh, of course. Please take it for her. She can wear it in the afternoon show."

That blue silk was nothing to me. I had no use for it, and Jemma had given me a pair of boots. But Jade's face broke into a broad smile.

"Thank you, Kara. You've a generous heart. We could never buy something like that." She grasped my hand. "I'm sorry for the way I've treated you. When Raven first brought you, I knew nothing of your past, and I thought he was…well, never mind what I thought. I was wrong, and he was right to place you in his own wagon. He always meant to put you in the show, and you needed a little extra privacy. I see that now."

This was quite a speech, and I didn't follow all of it, but her apology meant a great deal to me. To my mind, she had nothing to apologize for, but the fact that she cared to say these things touched me deeply.

"You've nothing to be sorry for," I said.

"I do, and when I think of that day you brought honey back from the market so Sean could have it on his bread, I'm ashamed of myself."

Unable to answer, I simply gripped her hand.

\* \* \* \*

The days passed.

I was part of the troupe, and yet I wasn't—because I planned to leave. We performed twice a day, and every few days, Raven had the stage moved to a new part of the city. Word of my stories began to spread, and as our crowds continued to grow, so did our profits.

But every time Raven gave me my share, I stowed the coins away, having some idea of their value now, and my plan never wavered. I couldn't remain with these people, and none of them knew it. Something about this pained me, but my lady needed me more.

Five days after arriving in Narbonnè, after the second show, I counted my coins. If I included the silver hair clips, I believed I would have enough to bribe some local man—with a horse—into riding to the de Marco estate with a message.

That afternoon, after the second show, once I'd changed into my wool dress and boots, Jade, Jemma, and I went to the market to buy supplies for dinner. When no one was watching, I purchased a quill, paper, and ink.

The merchant at the booth was middle-aged and soft-spoken.

Quietly, I asked him, "Sir, if I wished to send a written message north, where might I find someone to hire? I can pay."

"How far north?"

I wasn't precisely sure, so I answered, "To the de Marco vineyards, to the manor there. Do you know it?"

"I know *of* it," he said. His brows knitted. "I have a nephew, Stephen, who's paying off a debt. He's been working nights at the Iron Boar tavern, but for the right price, I think he'd take it for you. He can borrow a horse from me."

This was easier than I'd imagined. "Thank you. How might I speak to him?"

"Come to the Iron Boar tonight. You can speak to him there. Do you know it?"

I shook my head, and he gave me directions. The place was not far.

* * * *

That evening after dinner, as we sat around the fire, I asked Jade, "When we leave this city, where will we go next?"

Raven sat nearby, listening.

"To a town about a day downriver called Corlean."

"Will we stay long?"

"A few days."

I looked toward the small, white wagon. "Would you mind if I didn't help with clean-up tonight? I'm feeling tired."

She stood, seeming concerned. "Are you well?"

"I'm well, just a little weary."

"Yes, that ghost story you told this afternoon was long, but the audience loved it. Go and lie down."

My status in the group had changed over the past few days, and I didn't feel guilty leaving without helping to clean up. My act was bringing in more money than any of the others.

After saying goodnight, I went to the wagon and lit a candle.

Then I sat at Raven's table and wrote a letter to my lady, telling her what had happened to me and letting her know I would be in Narbonnè for another week, after which we would be traveling to Corlean. I sent her my love, and my certainty that we would be together again soon. Then I folded the message into quarters.

Blowing out the candle, I sat alone at the table…and I waited.

Later, I heard the sounds of water being splashed over the campfire, and the calls of people saying goodnight. Not long after, I heard Raven climb up onto the flat roof above me. Still, I waited until long after everything around me had fallen quiet.

Finally, I stood, donned my cloak, and slipped from the wagon, carrying the written message. All my money and the silver hair clips were stowed in the pocket of my cloak.

Though the thought of traveling into the city at night frightened me, I had no choice and hurried from the camp into the streets of Narbonnè. I knew the way to the market by now, and the merchant I'd spoken to had provided clear instructions for finding the Iron Boar from there.

Keeping my hood up, I walked swiftly, first to the market and then down a side street. Here I began passing soldiers and bargemen and women with painted faces and low-cut gowns. Trying to remain invisible, I continued on until at last I spotted a sign up ahead depicting a dark gray boar with tusks.

Once I reached the closed door to the tavern, the sounds of raucous laughter came from inside, and I hesitated. How would I do this? Go inside and ask for Stephen? That seemed the only option. Still hesitating, I held the note up to look at it under the dim light from a distant streetlamp.

There was no turning back now, and I reached out for the door latch.

I never touched it.

From nowhere, a hand came from the darkness and grabbed my wrist, pulling me around and pressing my arm up against the outer wall of the tavern. Wild fear coursed through me at the strength of the hand on my wrist. I nearly cried out...and then found myself looking up into Raven's black eyes. He snatched the message from my hand.

"What is this?"

After an instant of relief that it was Raven who held me—and not some stranger seeking to do me harm—despair set in. He'd followed me.

"Why don't you read it and see," I whispered.

"I can't read, but I probably don't need to read it to guess. You're trying to send a message to your lady?"

Dropping my gaze a few inches, I focused on his solid jaw line and didn't answer.

"Are you that much of a fool?" he asked. "You'd give your money to some man in a tavern, hoping he'll ride all the way north to de Marco lands? What's to stop him from just keeping the payment and tossing the message?"

I hadn't thought of that.

"Worse," he went on. "What if he does deliver it? What if your lady sends someone after you?"

"Then I would go home."

"For a day...maybe. Then Lord Jean would send word to the Capellos that you'd been recovered. He'd have to. Men like him can't be seen to renege on financial agreements, and he's already sold you to Royce Capello."

"No!" I cried. "My lady would protect me."

"Like she did before? She'd somehow be able to stop Lord Jean this time?"

Now, I was breathing fast as his words filled my head.

Leaning in, he said, "If you have that message sent, you'll be in Royce Capello's bed before winter."

I stood shaking. Everything he said was true. Everything. Why had I not seen it? My lady was forever lost to me, as I was lost to her. The truth of it all came crashing down, and I couldn't hold back a sob.

"Then I am alone."

Without warning, Raven grasped my head and pressed one side of my face up against his shoulder. His other arm wrapped around my back, and he held me so tightly I couldn't move. His mouth was close to my ear.

"You are not alone!" he whispered fiercely. "You have us. You're part of us now, and whether you know it or not, I…we have come to love you."

Held so tightly in his grip, I should have been frightened, but I wasn't. All I could feel was the warmth and strength of his body. I didn't want him to let go.

Reaching up with my free hand, I gripped his wool shirt.

We remained there for a long time, and then he said. "Can we go home?"

Home was our wagon.

I nodded.

# Chapter Eight

It took a few days for the truth of my present and future to completely sink in, that I was already home and these people were my family. I was a traveler now, a performer. I was lost to my lady, and she was lost to me. I must accept this. But to my surprise, once I did accept it, as opposed to sorrow, I began to slowly experience a sense of…liberation.

I worked hard preparing for my act. I helped Jade to mend costumes. I bought myself material to sew another wool dress, and we used my spare white muslin to make Emlee a new stage gown—adding some trim and a purple sash. We finished our tour of Narbonnè, putting on two shows a day, moving the stage about every three days to different parts of the city. Then we left. My friendships with both Jade and Jemma were deepening, and with some surprise, I found that I was content, almost looking forward to my life.

Only three things darkened my days.

First, upon reaching Corlean, we learned that word of my act, the lady in white, had already reached the town. The crowds were large, and people were coming to see me. Though Jade and Raven were elated by this development, something about it troubled me. I didn't know what… but something.

Second, since that night when Raven had forced me to see the truth, things between us had changed. Again, I didn't know what. I only knew that he often followed me with his eyes, and that at night, I was aware of him on the roof above, and I sensed he was aware of me just below him, just inside the wagon.

Third, Jade was growing more and more unhappy. She was always kind to me, and she worked hard on the show, but there was a haunted look in her eyes. I didn't know why, and I wanted to help. She was my friend.

We stayed two days in Corlean and then rolled onward to the next town. That night, after making camp along the road, Jemma and I carried buckets to a stream, to fetch water, and we had a few moments to ourselves.

"Jemma…" I began. "Do you know what troubles Jade? I know there's something wrong, but I don't know how to ask her."

Kneeling beside the stream, she nodded. "It's Raven. For years, those two have always been on and off. You must have wondered about the sleeping arrangements, with Sean, Tannen, and Badger in Jade's wagon. But if she and Raven wanted to sport around with each other, they always found a way…his wagon…or an inn if we were camped in a town…or they'd go off into the woods."

Although I was somewhat naïve in what happened between men and women in the bedroom, I wasn't entirely ignorant. More than once, Lord Jean had ordered me to leave my lady's apartments so that he might sleep there.

"Has my sleeping inside Raven's wagon become a problem?" I asked.

"Oh, no. That's not it. Trust me, if he wanted to go off somewhere alone with Jade, he'd find a way. But always before, those two would burn hot for a while, and then some tavern or town girl would catch his eye and he'd leave Jade alone, but he always went back to her. Always. I never understood her. She's proud. You've seen that, but she always takes him back. Then, this past summer, he stopped chasing other women around. He stopped looking at anyone but her, and this autumn, we all expected him to finally ask her to hand-fast."

"Why do you think he hasn't?"

"Well…first there was you. No, don't look at me like that. Everyone knows you're not sporting around with Raven. I may tease you a little, but except for Jade, Raven's never fished in his own pond. But he does have you sleeping in his wagon, and he's never done that, and Jade was angry. Once she understood why, the two of them started sitting and talking together like normal, and we all just figured they'd start to burn hot again, but they haven't."

"And she's wondering why?"

Jemma nodded. "I can't figure it out either. I think she'd feel better if he took up with some pretty tavern wench for a week or two because at least he'd be acting like himself. Then she could count on him coming back to her. But he's not sporting with anyone else, and she can't figure out why he hasn't come to her like he always does."

Turning away, I filled my water bucket. Instead of feeling better, I felt worse. Though I couldn't recognize it openly, in the back of my mind, I knew why Raven had not gone back to Jade.

* * * *

We played several more towns as the weather grew colder, and Jade told me that after one more city, we'd be heading back to the settlement for the winter.

"Before leaving though, we'll use most of the money Raven has saved in that brown pouch to buy supplies for our people back home: grain, lard, flour, sugar, cornmeal, wool cloth, canvas…other things they need but cannot produce themselves. Since we don't help with the harvest, this is our winter contribution."

Such an arrangement made sense to me, but I was concerned about going back, as I did not know what to expect at the settlement. Where would I fit in?

"Don't worry," Jade assured me. "Sean and I have our own little house. Sean's father built it, and there's room for you. You can winter with us, and we'll be on the road again in the spring."

This brought me comfort, and I liked the idea of living with Jade and Sean for a few months.

Traveling a road leading downriver, I sat beside Raven on the bench of our wagon until we rolled into the city of Lokeren. It was walled like Narbonnè, but not quite so large.

"How long will we stay?" I asked.

"Usually about a week, depending on the size of the crowds."

Once again, we set up camp near a large stable, and I took part in the now-familiar tasks.

* * * *

The next day, we found that word of the "lady in white" had spread throughout the city. The crowds were so large that Ash was having trouble being heard by everyone who'd gathered, and I worried that I'd soon need to raise my voice as well. I didn't like the idea of this, as it might affect my ability to act out the story properly while doing voices.

But we performed two shows a day and made good money.

Then, on the fourth day of our stay, something happened that changed everything.

At the afternoon show, Raven asked me to tell the story of the soldier who tries to fulfill the three tasks for the haughty lady and ends up falling in love with her maid.

"That one is a crowd pleaser," he said.

Out on the stage, as I acted out the tale, something tickled at the back of my neck, as if I was being watched. Such a feeling was ridiculous, as of course I was being watched, by hundreds of people.

I kept on with the story, but the feeling of discomfort continued to grow until I reached the end.

"The maid fell to her knees as well and accepted his love, for she had long loved him. And he took her to his family home and married her, and neither of them ever saw the haughty lady again."

Dropping my arms, I signaled the tale was done.

The crowd burst into applause, but I could see someone shuffling for a position closer to the stage. It was a tall, well-dressed man with dark blond hair. As I followed his movement, he stopped and stared at me.

My heart slowed as I looked straight into the face of Royce Capello.

Raven came out onto the stage, motioning to me as he always did. "The lady in white!"

People cheered. As I turned, he saw my face, and his brow furrowed.

But I walked past him, off the stage and behind the curtain, terrified beyond words. Raven announced Marcel, and as the final act started, Raven came back through the curtain, straight to me.

"What's wrong?"

"Royce…Royce is out there." The panic in my voice rose. "He's found me! He's come to get me!"

We never raised our voices backstage, and Jade came over with a frown. But Raven peered though the curtain, and alarm passed across his face when he spotted Royce. This did nothing to ease my fear, and I grasped hold of Jade.

"Don't let him take me."

Raven turned around. "He has no claim on you here, and no one is taking you anywhere." He spoke to Jade. "Get her back to the wagons while Marcel is still on stage. Tannen, Badger, and I will be there in a few minutes."

In a flash, Jade had a cloak over my head and was rushing me back toward our camp. I jogged along beside her, doing my best to keep up. Once there, she put me inside her own wagon.

"You stay inside," she ordered. "I have a few things to do out here."

I heard her running up another set of stairs, and then she was running about on the ground.

Moments later, I heard several sets of heavier footsteps followed by Raven's voice. "Badger, get up on my roof, but no one *do* anything yet. I'll try to talk us out of this."

Feeling helpless, but needing to know what was happening, I cracked the door so I could peer out. The only person I could see was Raven as he stood about ten paces from the back of our own wagon, and he appeared to be waiting.

Then I saw a group of men coming down the wide street toward us. Royce and a man wearing the green tabard of the Lokeren city constabulary were in the lead. Two of the Capello guards and four city guards followed.

"He's got Constable Bernardo with him," Raven said to someone I couldn't see from my vantage point. "That means he knows he can't just walk in and take her."

As the men approached, I had a good view of them. As always, Royce was hard to read, but he stopped cold at the sight of Raven. Masked or not, Raven was easily recognizable.

The constable appeared weary, as if he'd rather be anywhere but here. "Afternoon, Raven," he said and then turned to Royce. "Now, what is this about, sir? Some missing woman?"

"Not missing, but taken!" Royce spit out, pointing at Raven. "By *him* in a raid on my traveling party."

The constable raised one eyebrow. "Raven? In a raid? I don't think so. You must be mistaken. His troupe has traveled these roads for years and never caused a moment's trouble."

At this, Royce appeared nonplussed, and I knew why. Back on the northern estates, he had only to snap his fingers and any man of military or law enforcement would follow his orders. He commanded power there.

This did not seem to be the case in the southeast.

The constable asked Royce. "Are we talking about your wife? Sister?"

"No...she's not my wife."

"Then who is she to you?"

Royce shifted weight between his feet and didn't answer. He wouldn't want to admit that I was his property, that he'd traded a piece of land for me. What kind of man had to trade land for female company?

Constable Bernardo walked up to Raven. "Do you have any idea what he's after? He keeps saying you took a woman."

Raven smiled and glanced back behind himself. "Tannen, are we hiding any stolen women in the wagons?"

"Not that I know of," came Tannen's voice. "Jade, are you hiding any stolen women?"

Royce's face flushed red. "She was just on their stage! She cannot be missed. She has silver-blond hair and light blue eyes. The stories of her reached me, that she was performing with a group of travelers, and I came here to search. No one else looks like her."

Constable Bernardo turned toward him. "Are you talking about the lady in white?"

Royce was completely out of his element. He didn't know how to converse in any situation in which he was neither feared nor respected...and I knew what to do next. He'd heard tales of my performances and come to find me. He'd seen me that afternoon on stage telling a story, and now I needed to once again become "the lady in white."

Opening the door to the wagon, I descended the portable staircase. From out here, I could see Jade and Tannen to one side, and there were longbows and quivers leaning up against the outer wall. My hair was still loose, and I still wore my white silk gown. "Are you gentlemen discussing me?"

The constable sputtered once and offered a slight bow. "Forgive me, my lady. I didn't know this man was seeking you."

I became a character from one my stories: a heroine.

"No forgiveness is necessary, constable, but please tell me. How can I help you?"

He nodded toward Royce. "This man claims you belong with him, and that Raven stole you."

I smiled. "I am sorry, but I don't know this gentleman, and I can assure you that Raven did not steal me from anywhere. I see myself as most fortunate to be part of this company."

Both Royce and Raven were watching me as if I were a stranger.

But the constable turned to Royce. "The lady doesn't know you, sir. I suggest maybe you had too much ale today, and you saw her in the show? You might go somewhere to sleep it off."

Royce's features flattened. "Do you know who I am? My family owns half the lands in the northern territories, and I have the ear of the king."

"I don't care who you are," Constable Bernardo answered, motioning to his men as he walked away. "And the king doesn't grace us much with his presence here. But if you've an ounce of wisdom, I suggest you leave this lady in peace."

With that, the constable and his four men left us, walking away down the street. Within moments, they were gone.

Royce didn't move. His two guards both flanked him.

"Kara," Royce said. "I've come all this way to save you. I've had men from the king's army out searching for you."

Dropping my character, I turned back into myself. "I don't need to be saved, and I would like you to leave."

"But this man took you!" Royce pointed to Raven. "He stole you! He is a criminal."

How strange it was that he saw Raven as a criminal for taking me, but the same act had seemed perfectly acceptable for himself.

"I am not leaving with you," I answered. "Please go."

He drew a breath through his teeth. "I don't know what they've done to make you say these things, but you're coming out of here right now."

Then he was striding toward me, his face set in determination, and on instinct I drew back. But he didn't get far.

In flash, a dagger appeared in Raven's hand. Moving almost faster than I could see, he rushed Royce, slamming him up against the wall of our white wagon.

Startled, both guards moved after them, but a voice barked, "Don't!"

Looking up, I saw Badger on the roof, aiming a loaded longbow. The sight startled both guards, and Jade and Tannen flew into action. Almost instantly, they each had a bow loaded and aimed.

The guards froze.

Raven had Royce pinned with one forearm pressed against his throat and the dagger to his left eye.

"Don't touch her," Raven said.

His voice startled me, and I was not alone. Jade and Tannen's eyes widened. Raven's face was a mask of rage, as if he were fighting to hold himself back from ramming the dagger through Royce's eye.

"Or what?" Royce taunted. "You'll blind me?"

He had courage. I'd give him that.

"No, I won't injure you without legal cause," Raven answered. "But I will drag you to that constable and tell him you're still threatening Kara. I'll file a formal complaint, and he'll arrest you for assaulting a woman. Since he's the one who told you to leave her in peace, I don't think he'll look too kindly on you threatening to drag her off. You'll probably spend a month in jail."

Royce's expression flickered. For him, that would be the ultimate humiliation.

"How would you enjoy that?" Raven went on. "A month's labor...eating spoiled food...shitting in a bucket...criminals for company. Would that suit my *lord*?"

Again, the quality of his voice was too revealing. It dripped with hatred. He was not a leader protecting one of his people. He was a man protecting a woman. I could hear it, and I was sure Jade could hear it.

With one final shove against Royce's throat, Raven stepped back. "You come near her again, and I swear to all the gods I'll have you in prison."

Jade, Tannen, and Badger still had their bows aimed.

"Go," Badger ordered from the roof.

In some disbelief, Royce staggered sideways, holding his throat. Then one of his men hurried to him, and the three of them left us, walking in the same direction the constable had gone.

I stood there with no idea what to say.

But Jade looked to me and then to Raven, and her expression was stricken.

* * * *

That night, I couldn't sleep. As I lay in bed, sharply aware of Raven just above me on the roof, I kept seeing him pin Royce against the wall with his forearm, and I kept hearing his raw, jagged voice.

*Don't touch her!*

By now, I'd had time to reason out a few things—such as how Royce had found me. My nagging worries about the spreading word of "the lady in white" had not been unfounded. Eventually, word had reached him of a young woman with silver-blond hair and light-blue eyes, dressed in the white silk gown of a lady, performing with a traveling troupe. He'd come looking. The fact that he'd brought only two Capello guards suggested that Lord Trey had not supported the journey with much enthusiasm—which wasn't surprising.

But my new family had protected me—not only Raven, but Jade and Tannen and Badger. I was protected. This should have brought me peace, but here in the quiet, in the night, I could think only of Raven's reaction.

The air in the wagon felt cold, colder than ever before, and I rose from the bed to make sure the shutter was closed tightly. Outside, I saw something white and opened the shutter for a better look. Large flakes fell from the sky to land on the wagons and on the ground.

It was snowing.

And Raven was up on the roof.

Without thinking, I wrapped myself in my cloak, opened the door, and descended our set of stairs. Snow fell all around me, sticking to the ground, and in bare feet, I walked to the front of the wagon, near to the bench.

"Raven," I called up softly. "It's snowing."

No response came at first, and then he peered down at me, his head covered with a blanket. He said nothing.

"You'll freeze up there," I said. "Come inside. Please."

He didn't move.

"Please," I said again.

He vanished for a moment, and I heard him climbing down to the bench. From the bench, he jumped lightly to the ground, still wrapped in a blanket. Turning, I led the way inside, and he closed the door behind us.

Only then, did I see that he was shaking, and when I touched his hands, they were like ice.

"You're freezing."

"It's not much worse than it has been for the past few nights," he answered, teeth chattering.

"Come and sit on the bed." Taking the damp blanket from his shoulders, I wrapped him in mine. Then I sat beside him. "You've been suffering up there, in this kind of cold for several nights? Why didn't you just come inside?"

He shook his head. "I couldn't."

"Why not?"

But I knew. In the past few weeks, I'd turned from a girl into a woman, and I *knew*.

Sitting beside me, his eyes locked into mine with a question. I held his gaze.

"Kara?" he whispered.

Slowly enough to give me every chance to draw away, he leaned down and touched his mouth to mine.

His kiss was light at first, just a brush of his lips. Then I seemed to melt into him, as if this were the most natural thing in the world. When he opened his mouth, I opened mine in answer. When he touched me, I touched him in answer.

We knew what to do without speaking, but I could hear his breathing quicken. Still moving slowly, he pushed me beneath him, and I pulled the blanket over the top of us.

This felt right.

This wagon was our home.

He was my home.

* * * *

The next morning, in spite of the snow outside, I awoke feeling truly warm for the first time in weeks. I lay with my face on Raven's shoulder with his arms around me. He opened his eyes, and I kissed him softly.

"Kara," he breathed.

Our joining in the night had been gentle and desperate at the same time, and I could not bring myself to be sorry. Nothing had ever felt so right as when he touched me.

Outside, voices and footsteps sounded as the camp woke up around us.

"Winter's come," he said. "We'll need to start back today."

I didn't know what this would mean for the two of us, but I didn't think on it. Instead, I rose from the bed and pulled on my shift. He was dressed in a matter of moments and heading for the door. As he opened it, I wrapped myself in a cloak and followed him to the doorway to see how much snow had fallen.

When he opened the door, a world of white awaited us. The snow was perhaps a foot deep, but not enough to discourage travel. Halfway down the steps, Raven suddenly stopped. I wondered what was wrong and looked out past him. Then I saw what he saw.

Jade, Tannen, Ash, and Jemma were on the ground outside our wagon, trying to get a fire started.

They took in the sight of Raven coming from inside the wagon, with messy hair and somewhat disheveled clothing. They stared up at me, just behind him, wearing only my shift with a cloak wrapped around my shoulders.

Raven was not a man who explained his actions. He did as he pleased and walked away whenever someone questioned him. But this was different. For all his adventuring with women, he'd chosen tavern or town girls. Among the troupe, he'd always returned to Jade.

Tannen was Jade's brother, and Jemma was her friend…and I was her friend. The strong connections running between this family could be cracked, could be broken, if the next few moments were not handled correctly.

To save the group, I became a character in one of my stories: a trickster, a liar.

With an open smile, I leaned around Raven and spoke to Jemma. "I woke up last night when it began to snow, and I feared for him up on the roof. Stubborn as he is, I begged him to come inside and sleep on the floor lest we all have a snowman for a leader this morning."

In relief, she breathed out and smiled back. "Oh, of course. Good thinking. He certainly can't stay up there now. We'll need to figure something else out."

I don't know if everyone believed me, but my lightly spoken words broke the tension, and I could see how much Jade wanted to believe.

Raven stepped off the stairs. "We need to cancel today's shows and start heading back now. Jade, tell everyone to pack up."

# Chapter Nine

For me, the journey back to the settlement felt like a window of stolen time. In spite of Jemma's comment that something else should be considered for sleeping arrangements now that full winter had set in, Raven allowed no changes.

I spent each day sitting on the wagon bench beside him.

I spent each night joining my body with his under the warm blankets of our bed. We both knew what to do without speaking, bringing each other joy, pleasure, and a comfort that I'd never known existed. Sleeping in his arms was the most natural thing in the world.

One night, as we lay spent, I asked him, "Is it always like this between men and women? Do they all feel this joining as we do?"

At first, he didn't answer. Then he said, "No. I've never felt anything like this."

Somehow, this was the answer I'd expected.

Still, I knew Raven, and I knew his attentions did not last. As Jade had told me, right now, the sun rose and set about my head, but soon, it would rise and set around someone else's. I could accept that. I simply wanted this to go on as long as possible.

When I thought of Jade, my guilt was heavy. I loved her.

But I loved him more.

Regarding the troupe, I doubt we fooled anyone, but our attempt to pretend that nothing was happening, that nothing had changed, proved welcome to everyone—with the possible exception of Jade.

For this journey back to the settlement, the others were glad enough to get through the cold days with the normal familiar rhythms of life on the road. We stopped once in Narbonnè to buy all of the supplies to bring as our offering to the settlement, but we didn't stay long, and Raven seemed to keep us on the road as long as possible each day, as if he were in a hurry to get back.

Then, one afternoon, following days on end of travel, I was beside him on the bench when he pointed ahead.

"Look there, Kara. That's the turn off. That path leads to the chute. We're almost there."

Instead of bringing me happiness at the thought of warm indoor fires and the chance to stay in one place for a while, his words made me anxious. Our journey was over, and I didn't know what to expect next.

* * * *

When our wagons crested the top of the chute, someone called out. "Here they come!"

Of course the watchmen on the walls would know of our return, as Raven had whistled the signal, but now, it seemed everyone in the settlement was running to meet us. People in our own group began jumping off wagons to greet friends and relatives amid excited chatter.

"We've brought so much food back, Mama," Jemma said, hugging a middle-aged woman. "And some beautiful green wool for gowns and shirts. Wait until you see."

As Raven and I climbed down from our bench, Caine, Logan, and their grandfather came walking toward us. Caine's eyes were on me. I'd almost forgotten how tall he was...and the serious quality of his face. Jade had called him handsome. I supposed he was.

But Logan appeared tense and went straight to Raven.

"Did you make sure you weren't followed?" he demanded.

Raven blinked, "Followed? No, we weren't followed." He looked to Caine. "What is this?"

Jade came over to join us, listening.

"It's nothing," Caine answered, but his voice caught, suggesting this topic distressed him. "We had some trouble not long after you left. Some soldiers from the king's army followed one of our raiding parties home, and they found the chute. We let them get them get halfway up and killed them. The bodies are long buried. We've had no trouble since."

But I shivered inside my cloak, remembering Royce's words that he had men from the king's army out searching for me. Men had died because of me...because of Royce.

"It was *not* nothing!" Logan nearly spat, turning on Caine. "We cannot risk outsiders finding this place. We have enough stolen property here from the raids to get us all hanged."

Their grandfather held up his hand. "Raven and his people have just returned. They are most likely tired, cold, and hungry. Logan, you can see they were not followed. Let them eat and rest, and we will speak of these things tomorrow."

This was the moment I had dreaded. No longer part of the traveling show, where did I fit in now?

But Jade reached a hand out to me. "Kara, if you still wish, you can stay with Sean and me. We would be glad to have you."

Caine cast her a grateful look, as if he approved this suggestion, and I began reaching toward her hand. At least I had somewhere to live, and of anyone here, Jade was the only one who might understand my feelings.

"No," Raven said, pushing my hand down. "Kara stays with me. She'll live with me."

Everyone went still, and color drained from Caine's face.

"With you?" Caine said. "In your house? Raven, you don't even let people visit when…" He trailed off, looking from Raven to Jade.

Turning abruptly, Jade walked away.

\* \* \* \*

Raven had a small, two-room house on the outskirts of the settlement. Once our horses had been settled, he took me there alone.

"I built it myself," he said, "so I wouldn't have to live with anyone." He hesitated before opening the door. "It's not much, but I'm only here a few months out of the year."

"I don't care."

I didn't. I cared only that he hadn't sent me away, that he'd kept me with him. Inside, I found a dusty table, one chair, a set of cupboards, a wood stove, and a bed. There were spider webs in the corners, and an empty bird's nest above the single window.

"I'll get a fire going," he said, moving toward the stove.

"You don't let other people in here?" I asked.

"No. Not until now."

Walking over, I looked down at the dust-covered bed. "We'll need clean blankets before we can sleep."

Leaving the stove, he walked to me and grasped my face with both his hands. "Marry me. Tonight. I want to wake up every day and see you for the rest of my life."

I knew our actions would hurt other people. I knew we would hurt Jade. The thought pained me.

I loved Jade.

But I loved him more.

"Will you?" he asked.

"Yes."

* * * *

In the late afternoon, the women of the settlement began putting together a feast to recognize the return of our group. They put the lard, flour, and sugar we'd brought to good use, making sweet rolls and apple tarts. The common house was a vast one-room building built from logs. One wall boasted a great stone hearth, and another wall boasted a cooking stove. Tonight, everyone gathered at this common house after dusk, and the mood was one of celebration.

Cheers sounded when Raven had a large cask of wine rolled in.

I stood a good distance from the doorway, not knowing what to do or say. There were so many people. Logan and his wife Brida greeted everyone as they entered. Across the room, Caine stood apart from everyone else, like me. He spotted me watching him, and we made eye contact for a few seconds before I dropped my gaze. Jade was near the table laden with food, but there was no joy or celebration in her face.

Raven's grandfather helped him to open the cask of wine.

As soon as they finished, Raven jumped up onto a bench.

"My friends!" he called, sounding again like the master of the stage. "I have an announcement that will help us celebrate far into the night." He smiled at me. "I've asked Kara to hand-fast with me, and she has agreed. Grandfather has given his permission, and he will marry us before dinner."

For a moment, most of the people appeared dumbfounded. Some looked to Jade and then to me.

"To Kara?" Brida asked, and for some reason I could not fathom, she seemed beyond pleased. Her goblet was still empty, but she raised it high. "We will drink a toast to you and Kara."

Then a number of people began offering congratulations. Jemma, Tannen, Badger, and Marcel still appeared dumbfounded. Caine's jaw was tight, and he remained silent. Jade's eyes were bleak.

Raven's grandfather came to me. His face was lined, and his hair was gray. I'd not spoken to him before, but he grasped my hand gently. "I am Tristan," he said.

Somehow the name didn't quite fit. From the stories I'd read, I'd always thought of Tristan as a young man's name. But when I looked into his eyes, I saw a young man there, and I grasped his hand back. It felt like touching Raven, natural and easy.

"If you'll come with me now, I'll perform the hand-fast if you wish," he said. "Is this what you wish?"

When he asked this question, the weight of what I was about to do hung over me. But I looked at Raven, who stood waiting.

"Yes. It is what I wish."

*  *  *  *

Near the mid of night, people were still eating and drinking.

I was married.

The ceremony itself had been brief. Our hands were tied together with a ribbon. This was followed by our promises to join for life, followed by Tristan blessing our union.

That was it.

But I didn't care for lavish accoutrements or displays. I only cared that Raven and I were sworn to each other. For my part, after that, I had wanted the evening to end, so that we might go home to our two-room house and arrange some clean blankets.

And yet, the night had gone on and on. I smiled and nodded until my face hurt.

Then, at some point, I realized I'd not seen Raven in a while, that he was no longer inside the common house. Looking around, I saw that Jade was not here either. At first, I wondered if she'd taken Sean and gone home, but I spotted Sean with Ash and Lizbeth.

The backdoor to the common house was partially open, and I crossed the room to slip outside into the cold night, looking both ways. There was no one in view, but an anguished voice reached me.

"To announce it like that, in front of everyone! Could you have been more selfish and cruel?"

It was Jade.

Walking towards her voice, to the edge of the common house, I stopped. Though I could not see her, she must have been just around the corner.

"I'd never hurt you on purpose," Raven answered.

"Hurt me?" she cried. "All you have ever done is hurt me! And I let you. All these years, Raven…I've let you in and out of my bed because we both knew we were meant to be together, and I was the one who'd ruined it when we were young by getting impatient and marrying someone else. I understand that we all make mistakes and pay prices." She let out a sound like an animal in pain. "But this! For you to marry Kara? She doesn't know any better. How could you do this to her? To us?"

"You don't understand."

"No! I don't. Why would you do this?"

"For some peace! For some stillness in my soul."

"Oh, stop talking nonsense."

"Jade, if there was any way I could choose you, I would. But I can't. I choose Kara. She is my choice."

"You and your talk of choices. You cling to your preaching of choices like a religion, but in truth, it's just an excuse for you to do what you please instead of doing what is right."

Flinching, I drew away, not wanting to hear anymore.

Jade was in pain, and I had helped to hurt her. Moreover, in my heart, I knew she was not wrong about Raven and his talk of choices.

Quickly, I went back inside, and among the crowd, I saw Caine sitting alone at a small table near the far wall, drinking. I did not know him, and we weren't friends, but there was no one else with whom I wished to sit while waiting for Raven. Crossing to him, I pointed to a chair.

"May I?"

His eyes were bloodshot, and he had a half-empty pitcher of wine on the table. He'd been drinking quite a bit. But he nodded.

I sat.

"Where's Raven?" he asked.

"Out fighting with Jade."

"Oh…that's to be expected. He's been fighting with Jade since they were six years old. It's what they do."

This only reminded me that these people all had a history in which I did not share.

The loneliness of this made me brave, thinking on how I'd come to be here in the first place. "Why did you take me from Royce?"

He lifted his goblet for another long drink. "Do you really want to know?" His words were slurred.

"Yes."

Laughing once without humor, he said, "A prophecy."

I shook my head, not understanding.

Sighing, he took another long drink. "I swore to myself I'd never tell anyone, certainly not you. But there's no point now, is there?"

"No point to what?"

"To silence." He looked into his empty goblet but didn't pour any more wine. "My grandfather made it clear that I'll need to be married if I want to succeed him as tórnya. He thinks family men, with something to lose, make better leaders. Perhaps he's not wrong. But I…I don't connect well with other people. I don't want to be miserable or make someone else miserable."

"Well, I think you're wise not to marry until you find the right person."

He looked up from the goblet. "Do you? I took a journey north, to visit a seer. She's a true seer, not someone like Ash. Her prophecies have come to pass. When I asked her who I should marry, she told me to wait for the day I saw a girl the color of a white winter morning, that I would know her when I saw her, and only with her could I make a success out of a marriage."

"Oh, Caine."

"I came home, and I waited. Then on that raid, I saw you."

"But there's no way to know this prophesy meant me."

He poured another goblet. "Isn't there? Well, there's no way to know anymore."

I had no idea what to say, and Raven came through the back door looking shaken. I wanted this conversation to end.

Standing, I said to Caine. "I do hope you find her." Then I hurried across the room to Raven. "Might we go home now?"

He nodded. "Yes. Let's go home."

\* \* \* \*

The days began to pass.

I cleaned every inch of our house and spent several weeks turning it into a comfortable temporary home. Though the weather was cold, the people of the settlement were not idle, and there was much work to be done. The men cared for livestock and repaired dwellings or other structures. They hunted in the forest. They chopped and stacked firewood.

The women minded children, prepared food, and sewed clothing from the material our group had brought back.

Though families sometimes ate meals at home, the women did a good deal of communal cooking at the common house, and we often ate meals together. At first, relations with other members of our traveling group were strained, but the connections between myself, Jemma, Tannen, Badger, Lizbeth, Ash, Marcel, and the others had grown deep while performing out on the road, and soon, they accepted Raven's choice. Jade was subdued but kind to me. She seemed to blame Raven entirely for what had happened. While I found this somewhat unfair, we never spoke of such things.

I do think people watched us to see what would happen when Raven began to tire of me.

He did not.

For myself, I spent my nights under the blankets with him, both warm and in love. If anything, we found only more joy and wonder in each other as the winter passed. Joining my body with Raven's, knowing how to touch him, how to kiss him, came as easy as breathing.

Only one thing troubled me; I missed the road.

I was not unhappy here, but I longed to be living again with him in the wagon, putting on the show, shopping for dinner in the markets, and moving from place to place. He must have sensed this in me, and one night he whispered, "We're just here until spring. We'll leave again once it thaws and the trees bud."

The women of the settlement were polite to me, and I became fond of Jemma's mother, Doris. She was always friendly. As we cooked or sewed together, I listened and learned about some of the issues here. There had been some talk of stopping the autumn raids. Logan had been pushing for this, and his grandfather, Tristan, was showing signs of agreement. Apparently, the raids were more of a tradition left over from the days of Tristan's father, when all of the people were travelers, and each autumn, the men would conduct raids for goods and supplies to see everyone through the winter. Now…it seemed the risks these raids brought outweighed their possible value.

While I helped the women in their work, Logan's wife, Brida, was also friendly to me. She was not a pretty woman, with a square build and a square face, and she liked to tell other women what to do. I never minded this. But one morning, when I was in the common house helping with the baking, Brida came striding over to Jemma, who was kneading a loaf of bread.

"Mind what you're doing girl!" Brida admonished her. "You've far too much flour in that dough. It's wasteful and that loaf will be tough."

As she walked away, Jemma scowled and said, "Dried up trout. She thinks she already rules here."

"She is always kind to me."

Jemma snorted. "Of course she is. She's thrilled with you. When Caine first brought you home, she was terrified he'd marry you. Now, you're safely sworn to Raven."

Remembering Caine's story on the night of my wedding, I stopped talking. I didn't wish to speak or think of such things. What I wanted was to leave this place and go back on the road.

For entertainment after dark, people often gathered in the common hall to drink ale or play at cards or games of dice. Some nights, Bonham and Marcel played their violins, and people would dance.

One evening, after we'd been back about a month, Tristan asked if our group would put on the same show we did on the road. He felt that some lively entertainment would be good for everyone's spirits.

Raven agreed readily. He told me to don my white silk and be ready to tell the story of the young man who falls in love with the haughty lady and ends up falling in love with her maid—as that was his favorite.

But I didn't want to do this.

I didn't want to wear my silk gown and become "the lady in white" and perform for people who knew me mainly as Raven's quiet wife. It would be different from performing for crowds of strangers.

But I could not argue with Raven. I couldn't tell him no.

The men set up a stage with a curtain in the common house, directly in front of the back door, so that we could enter and hide behind the curtain without being seen by the audience. Well after dark, our troupe gathered out at the back of the common house in our costumes. Jemma had laced me up and curled my hair. She was in high spirits, happy to wear the ice blue silk I'd given her—and to have a chance to dance for her family and friends.

"Have the people here never seen the group perform?" I asked quietly.

"Oh, of course," she answered. "But not for a year, and the show has changed. I think it's better than ever."

Jade stood quietly in her emerald green gown. I don't think she wanted to do this any more than I did. The children from our group were already inside, with the audience, and Marcel was having trouble keeping his dogs quiet.

Raven was also inside, and finally, he opened the back door and stuck his head out. "Everyone ready?"

I tried to smile.

Motioning with his hand, he brought us in, and we hid behind the curtain. Then he stepped through the break in the curtain and out onto the stage.

"Welcome my friends!" he called. "To the finest show in all of Samourè."

I heard laughter and moved to usual my place downstage to peek out. The faces of the people were bright and happy. They liked that Raven was doing exactly what he would have done in a city or town.

He announced Jemma's dance of the sprite, and Marcel and Bonham ran out onto the stage. People were already applauding. Perhaps this amusement had been a good idea on Tristan's part.

The show went on, and Ash's act was more comic than anything else, since he knew everyone so well, and he spilled a few innocent secrets. From where I stood, I could see how much everyone in the audience was enjoying themselves. Tristan smiled broadly. Even Caine was there, and his expression hinted at amusement. Then…my gaze settled on Logan and Brida. They stood slightly apart from everyone else, and two small boys stood in front of them. The boys were delighted, but Logan's expression was tight, and his arms were crossed.

When it came time for my act, Raven announced me.

"And now for something special," he called. "A tale to pull at your heart strings. May I present, the lady in white."

As he stepped back, I stepped out, and as I expected, the room went silent. Of course they had all seen me before, but they'd never seen me like this—like a mix between a noblewoman and a winter fairy. For once, I did not make eye contact with my audience. Instead, I shut everything out, and for first time in months, I thought on my lady, and pretended I was telling the story for her.

"There once was a soldier," I began, "who fell in love with the proud and beautiful daughter of a nobleman. She was tall and slender, with eyes of green and locks of waving red hair. She wore the finest gowns of satin and velvet. Though the girl was set above him, the soldier was of good name and family, and he found her alone in her family's garden. There he fell to his knees, begging for her hand."

I went on to act out the various tasks he was set, and near the end of the tale, I could not help but notice that Logan's eldest son—perhaps seven years old—had moved forward and was hanging on my every word.

When I finished and dropped my arms to signal the tale was done, there was the usual moment of silence, and then applause.

When Raven stepped back out, I could see the pride on his face. "The lady in white!"

Before taking my bow, I couldn't help looking at Caine. He stared back at me in shock, and I turned away quickly, hurrying through the curtain. I barely heard Marcel's act with the dogs.

However, after taking our final group bow, no one went backstage again. Instead, they hurried forward—still in costume—to join friends and family.

"Wonderful!" Doris said, hugging Jemma.

And then I realized I'd need to mingle, still wearing this gown that made me look so otherworldly. Even with Raven at my side, I wondered how I would be received.

I never found out.

Logan's son, who'd been watching me so intently, came running over to Raven. "Uncle," he said. "When you leave to go on your travels, can I come with you?"

Raven smiled down at him, but Logan was close on his son's heels. "You see what you've done!" he shouted at Raven. "This is the last time. No more of these...performances here at home. You breed unrest! You make it look as if rolling from town to city is some great adventure." He glanced down at his son and lowered his voice. "They can't understand what it's really like."

Had he traveled as a boy and been unhappy on the road? There was so little I knew.

But everyone had heard him shouting. Tristan frowned from where he stood, and soon, people began to slip away and go home.

* * * *

Just when I thought it might never happen, the air began to warm, the ground thawed and the trees began budding with leaves. Yellow and purple flowers came up from the ground, and I rejoiced in the knowledge that we would soon be on the road again.

Raven felt my joy, and he began inspecting wagons, seeing to any repairs that might be necessary.

The people of the settlement began inspecting both their gardens and the cleared lands near the orchards in preparation to till and plant new crops. I was glad for them too, as we were approaching the last of our flour, sugar, and oats. The onions, potatoes, and carrots stowed from last year's harvest were nearing the bottoms of barrels. But no one worried. There were chickens, eggs, goat's milk, pigs, and fish from the stream. Soon, the people here would be planting, and I knew Raven still had money, so our group could re-supply on the road.

A week before we were scheduled to leave, Caine brought down a large buck deer with his bow. Raven built a fire outside and set up a spit, and the men roasted the venison. That evening, everyone gathered in the common house. Brida had ordered a rationing of bread, but there was plenty of roasted meat.

Inside the common house, Raven and I sat with Tristan, Logan, Brida, their sons, and Caine.

Tristan took a bite of meat and raised his cup to Caine. "Fine venison," he said. "Rich and tender."

But he did not take another bite. Instead, one side of his face twitched, and then his entire body jerked as he fell off his chair. Raven was on his feet first, his expression wild with alarm.

"Grandfather!"

Everyone was up, but Tristan lay on the floor with the side of his face still twitching.

"Raven, help me," Caine said. "We have to get him home."

* * * *

I knew that Tristan and Caine lived together in a large house—which had once been populated by more than just them—but I'd not been inside. It could not have been more different from the house I shared with Raven, as it was stocked with polished furniture, thick rugs on the floors, and curtains on the windows.

That night, the family held vigil around Tristan's bed.

Near the mid of night, he awoke and looked around.

"Grandfather," Raven said, kneeling to grasp Tristan's hand.

"Where am I?" Tristan asked, but he seemed to have difficulty speaking.

"In your room. You collapsed."

I got him a cup of water, but Brida took it from me and moved to the other side of the bed to help him sip. "You are ill," she said to him. "I know it seems unfeeling to speak of such things, but what if you do not recover? Who will be tórnya? You must name a successor."

Aghast, Raven jumped up. "Brida!"

But neither Caine nor Logan reacted. Instead, they both looked to Tristan.

His eyes were sad, but he pointed to Logan.

"Logan."

This was the only word he managed to say. Then his body jerked again, the side of his face twitching more fiercely. He went stiff from the force of it, and then he went still.

"No!" Raven cried, dropping to his knees again. The sight broke my heart, as he was weeping.

But Tristan's eyes were closed, and he did not breathe. He was dead.

The room was silent but for the sounds of Raven's sorrow.

Then Logan said, "You heard him. You all heard him."

\* \* \* \*

The following night, even before Tristan's funeral, Logan called everyone to the common house. I sat with Raven, who was still openly suffering from Tristan's sudden death.

Logan stood near the hearth, with Brida beside him. Caine stood nearby.

"My grandfather has passed on," Logan said in a voice that carried. "We all mourn him, as he was our leader for as long as most of us remember. But he named me tórnya before he died, and I must now do what I think best for our people. First, there will be no more autumn raids. We don't need the luxuries those raids provide, and we cannot risk any more soldiers following our men home and finding the chute."

No one appeared surprised by this announcement. Even in their sorrow at the loss of Tristan, many nodded their agreement with Logan's decree.

"Second," he called, "there will be no more of us traveling through parts of the year. Everyone will remain here. We'll dismantle the homes on the wagons and use the wagons for other needs."

"No!" Raven shouted jumping to his feet.

Caine started in shock and stepped toward Logan. "You can't do that."

Logan didn't flinch. "I'm tórnya here now, and there is too much danger of our travelers being followed home."

Doris stood. "But Logan…what about the supplies Raven's troupe brings back every winter? We cannot produce everything we need here."

"We will learn to survive with what we *can* produce here," he answered. "We are strong. We need no one and nothing else."

Raven crossed the room to face him. "Those wagons are mine. Father left them to me. I couldn't care less if you rule here, but my group leaves on schedule."

Logan met his eyes. "If you leave, you will not be allowed back, and if you try to return, I'll order our men on the walls of the cliffs to shoot."

People about the common hall gasped.

But Logan was tórnya now.

\* \* \* \*

I never feared that we would stay, but I knew it would take several days for the reality of Logan's decree to set in. At first, Raven and those of our troupe believed he might be swayed, but I knew full well that this would not happen either.

Logan was an isolationist. I never used this term to Raven, but I'd read of such men in my lady's books. He would not relent. He'd most likely been waiting for years to cut the settlement off from any outside influence.

In the end, Raven called our group to meet at the wagons.

Between his grandfather's death and this agonized decision, his face was etched with pain.

"I cannot live here year-round," he announced. "Kara and I are leaving tomorrow. We'll take anyone who wants to come, but there will be no blame if you stay. Many of you have family here…I have family here. Also, you are welcome to ask anyone who might want to come with us. We'll make room somehow, and if need be, we'll buy more wagons."

"What will we do in winter?" Ash asked.

"We'll take the money we would have used for supplies for the settlement, and I'll rent us space for the wagons in Narbonnè or Lokeren."

"Marcel and I are coming with you," Jemma said. "My parents might wish to come too. They fear staying here with Logan as leader."

Raven nodded.

One by one, from to Ash to Tannen to Emilee and Bonham and onward, everyone stated they were coming.

Then Jade said, "Sean and I will stay."

Raven frowned as if he hadn't heard her correctly.

"What?" Tannen asked. "You can't mean that."

But I rushed forward and grabbed her hands. "Don't say that. You must come. We cannot be without you, and you will regret this. Jade, we're not coming back!"

How could she not understand this?

Gripping gently on my fingers, she said, "I can't come, Kara. I can't."

* * * *

That night, the last night at our house, Raven nearly broke down. It had all been too much.

"How can we do this without Jade?" he asked. "Who will plan the costumes and do the girls' hair and call cues when I'm on stage?"

I ached for Jade to come with us, but I wouldn't stay here for her.

Walking to him, I touched his face. "I can plan costumes and do the girls' hair and call cues when you are on stage."

He looked down at me and exhaled. "Of course. You can do all of that, can't you?"

"Yes."

\* \* \* \*

In the end, Jemma's parents decided to join us. Badger tried once more to convince Jade to come, but she would not. She did not even come to see us off.

On the day we left, Caine grabbed hold of Raven and held him for a long time. But Caine would never leave the settlement. His place was here.

After tears and goodbyes, we climbed up on the wagons, knowing we would not return.

Logan stood with his arms crossed, but he was pale. I think in his heart, he didn't believe Raven would actually leave.

He did not know his brother.

As we rolled down the chute that day, I looked ahead at my life of traveling and performing and living in the wagon with Raven.

I had love…and I had freedom.

\* \* \* \*

The chute around me disappeared and I found myself once again inside the small shack, kneeling by the hearth and staring into the right panel of the three-tiered mirror.

Fighting to take in air, I thought on all that I had just lived through.

But the dark-haired woman was now looking out from the center panel.

"What was that?" I cried.

"That would be the outcome of the first choice," she answered. "But now those memories will vanish, and you'll go back to the beginning, to the moment of the crisis, to live out the second choice."

"Wait!" I cried. "I won't remember anything of what I just saw?"

"Back to the beginning once more," she answered. "To live out the second choice."

My mind went blank, and the interior of the shack vanished.

# The Second Choice
# Flight

# Chapter Ten

I was standing in the darkness just outside the door of the shack, feeling dizzy and disoriented, as if I'd forgotten something and needed to remember. What was I doing out here?

Then I remembered that Raven had just left me—with the door unlocked—and I had a decision to make. Looking to the left, I saw the long tree line stretching along the backs of several dwellings.

Raven had given me the choice of leaving with his troupe in the morning or staying here and taking my chances—or I could escape the settlement, make my way down the chute, and try to get back to my lady.

The thought of attempting to flee this place and then navigating the forest on my own was terrifying. But I didn't know Raven well enough to leave with him. He had shown moments of kindness, but I'd only met him two nights before. And Caine…he wanted something from me. I didn't know what, only that he did.

I had no choice but to run.

Looking down the tree line, I forced myself into motion, slipping down the backs of buildings all the way to the edge of the settlement nearest to the chute. At the last dwelling, I peered around the corner and saw no one.

Where was everyone?

Perhaps they had all gathered somewhere, but this didn't matter. From where I stood, I had a clear line to the entrance to the chute. Breathing fast, I still hesitated. What if while I was on my way down, one of the men out on watch on the cliffs spotted movement and took the shot?

There were worse things than death, and I braced myself, taking one more look before dashing out into the open, across the space between the dwellings and the top of the chute. On the way, I passed a collection of six wagons with houses built on top, but they were quiet and dark, with no horses harnessed.

Reaching the mouth of the chute, I pressed my body up against the near side, panting—somewhat surprised that I'd made it this far. Then, slowly, I began to creep downward in the darkness, keeping myself up against the cliff wall as Raven had instructed.

The journey was slow.

I never once looked up.

The moon provided my only light, but it was easy for me to follow the path down, always pressed to the wall. Near the bottom, I tripped over some loose stones, sending them skittering, and I froze at the sound they made, but no arrows rained down from above.

Shaken, I remained where I was for long moments and then ran from the bottom of the chute, back through the brush that hid its lower mouth… and found myself alone, in the dark, in the forest.

I'd escaped the settlement.

The way back was to the west, but I didn't know how to navigate by the moon, only the sun. At first, I thought it best to hide someplace nearby until morning when I could gauge my path. But then I feared what might happen should Caine go to check on me in the shack and find me gone.

He'd come searching, and he knew this forest. He would find me.

An open plain stretched out on my left, and I remembered that Raven had led us in through the forest. Turning right, I headed into the forest, following the straightest line possible. I would travel only far enough to evade possible pursuit by Caine, and then I would rest.

\* \* \* \*

The next morning, I woke up huddled beside a large tree and wrapped in my cloak. The morning air was cold, and I shivered. I was hungry and thirsty.

Worse, in daylight, above the thick trees, I could see the open sky and feel it pressing down upon me. But I could also see the sun rising directly behind me, and knew I'd been traveling in the correct direction. I simply had to keep my eyes off the sky as much as possible and continue making my way west until I reached the wide, main road through the estate land. Then I would turn north. Once back at the de Marco manor, I could tell my lady what happened. By now, I believed Lord Jean would regret having taken me from her, and she could sway him into allowing me to stay.

Thinking of all the space and distance above and around me was nearly paralyzing, and at first, I couldn't move. Then I dragged one foot forward and began to walk.

Within several hours, the thirst began affecting me more than the sky, and I'd crossed no streams or water sources. By early afternoon, even in the cold air, I grew warm enough to begin sweating inside my cloak. I had never walked like this, on and on. The world began to spin around me, and I'd still crossed no stream. Birds chirped and sang from the trees, and several squirrels darted across my path.

Soon, I stumbled from near exhaustion, and the cloak and hem of my gown caught on a patch of brush around my feet. Jerking them free, I stumbled onward, but the fabric of my clothing was ripped and torn. I was hot now…so hot that my fingers pulled at the tie on my cloak, and I pulled my cloak from my shoulders, letting it drop to the ground and leaving it behind as I stumbled on.

By late afternoon, I was dizzy and having trouble staying on my feet.

In my mind, I heard Lady Giselle's voice. "Kara! Where are you?"

I couldn't answer her. The tissues of my mouth were too dry.

Then, up ahead, I heard the sound of rushing water and stumbled forward in wild hope.

But I stopped.

There, about six trees away, stood a man wearing armor and the purple and orange tabard of the king's army. He jumped at the sight of me, as if I were a ghost emerging from the forest. Was I real?

Was he real?

The world spun all around me.

I didn't want to be found by the king's army, but…on the edge of my awareness, I knew I needed help. Maybe he would help me. Maybe he would take me to my lady.

Turning his head, he called out, "My lord?"

Footsteps sounded in the brush, and another man stepped into view. At the sight of him, I tried to cry out in despair, but no sound came from my throat.

It was Royce Capello.

His eyes widened. "Kara!"

I ran.

Whirling, I tried to escape through the trees, but in seconds he had a hold of my arm and drew me around, pulling me against his chest. Struggling wildly, I made a fist and hit his shoulder several times until he had me fully pinned against him.

"It's me," he said. "Kara, it's me. You're safe."

My strength gave way, and I sagged in his grip.

"It's me," he said again, his mouth close to my ear. "You're all right. I've found you, and you're safe."

Leaning down, he slipped one arm under the backs of my knees and lifted me. As my feet left the ground, the world spun faster, and I couldn't help clinging to him now.

"Captain!" he called. "She's burning up. Get me a horse!"

He began striding forward, and that was the last thing I remembered as everything around me went dark.

\* \* \* \*

When I came to awareness and opened my eyes, I was lying in a soft bed, covered by a thick blanket, with my head on a pillow...feeling so weak I didn't try to sit up. But I wore a clean nightgown. From where I lay, the room around me appeared lavish, with cream walls, long lace curtains on the windows, and a large still-life painting on the wall—of pink roses and green apples.

There was a silk screen at the end of the bed, so I could not see far.

From beyond the screen, a man's voice spoke.

"Well for the girl's sake, of course I'm glad he found her, but that doesn't solve our problem here."

The voice was familiar: Lord Trey.

A woman laughed, and the soft sound was like music. "Really, my dear. You worry too much."

"You've not met her, Adina, and I'm not joking. She's defenseless, and Loraine will *not* be happy with Royce's choice."

"Loraine won't be home for months, and after all this time, Royce must have chosen the girl for a reason. What is her name again?"

"Kara." He sighed. "I told him to choose someone clever, witty, and strong. But this Kara is nearly silent and afraid of her own shadow."

"Well, she must have some strength if she escaped from brigands and made it through the forest on her own."

"Oh, and that's another thing. He can't stop talking about how he saved her. He sees himself as her hero. There'll be no sending her back to de Marco now."

Soft footsteps sounded, as if someone light crossed the room. "Tut, tut, my darling. Surely, you don't want him to send her back? At least now he'll have someone to keep *him* happy, to focus on his needs. Isn't that what we've both wanted?"

"Yes...perhaps it will work out. But she'll need to learn to handle his moods, and I still think Loraine will throw a fit. She's known Royce was getting close to choosing a companion for some time now, but she'll expect a grasping, ambitious girl from court, not some pretty, timid little nobody he might actually care for."

The musical laugh sounded again. "Let me see what can be done. Off with you now, so I can check on the invalid. I'll give you a full report at dinner."

"All right. You know best in these matters, but don't say I didn't warn you."

Heavier footsteps sounded, followed by a door opening and closing.

Beneath the blankets, I tensed as the lighter footsteps came toward me...but then *she* came around the screen, and I saw her.

She was perhaps thirty years old, wearing a peach silk gown. Her eyes were lavender and her hair was a shade of light brown with blond flecks. It was elaborately curled, with much of it piled on top of her head and long, wavy strands hanging down over her shoulders. She had a hint of kohl painted around her eyes, and her heart-shaped mouth was tinted red.

She was the most beautiful woman I'd ever seen.

"Oh, my dear," she said. "You are awake."

Going to a side table, she simultaneously poured a glass of water and pulled on a bell rope.

Instantly, a maid called in, "Yes, my lady?"

"I want tea, toast, and warm beef broth brought in immediately."

"Yes, my lady."

The beautiful woman walked to me and sat on the bed, putting one hand gently behind my head. "Sip this, my dear."

I drank the water gratefully and let her settle me back on the pillow.

For the first time, she really looked at me, taking in my face and eyes. "Goodness," she said. "No wonder Royce has lost his head."

I had no response.

"I am Adina," she said, as if this would explain everything.

"Where am I?" I managed to whisper.

"Where are you? You're home of course. Royce found you. Don't you remember? He carried you last night, nearly exhausted himself." She touched my forehead. "Your fever is broken, but you need rest. I think you'd gone too long without water."

She had me take a few more sips, and her expression grew more serious.

"My dear. How did you escape from those thieves? Lord Trey would like to know."

Her eyes were kind, and her concern for me was genuine. I could see this much for myself, and I was hungrier for the kindness of a woman than I was for food. My first instinct was to tell her everything, but a warning bell went off in the back of my mind.

She would tell Lord Trey what I told her, and for some reason, I didn't want Trey or Royce to know about the settlement. I could still see the women and children there. I could see the houses and gardens.

"They let me go," I said. This was not entirely a lie. Raven had let me go.

"Let you go?" she repeated.

Remembering the argument between Caine and Raven not long after they had taken me, I said, "Only one of the men wanted to take me. The others did not, and Royce had threatened to send the king's soldiers after them, so they put me off the horse and left me."

This was a lie.

Her expression shifted to sympathy. "Oh, my dear. How awful. It's a good thing Royce was out looking."

Was it? I wasn't sure.

I was glad for this woman's presence, more than I could tell her. But who was she? She had called herself Adina, yet that meant little to me. I knew nothing of the family dynamics. As she was about the same age as Royce, she could not be his mother. Perhaps Royce's mother was dead, and Adina was his stepmother.

"Are you Lord Trey's wife?"

She laughed. "Goodness, no. I am companion to him, as you will be companion to Royce."

A serving woman entered the room and carried a tray around the side of the silk screen.

"Set it here beside the bed and then leave us," Adina ordered.

She had me sip some tea. Then she soaked bits of toast in beef broth and fed them to me. I had never tasted anything so good. When I was finished, Adina had me lay back against the pillows.

"Sleep now. You need rest. I'll be in again later."

Comfortable for the first time in days, I closed my eyes.

\* \* \* \*

I remained in bed that night and through part of the next day.

In the late afternoon—or perhaps early evening—I felt well enough to rise and explore my immediate surroundings, walking around the silk screen to better see the room. It was lovely, and much larger than I'd expected. As with the area near the bed, all the walls were painted in a soft cream. The burgundy carpet beneath my bare feet was thick, and the far wall sported a small hearth. There were low tables and long couches with velvet upholstery. The paintings were all still-lifes of flowers, from peonies to gladiolas.

Even I could see the furnishings were finer than anything in Lady Giselle's apartments.

The door opened, and Adina entered with a graceful walk—carrying an armload of towels. She stopped at the sight of me standing there in my nightgown. Then she smiled.

"You're up. I'm so glad. Royce is insistent you join us at the dinner table tonight, and I wasn't sure what to tell him."

My stomach tightened. "Dinner?"

"Yes, he's not seen you since he carried you through the front doors." Without noticing my anxiety, she set the towels near the hearth. "Do you like your room? There were several choices, but I thought this one best."

"My room?"

So little of what this woman said made any sense.

"Of course," she answered. "You must have a room. If you don't care for this one, I can show you a few others."

For the moment, this room felt safe. "No. I like this one."

Before either one of us could speak again, the door opened, and two serving women carried in a tub. Several others followed with buckets of steaming water.

"I thought you'd like a bath," Adina offered.

As I could hardly argue with her, I let myself be swept along. Once the tub was ready, she sent everyone else out. I bathed myself, and then Adina washed my hair. Once I stepped out of the water, she wrapped me in a thick blanket, and she towel-dried my hair.

Then she combed it out.

"Sit here on this couch while we wait for it to dry," she said.

As I sat, something occurred to me. "Oh...Adina. I don't have anything to wear at dinner. My trunk was taken."

"I know. But I have more gowns than I can count, and I've had maids working on hemming enough of them to get you by until we can bring in a proper seamstress and order your wardrobe. Royce was surprisingly particular. Normally, he couldn't care a fig about gowns, but he says he likes you in white, and a particular shade of very light blue."

Something about this last part bothered me, but I wasn't sure what.

"Don't worry, my dear," she went on. "I have several gowns ready for you, and dinner will be a simple family affair."

This gave me an opening. "Who will be there?"

"Only you and I and Lord Trey and Royce."

From yesterday, I remembered Lord Trey saying that Royce's wife would be away for several months, but what about Trey's wife?

Adina was watching my face. "What do you know of the family?"

"Nothing. Is Lord Trey married?"

She sat down beside me, fluffing my hair as it dried. "He was...to Royce's mother." I heard pain in her voice. "We lost sweet Marianne five years ago."

This didn't help me much. "How long have you been here?"

"Me? Goodness. Since I was about your age." She suddenly seemed to understand that I truly knew nothing of the family. Perhaps she believed they were so well known that everyone knew their story. "Trey and Marianne married young, and he adored her. Everyone adored her. She had a wonderful warmth about her. Royce was born soon after, but Marianne was never strong, and no more children followed. Around the time Royce became a man, Trey decided to take on a formal companion—and Marianne fully approved. Many girls from the noble families were hopeful, but my father is Pierre des Brumes, and Trey made an arrangement with him."

I followed only about half of what she said, but it appeared that she had been Trey's mistress since around the age of eighteen, and her position was envied.

"You were happy?" I asked.

"Oh, very. Marianne was kind to me, and we all did quite well here together until Royce married Loraine...and then things were not quite as before."

"Why?"

She hesitated. "You still have much to learn here, and I shouldn't say too much. But five years ago, Trey hosted a hunting party, and Marianne insisted on riding. She fell from her horse over a jump and was killed. The house went into a kind of mourning I'd never known. It took us over a year to recover."

Adina closed her eyes, and I could see how fond she'd been of Royce's mother. But the story was oddly close to home for me. My own father had died falling from a horse. Even though I'd never known him, this seemed to make for an unexpected connection between Royce and myself.

Opening her eyes, Adina stood. "So, that is our story." Leaning down, she touched my hand. "I have been happy here, and I hope you will be too. But I do fear Royce may be a bit more of a challenge than his father."

I wanted her to elaborate on that last part.

The door opened, and a young woman, perhaps a few years older than me walked in carrying a white silk gown. Adina went to her. "Yes, Abigail. That's the gown. Bring it in." Turning back to me, she said, "This is Abigail. She will be your personal maid. You don't need to worry. She's very skilled. I trained her myself."

A personal maid? For me?

Before I could speak, Adina walked to the door. "Now, I must go and dress for dinner myself. Kara, I'll meet you in the dining room. Abigail will show you the way."

Then she was gone, and I was alone with Abigail. She was pretty, with a smattering of freckles. Her red hair was pulled into a bun at the nape of her neck.

"May I get you dressed, my lady?" she asked.

I was not a lady. I was the illegitimate daughter of a lady's maid. But I had no idea what was happening here, and so I simply stood up.

I let Abigail help get me into my undergarments, and then I stepped into the gown so she might lace me in. After this, she heated a round iron and curled my hair, leaving it down.

But then...she leaned in to paint kohl at the corners of my eyes.

"Oh, no," I said. "I don't wear any kind of makeup."

Lord Jean had always disapproved.

"Lady Adina was most particular in her instructions," Abigail answered.

Not knowing my power here, I let her paint the kohl at the corners of my eyes, and she tinted my mouth red. Finally, she hung a crystal pendant around my neck and helped me into a pair of slippers.

I was ready.

"May I show you to the dining room, my lady?" she asked.

* * * *

The journey down took longer than I anticipated, and I was beginning to gain an understanding of the sheer size of the house. My room was on the third floor.

We descended three flights of stairs, past countless paintings and wall sconces—and two suits of armor. On the main floor, Abigail led me down a long, wide wall, and I could see an open arch up ahead.

"Through there, my lady," she said.

Clearly, she was not going any farther.

With a nod, I walked forward, passing through the archway into a vast dining room. The table would have easily seated thirty people. In here, the walls were painted red, and the paintings depicted images of noblemen on horseback.

Royce, Trey, and Adina all stood near the far end of the table sipping glasses of wine.

When I entered, Royce turned and took in the sight of me.

Striding to me quickly he took my hand. There was a dark bruise from his left temple to the outside of his jaw. I hadn't noticed this in the forest when he found me, but I now remembered that Caine had kicked him in the head. I could not imagine what it would feel like to be kicked by Caine.

"Kara," Royce said. "Are you well? Adina told me those men released you, but I hope you did not suffer long. I found you as quickly as I could."

He and I hadn't spoken much. As he looked down at me intently, I sensed he wanted something, but I had no idea what.

Trey and Adina were coming to join us, so I simply answered Royce, "No, I did not suffer long."

His expression shifted to disappointment. I'd not given the correct response.

"I did find you as soon as possible," he said.

"Royce," Adina said. "Please fetch Kara some wine. She is still recovering from her ordeal."

With a stiff nod, he walked away. What had I done wrong?

Slightly alarmed, Adina leaned in toward me. "Thank him."

I shook my head at her, confused. Thank him? For what?

"For rescuing you," she whispered.

Had it not been for Royce wrenching me away from my lady and lifting onto the back of a horse, I would never have been out in a forest near nightfall at all. I would never have been exposed to an attack from thieves in the first place.

But then I understood. Yesterday, Trey had mentioned that Royce saw himself as my hero. Though I did not see things quite the same, if Adina was alarmed, I needed to act. I had much practice at meeting the emotional needs of someone else, and I knew what to do.

When Royce returned with a goblet of wine, I said to him, "My lord. Thank you for finding me. Thank you for saving me. I was frightened and near the end of my wits."

His features softened. "Of course. I started after you as soon as possible."

Lord Trey appeared somewhat bored with this discussion, but I thought back to what had happened on the road that night. When I was taken, Royce had been unconscious on the ground, but I did not mention this.

"Your guards were all injured. What did you do?" I asked.

"Oh," Royce answered. "Father brought me around, but we were the only two still on our feet. The manor wasn't too far, so we came home for help. There is a contingent of the king's soldiers stationed a few miles from the manor, so I sent a message off to them, and then we gathered some of our own guards and several wagons to go back and help our men."

Adina listened with interest.

"That was wise of you," I said, and I meant it. "And good of you to worry so for your men."

Trey nodded, warming to the topic now. "A few were badly hurt, but once home, we had the arrows removed and the wounds dressed."

"Soon after that," Royce finished, "twenty of the king's soldiers arrived, and I took them and set off in search of you."

When he told the story, he did sound like a hero, and from his perspective, he was. I'd been stolen by raiders, and he'd done everything he could to recover me.

"Thank you," I said again.

Several servants carried in trays of food.

"Shall we sit?" Adina suggested.

There were four place settings at the far end of the table. Trey sat at the head. Royce sat on one side, and Adina and I sat on the other. The table was so long that I could see why they preferred this arrangement.

As servants served the soup course, Adina asked, "Royce, where did that bruise on your head come from?"

"He was protecting me," I said.

At the flash of pleasure on Royce's face, I knew I'd said the exact right thing.

"We were simply outnumbered," Trey answered. Again, he seemed more interested now that the story had moved beyond Royce finding me in the forest. "Until that point, we'd managed to keep a steady head. Royce only took action when it became clear they meant to take Kara."

Adina nodded. "Tell me from the beginning. I've not had a moment to hear the entire tale since your return."

At her prompting, both men began to alternately tell the story of their adventure. Now that everyone was safe, they seemed to be enjoying themselves.

Adina intently listened to every word, and I followed her example.

Dinner conversation proved easy. The men simply needed an audience.

\* \* \* \*

Later that night, upon finally being allowed to retire, I was beyond relieved when Abigail helped me out of my dinner gown and into a white lace nightgown. Perhaps I'd not fully recovered from my flight through the forest, and I felt somewhat weary.

Dinner had not been an awful experience, only tiring, and I looked forward to crawling into bed. I tried not to think on my lady and how alone she must feel. I hoped Lord Jean might spend some time with her and try to offer comfort.

Would I be allowed to write to her? I would ask Adina in the morning.

"Is there anything else you need, my lady?" Abigail asked.

I wished she would stop calling me that. It made me feel like a fraud. But I had no wish to seem disagreeable either. My place in this household was still unclear to me.

"No, thank you. I should like to sleep now."

Nodding, she turned to leave, but as she reached for the door, it opened. Royce stood on the other side.

Wearing nothing but a thin lace nightgown, I cast around for a blanket or something to cover myself. There was nothing.

"My lord," she said, hurrying out past him.

To my surprise, he stepped inside and closed the door.

As he looked at me, I recognized his hunger and stepped back.

"Kara," he breathed.

"My lord…" I began, wondering how I might make him leave without giving offense. "It is late."

"I've brought you something."

Looking down, I saw a velvet box in his hand. He carried it over to me and opened it. Inside lay a diamond necklace. It was beautiful but looked as if it would be heavy to wear.

"This is for you," he said.

I didn't understand him. Though I knew little of the value of precious stones, even I could see this was an object of great value. Why would he give it to me? Perhaps I could ask Adina tomorrow. But for the moment, I was on uncertain ground. "Thank you."

His face flickered in disappointment, and I didn't know what he wanted. He set the box on a table. "I know you must be overwhelmed with gratitude, being taken from obscurity and given a place in the Capello family, but you don't need to hide your feelings from me. We're alone. You can show me how you feel."

Reaching out, he touched my face. Startled, I shrank away, and his eyes clouded. Without warning, he grabbed the back of my head and pulled me up against him, pressing his mouth down onto mine.

The sensation was shocking, foreign, and invasive. For an instant, his grip loosened, and I wrenched away from him, trying to run for the door, but he came behind me, and I veered toward the silk screen, knocking it over. It fell into a table.

Near the bed, Royce caught me, grabbing my left arm. I swung with my right fist, hitting him in the chest.

"Kara!" he shouted. Grabbing my wrist, he jerked me up against him. Now he was angry. "I took you from nothing! I scoured the forest with no sleep for days in search of you, and *this* is how you repay me? You are not what I thought."

Then his mouth was pressing against mine again, and he pushed his tongue between my teeth. Fear turned to panic. I fought and struggled, but he was so much stronger. Dropping his weight on top of me, he pinned me to the bed, and I began to weep.

"Please, stop," I begged. "Please."

He didn't stop.

# Chapter Eleven

The next day, upon waking, I was in so much pain I wasn't sure I could move.

At least I was alone.

Royce had left me at some point. My mind would only allow in small bits of what he'd done to me in the night, and it rejected some of the memories fighting to surface. Slowly, I tried to rise from the bed, ignoring the small spatters of blood on the sheets.

Making my way to the water basin, I hoped there was still water inside.

The door to my room opened, and I froze in terror, fearing he'd come back.

But it was Adina, her face awash in concern. "Kara, what happened last night? Royce just came downstairs with a face like thunder, and he walked through the house without speaking to anyone. I've never seen him so angry."

Then she took a look at me. "Oh, Kara…what have you done? You didn't try to refuse him, did you?" She saw the fallen silk screen, and her eyes widened in alarm. "You could not possibly have…Didn't Lady Giselle teach you anything?"

I barely followed what she said.

Moving closer, she took my arm, and the alarm on her face turned to fear. "Did you try to resist him? Don't you understand? He views himself as your savior, your protector. That is why he values you. If you lose that, you'll lose him."

Her eyes shifted back and forth, but I still barely heard her words and pulled away, cupping water into my hands and drinking several mouthfuls.

"Listen to me!" she said urgently. "There's still time, but you have to do exactly as I say. He's out riding, as he always does at this time of day. He'll come in later for lunch. You need to get dressed and meet him out back in the rose garden as he's walking in. His mother planted it, and it's one of his favorite places. Kara, are you hearing me? Ask his forgiveness. Plead your innocence and ignorance. He'll understand that...He may even like it. But you *must* convince him how grateful you are to him for both giving you this position and rescuing you from those brigands. You must make him feel like your savior."

What was she saying? She wanted me to go to Royce and ask his forgiveness, when last night he'd forced himself on me as I wept and begged him to stop?

"No," I said. "I won't do that."

"Then you're lost! You have one chance to turn this around, and if you can't, he could lose his value of you."

"Good. He'll send me back to my lady."

"Back to your lady? Kara, he lost a thousand pieces of silver on a land deal to purchase you. Do you think he'll give that up? He'll sell you to another nobleman who might not view you as an honored companion, or he'll sell you to..." She trailed off and then said. "There are far worse things in this world than flattering and catering to the needs of one man."

I stared at her, finally listening. She was frightened for me.

"You have one chance," she repeated, "while he would still prefer to keep you. Win his affections back this morning, and then never displease him again. In most ways, Royce is not a complicated man. He simply needs to feel that you need him, and I know you can do that, but if you don't..."

Her fear was infectious, as were her words of what Royce might do should he lose his value of me.

"How long will he ride?" I asked.

"At least an hour. We need to get you dressed."

\* \* \* \*

Not quite an hour later, I stood in a doorway out the back of the manor. I wore a light blue muslin day-dress similar to the one I'd worn the morning Royce had bought me from Lord Jean. I wore no kohl on my eyes and no tint on my mouth.

My hair hung in loose waves down my back.

I needed to prompt images in his mind of why he'd wanted me in the first place. I hated this and was humiliated at the thought of what I was about to do. But Adina's fear was real, and if she said there were far worse things than catering to Royce, I believed her.

Before me, a rose garden stretched out. Most of the buds were gone by now, but a few autumn roses remained, in shades of pink and yellow, making for a pretty scene.

I waited.

Then...I saw him striding toward me from the stables. He wore canvas pants, high boots, and a burgundy tunic. His hair blew in the morning breeze. His eyes were brooding, and his mood was still dark.

Taking a breath, I walked out through the roses to meet him.

"My lord."

He stopped. But his gaze passed from my dress to my face, and I could see he was moved, as always, by my physical appearance. I needed to act quickly.

"My lord," I said again, making my tone to sound deferential. "Please forgive me for last night. I didn't understand your actions, and in my ignorance, I was frightened. Lady Giselle always kept me to herself, and she never told me of such..."

Looking down at me, his expression softened as he listened. I'd read my lady's face a thousand times and always knew when I'd struck the right note to please her. I had a good deal of practice with this skill.

Whether Royce knew it or not, my words were exactly what he wanted to hear.

"Please forgive me," I said again.

He shook his head, "I should have realized you knew nothing of..." Reaching out, he touched my hair.

Somehow, I managed not to shiver. "I am so grateful to you for bringing me here, for saving and protecting me."

His eyes filled with warmth, and even mild regret. "I was too rough last night, but I didn't understand either. I hope you will forgive me."

This made me cautious. If I verbally granted forgiveness, it would suggest he'd done something wrong, and I was beginning to understand that Royce did not like to be faulted.

"There is nothing to forgive," I answered. "The fault was mine."

Of course I would never forgive him, and I'd never forget his brutality. But I feared Adina's warnings more than I feared him.

"And you are glad to be here with me?" he asked.

"I am so glad, and I am so grateful."

He breathed in with a satisfied sound, as if he were hungry and I'd fed him exactly what he needed. Leaning down, he kissed my forehead gently. "Have you had breakfast? I know it's almost lunchtime, but I've not had a bite."

He offered me his arm.

I took it.

\* \* \* \*

Royce spent much of the day with me.

Together, at the table in the dining room, we had eggs, bacon, and tea for lunch, and then I suggested a game of chess.

"You play?" he asked, clearly pleased.

The manor was large and lavish, and he led me to a parlor that nearly left me speechless. The hearth was built from white bricks, and the thick carpets were blue with a pattern of white diamonds. The velvet-covered chairs and couches were also blue, and the paintings in here depicted seascapes of waves crashing into shores. There were polished cabinets with glass doors filled with crystal or porcelain vases.

He watched my reaction when we entered, and he smiled.

This was the first time I'd seen him smile.

"Even the king does not have so fine a sitting room," he said. "Wait until you see the library. There are twenty girls at court who would give up the thumb of their right hand to trade places with you."

Not knowing how to answer this, I nodded.

A chess set sat on a cherrywood table near a long window. Royce motioned to a chair. "You play white."

Here, I gauged him again. I knew he would not like to lose, but neither would he enjoy an easy win.

He opened with a foolish gambit, leaving his queen partially exposed, but I ignored this. Later though, I had him in check several times before purposefully moving a knight out of his way, and letting his bishop cross the board to place me in check mate.

He was quite pleased by the game.

"Well done!" he said. "I'd no idea you would be so skilled. You nearly had me."

This time, I smiled at him, and he went still at the sight. Though I could never discount his potential for violence, I was beginning to understand him. So long as he felt both superior and magnanimous, he could be kind.

\* \* \* \*

That night at dinner, I wore a shimmering white silk gown with tiny pearls sewn into the neckline. Royce had me sit next to him, and he was attentive to me even as he discussed crops and taxes with his father.

"The Dulcimer village had fever pass through over the summer," Trey said. "They lost men and have been slow bringing in the harvest. I want to give them extra time to pay us their taxes."

Royce nodded. "If you think so, but will that leave us in a position to pay our own?" Using his knife and fork, he cut the most tender portion of meat from the roast beef on his plate and moved it over to mine.

"I'll let the king know," Trey answered. "He has sympathy for villages who suffer from fever."

But Adina had been watching Royce, and when he gave me his best cut of his beef, she nodded to me almost imperceptibly in approval. Again, at dinner, Adina and I were not expected to speak much.

Once dessert was over, she stood. "We will leave you gentlemen to your port now. When you're ready, come meet us in the sitting room."

Last night, as I'd been tired, she had excused me to go upstairs right after dinner, but it seemed tonight I would be expected to remain downstairs. I followed her from the dining room, down the hall toward the front of the manor and into the lavish sitting room.

"Would you like tea?" she asked.

I'd struggled to finish my dinner and was too full for even a sip of water. "No, thank you."

The hearth was burning, and we sat by the fire.

"Whatever you did this morning, my dear," she said, "you did it well, and I can see that you're beginning to understand your role here. You have one job and one job only, to make Royce happy. So long as you keep him pleased, you'll have a safe and comfortable life."

And what if I couldn't?

As always, she read my face. "You can. I see that you can. He's already besotted with you. Make him feel generous, and he'll be clay in your hands."

I was about to ask her more when Trey and Royce both walked in.

"The port doesn't call to us tonight," Trey said. "Nor does the company of only each other. Royce has told me Kara is quite skilled at chess. What about a game?"

Adina leaned back in her chair and rolled her eyes. "Goodness no. Chess bores me to tears when I have to play it, much less having to watch you both play it."

I tensed, wondering how he would react.

But he laughed. "And what doesn't bore you besides spending money?"

Tilting her head, she smiled at him. "I can think of a few things, but they aren't fit for polite company. What about a game of cards? Spades perhaps? Now that there are four of us, we could play teams?"

Royce looked to me. "Do you enjoy cards?"

Though I would have agreed to anything, I answered honestly, "I do, but I've never played in a game with teams. My lady and I played only games for two people."

"This one is simple," he said. "I can teach you. Shall we play as a team?"

"No," Adina said. "She'll be on my team. I say women against men."

Again, Trey laughed.

As we sat down around a small table, another piece of the puzzle here fell into place. For Adina and me, our roles were quite different here given the natures of these two men. If it was my job to make Royce feel generous, it was her job to make Trey laugh.

\* \* \* \*

That night, when I went to my room, the silk screen was back in place, the sheets had been changed and all evidence of what had happened was gone. The only reminder was the black velvet case containing the diamond necklace, and this had been moved to my dressing table.

I put it in the top drawer.

Abigail entered the room, carrying a clean nightgown.

"A pleasant evening, my lady?" she asked.

With no idea how else to answer, I nodded. "Yes."

She unlaced me and helped me step out of the gown. Then she slipped the nightgown over my head. This one was too long, but otherwise it fit well.

"Come sit, and I'll brush your hair," she said.

As I sat down, the door opened and Royce walked in. Though I'd hoped he'd not come here again so soon, I wasn't surprised to see him. It seemed he was not required to knock or ask permission to enter my room.

But he appeared more at ease tonight and dropped into a chair, motioning to Abigail with one hand. "Carry on."

He sat watching as she brushed my hair.

When she finished, he nodded with his head toward the door. "Out."

Quickly, she gathered the silk gown and fled the room.

But Royce remained in his chair. "You looked beautiful at dinner tonight. Did you enjoy the card game afterward?"

"I did. Did you?"

"Yes. The whole evening reminded me of days long past, when my mother still lived."

This took me aback. It was the first time he'd tried speaking to me about anything that mattered. "You miss her?"

He nodded. "When she left us, the life seemed to go out of the house, but tonight...I didn't feel so alone."

Was that Royce's great secret? He was lonely?

Standing, he came over to me, drawing me to my feet. My eyes were level with his collarbones, and I couldn't help my rising fear. But I kept my expression calm, even when he tilted my head up and kissed me. Again, the feeling was foreign and invasive, and I had no idea what to do—only that I couldn't try to push him away or resist him.

Thankfully, he wasn't offended by my lack of response and whispered. "Just move your mouth with mine."

When he kissed me again, I tried to respond.

* * * *

As the weeks passed, I began to find my place inside the household, and the days took on a somewhat familiar rhythm. Royce began to stay all night in my room. He asked me to call him by his name in private, as it was more intimate than "my lord."

We slept until mid morning and then had a light meal of rolls and hot chocolate. After this, he either went riding on his own or he and Trey would ride out to visit some of the villages on their estate lands—checking on crops or taxes.

Adina and I were never idle. She ran the house and managed the servants and went over menus with the cook. She was only too happy for my inclusion in these tasks, and because I'd worked with my lady back home, I knew something of how a great house was run.

I also had gown fittings several times a week. Adina oversaw these as well, and at one point, she launched into an argument with Royce after he'd insisted all my gowns be made from fabrics of either white or ice blue.

"Surely, you'd like to see her in some other color on occasion?" Adina asked. "What about a soft shade of oyster-shell pink?"

"No."

On this point—as with most points—he was firm. I never questioned him. My lady had liked me only in those two shades as well, so I was accustomed. However, as the days passed, I became uncomfortably aware of many similarities between my relationship to my lady and my relationship to Royce.

I watched his face and listened carefully to the cadence of his voice. I tried to anticipate his needs and moods and to find ways to please or entertain him. So long as I showed him my gratitude, never argued with him, and made him feel like my savior and protector, he was the soul of kindness.

We often ate a late lunch in the dining room, and then we would spend much of the afternoon together. Sometimes he liked to play chess, but often, he liked for me to walk the manor grounds with him. This was difficult for me at first, as I still feared the open sky, but I learned to hold his arm and keep my eyes down and let him lead. This didn't offend him, and he even seemed to enjoy my need of keeping his arm.

The grounds were beautiful, even as we moved into late fall. Lord Trey employed three gardeners to trim hedges, trees, and holly berry bushes. Royce liked for me to have a good view of the manor itself as well. Although my experience was limited, even I could see the Capello manor was magnificent: four stories of tan brick with ivy and climbing roses. The numerous windows contained clear glass. The slanted roof was of red tile, and the front doors were enormous, painted white with a gold knocker in the shape of a lion's head.

"It's been in my family for six generations," he said one day as we walked.

As he seemed willing to speak of his family and the past, I found myself on the edge of asking him a question I'd been longing to pose. My face must have given something away because he asked, "What is it?"

Still, I hesitated. "I have been wondering…wondering about your wife. Why is she not here?"

He stopped walking, and I was poised to change the subject instantly should I have tread on dangerous ground.

But he sighed. "She is away in Kerago, in the south, at the baths there. Do you know of them?"

I didn't know much about these baths, but I had heard of a place called Kerago where nobles and merchants went on holiday. The town boasted underground springs that had been piped up into indoor baths and were said to heal many ailments.

"Is your wife ill?"

"No, not ill, but she has never been completely well either. I finally convinced her to try the baths and remain in Kerago for a few months."

When he said this, the relief in his voice was unmistakable.

"She does not like to be away from you?"

"No, she does not. I sometimes travel without her...but she does not care to travel without me, and we've never been apart for an entire season."

From that morning back at Lord Jean's table when Royce had bought me, I remembered my lady having said that Royce had been married for eight years. As he was perhaps thirty now, that meant he'd married young for a man.

"Forgive my questions," I said. "But I don't know your customs, and sometimes feel at a loss. What you and I have...what Trey and Adina have, this is normal among most nobles? For a man to take a formal mistress?"

"Yes, in some houses it's even expected. We tend to use the word companion, but I suppose it's a euphemism."

"Before me, had you ever taken a companion?"

Here, he hesitated, and beneath my hands, the muscles in his arm tightened. "No."

This was my cue to change the subject. "How was your ride this morning. Did you go into the orchards? Are there any apples left on the trees?"

His arm relaxed, and he began walking again, leading me onward. "Yes, I did ride to the orchards, but the trees are bare."

We walked onward, speaking of insignificant things, but my thoughts churned with revelations of our brief discussion. First, Royce had made an effort to get his wife to leave and go to the baths without him. Second, this was their first lengthy separation in an eight-year marriage. Third, he was clearly relieved at her absence...and fourth, he'd used the opportunity to acquire his first formal mistress.

I did not know what the ultimate ramifications of all this would be, only that there would be ramifications.

# Chapter Twelve

A week later, we had an important visitor arriving, and the household was aflutter. King Amandine's brother, Alexi, would be stopping for the night. Even Lord Trey was unusually particular about the dinner menu and asked Adina to go over it with him several times. He had a fine cask of wine, aged twenty years, brought up from the cellar.

Only Royce appeared unaffected.

"Father always makes a fuss," he said in private. "But Alexi passes through several times a year and stays with us. Give him a decent dinner and a game of cards and he'll be content."

Still, in spite of his assurances, I sensed the evening was important to him when he told me to wear the diamond necklace.

That night, I wore an ice blue silk and the necklace. Abigail spent a good deal of time on my hair, arranging it into long curls. She put kohl under my eyes and tinted my mouth. The hint of black beneath my eyes made them glow even more than usual

"You look lovely, my lady," she said.

I found myself wishing I could feign a headache, but I could not. Royce was expecting me.

Leaving my room, I headed downstairs and toward the dining hall, hearing voices well before I arrived.

"I hadn't intended to stop," a man said, "but then I heard Loraine wasn't in residence and found I couldn't resist."

Another man laughed, but I didn't recognize that voice either.

Stopping in the archway, I realized I was the last to arrive. Adina, Trey, and Royce were all present. Adina looked beautiful in a straight-cut gown of light pink satin. Royce wore a black sleeveless tunic. Candle lanterns glowed from all about the room and on the table.

The other two men in the room were strangers. The one nearest to me was slender with dark hair and a goatee around his mouth. He was perhaps five or six years older than Royce. The other man was smooth shaven with thick, reddish brown hair. Both men wore tall boots, black pants, and silk tunics.

The dark-haired man exuded an aura of confidence. "Oh, and I'd heard rumors that Royce has finally taken on a companion? Could it be true? If so, I wanted a glimpse of the brave lady."

As if on cue, I walked through the archway, and Royce came toward me. "Alexi," he said, "let me present Kara."

With an amused smile, the dark-haired man turned, but when he saw me, the smile faded. On instinct, I moved closer to Royce, and at this, Alexi's smile returned.

"Good gods, Royce," he said. "Who is this? Where did you find her?"

"She was Jean de Marco's ward," Royce answered.

"No?" Alexi said and then turned. "Francis, do you see this?"

Reaching up, I took Royce's arm.

"I could hardly miss it," said the other man, walking over.

"Kara," Royce said, "may I present King Amandine's brother, Alexi, and his good friend, Francis Le Trou."

I bowed my head politely.

"At your service, I assure you," Alexi said with a laugh.

I was out of my element and growing more nervous. But Royce seemed to sense this and led me to the table. Everyone took a chair. I knew it would be considered poor manners for him to seat me beside himself, but he did anyway, and I was grateful.

Adina smiled at me from across the table. "I fear we are outnumbered by the men."

"So long as Loraine is absent, we'll be a merry party," Alexi said, taking a long drink of wine. He looked to me. "Have you met my dear cousin?"

I wasn't sure what he was asking me and did not know how to answer.

"Does she ever speak?" Francis asked.

Adina did not appear to be enjoying the way they spoke around me and explained, "Kara, the lady Loraine is Alexi's first cousin. They are not fond of each other."

Alexi laughed again, but I absorbed this information—which Royce had neglected to share. If Alexi was Amandine's brother, then Loraine was first cousin to the king. Royce ignored all of Alexi's slights upon Loraine.

"Where are you off to after this?" he asked.

The conversation flowed to Alexi and Francis's coming travels, and I felt myself begin to relax. Thankfully, no one expected me to speak through the rest of dinner, but I did notice Royce drank three goblets of wine, when he normally stopped at one. I was beyond glad when dessert was finished and Adina stood.

"Gentlemen," she said, "it's time we leave you to your port."

Perhaps she and I would have a short reprieve.

To my disappointment, Alexi stood up as well. "I've no taste for port tonight." He looked to Royce. "And I'd rather join the ladies. This little thing of yours has yet to say a word. Does she play any games?"

"She's quite good at chess."

"No? Really?"

Coming over to me, Alexi offered his arm. "Lead on to the sitting room. I challenge you to a game."

I glanced at Royce, and he nodded.

This appeared to amuse Alexi greatly. "Did she just ask your permission to take my arm? My gods, I wish I'd visited de Marco first."

With little choice, I took his arm.

Everyone moved to follow us, but Royce brought a full decanter of wine from the table.

Once we reached the sitting room, Alexi headed toward the chessboard. Numerous candle lanterns and wall sconces provided light.

"Kara," Lord Trey said. "I'm having trouble with my collar."

Letting go of Alexi, I saw Trey pulling at the collar of his tunic and went to help. Perhaps it was too tight and would need to be loosened.

But as I reached him, he leaned down and whispered. "Don't let him win."

I looked into his eyes. Did he know I let Royce win?

"He's better than Royce," Trey whispered, "but take his king as quickly as you can."

Not only did he know, he was giving me permission to really play.

I nodded.

A few moments later, Alexi and I were seated at the board. Adina and Trey played a game of cards while Royce and Francis chose to watch the chess match. Royce poured himself a full goblet of wine and offered one to Francis.

"Ladies first," Alexi said, waving a hand over the board.

As Trey had warned me that he was better than Royce, I started by setting up a careful defense. Four moves in, he saw what I was doing and raised an eyebrow.

"Who taught you to play?"

"Lady Giselle," I answered with just enough voice to be heard. It was the first thing I'd said all night.

The sound of my voice seemed to affect him. "I'm not going to bite you." Royce took a long swallow of wine.

Lord Trey had not been wrong. Alexi was a skilled player, but he was also overly aggressive, and less than hour in, he left an opening with his king cornered. I moved a knight to block any escape.

"Checkmate."

Sitting straight, he looked down at what I'd done, and I waited tensely for his reaction. Thankfully, he was not annoyed, only surprised.

Then he laughed. "I've not lost a game in four years." Turning to Royce, he asked, "What kind of arrangement did you make with de Marco. What were his terms for her care and future?"

By this point, Royce was nearly drunk, slumped in his chair. But I could see his amusement that I'd beaten Alexi at chess.

"No terms at all," he said, sounding as if he was boasting. "I bought her."

"What do you mean?" Francis asked. He'd been growing bored but was at full attention now.

Royce shrugged. "He's been after me for a piece of land for years. You know the one, on our northern border? They called the girl their 'ward' but she's the daughter of Lady Giselle's brother and some maid. De Marco offered me twenty-five hundred silvers for the land. I told him I'd take fifteen hundred and the girl. He agreed. She's mine."

My face flushed with shame. Again, I was "the girl."

"She's of no family?" Alexi asked, leaning forward. "And she's property?"

"I'll give you a draft for three thousand silvers for her tonight," Francis said.

"Four thousand," Alexi countered.

My hands began to tremble.

But Royce came to his senses. "No, my lord," he said to Alexi. "She's not for sale."

"Five thousand," Alexi offered. "And I'll make sure you have an invitation to next year's council gathering."

Royce's body stiffened. "She's not for sale."

"*Gentlemen*," Adina said, rising from the card table. "Surely you can see this vulgar display is distressing Kara. I suggest if you wish to make bids on each other's property, you go out to the stable and look at horses."

Both Alexi and Francis had the good taste to appear chagrined.

Reaching out to me, she looked back to Trey. "Might the ladies be excused for the evening?"

"Yes, of course," he answered.

I looked to Royce, and he nodded.

Taking Adina's hand, I fled the sitting room.

\* \* \* \*

About two hours later, Royce came to my room. I was in my nightgown and dressing robe, but I knew he'd be coming and would want me to wait. I didn't mind having to stay up and was simply glad for the two hours of privacy behind a closed door.

He appeared more sober, so he must have stopped drinking, but he was troubled.

"Kara," he said upon closing the door. "I'm sorry about what happened down there. I did not mean for that to happen. Adina was right, and I could see you were distressed."

Though Royce had once before mentioned hoping for my forgiveness, this was the first time he'd ever said he was sorry. He had indeed shamed me, and his thoughtlessness had prompted those two men to start bidding. But the apology was another quagmire for me. If I offered my forgiveness, it would suggest he was at fault. He might blame himself, but no matter how much regret he might feel, he would not want blame from me.

"You couldn't have known how they'd behave," I said. "And you put a stop to all that rough talk quickly."

His body relaxed, and his eyes drifted as if he thought back to the conversation. "Yes," he said. "I did stop it."

Again, he was my hero, my protector, and he came to me, touching my face. "For all Alexi's power and money, he doesn't have anything like you. He's always envied us this manor, and now he envies me for you."

He was pleased, and any potential crisis was past.

Leaning down, he kissed me.

Dutifully, I kissed him back.

\* \* \* \*

The next day, we served our guests a late breakfast and then walked them out to the courtyard to say goodbye. Several wagons of luggage and at least twenty royal guards were waiting.

"Keep an eye out if you're on the road near dusk," Trey told Francis. "We were attacked not three miles north of here."

Alexi kissed Adina's hand and thanked her for the pleasant stay. Both men were on their best behavior this morning, perhaps even somewhat embarrassed by the events that had followed the chess match. I supposed, in their defense, they had been drinking.

As I stood halfway behind Royce, Alexi did not attempt to kiss my hand. But he glanced at me and said to Royce, "If you ever change your mind..."

"I won't," Royce answered. "But come back soon. You're always welcome at our table."

The men mounted up, and we waved our goodbyes. I was not sorry to see them go.

As I started back for the front doors, Royce stopped me.

"I need to ride out on an errand," he said. "And I won't be home until mid-afternoon."

I knew better than to ask him about his business. "Would you like me to wait until you return before having lunch served?"

"No, you go ahead and eat. I don't know how long this will take."

With that, he strode off for the stables, and I walked back through the manor doors with Trey and Adina.

"I'm going to make sure the guest rooms are cleaned," Adina said. "Kara, would you like to come?"

As I was about to agree, Trey interrupted. "I'd like Kara to come to the sitting room."

"Goodness. Whatever for?" she asked.

He smiled. "I'd like her to play a game of chess with me."

Shaking her head, Adina started toward the stairs. "Whatever you like, but it's far too early in the day for chess."

Trey looked to me. "Do you mind?"

"Of course not."

Together, we walked to the sitting room. The fire in the hearth had been lit, and the air was comfortably warm. I liked the way the daylight streamed in through the windows.

Trey said, "I'm not Royce. Play your best game."

Sitting at the game board, I asked, "How do you know I let Royce win?"

"I'm no fool, and I've watched you. You lose too skillfully." He sat. "I've not done enough to make you feel welcome here. I was worried at first and thought Royce had made a mistake in choosing you. But he didn't. No one could handle him better than you. I've never seen him so at ease with himself, and I'm well aware what this must cost you."

Dropping my gaze, I didn't trust myself to answer. He knew. He knew a good deal more than he'd let on.

"You are welcome here," he added, "and wanted here. Adina adores you, and in all areas but one, you have my protection."

Lifting my head, I assumed the caveat meant that he could not protect me from Royce. Still, his promise moved me. I'd never had Lord Jean's protection.

Trey motioned to the board. "You play white."

\* \* \* \*

I won the first game, but he beat me fairly on the second, and I enjoyed myself immensely. With Lord Trey, I could drop all pretense and be myself.

Adina came to join us, bringing both my embroidery and hers. The servants brought us lunch and tea in the sitting room. After lunch, Trey offered to read a novel aloud while we did needlework, and the three of us passed half the afternoon in quiet companionship. I could not remember having been this close to feeling peace or contentment since my arrival.

In the late afternoon, Royce came home and stuck his head in the door, but he didn't enter. "Are you all in here?"

"Where have you been?" Trey asked. "Kara said you went off on some errand."

Still not entering, Royce answered, "I did. But I've brought a gift for her."

My heart sank. I hoped I would not have to feign pleasure over some gaudy piece of jewelry. The afternoon had been so enjoyable.

"Are you ready?" Royce asked.

"What are you up to?" Adina asked.

Royce entered, wearing a full cloak, but I could see he carried something beneath it in one hand. As he approached, he drew his hand out to show me the gift.

I took a quick breath.

It was a puppy, perhaps twelve weeks old.

"I've been told her name is Lily," he said. "But you can change it."

I dropped out of my chair onto the floor as he set her down, and she ran to me, wriggling in my arms and licking my face. She was white, with soft fur, and I was overwhelmed. I'd never had a dog, and she already appeared fond of me. Her small body was warm as she whined and licked my face again.

"Do you like her?" Royce asked. "I could see you've little interest in jewels, but I wasn't sure what else to buy you."

I couldn't answer, and my eyes were wet. I did not just like her. I loved her. He had brought me sweet company, something of my own to care for.

"Kara?" he knelt down and saw the tears on my face. "What's wrong?"

He sounded tense now, as if he'd guessed wrongly, but I rushed to say, "Nothing is wrong. She's perfect. Thank you so much."

My voice shook, and he then seemed troubled that I was too moved by his gift.

Perhaps he had not known that I'd been lonely.

That night, when he came to my room, I had Lily with me. I'd arranged for bowls of milk and water and had been feeding her small bits of meat. I asked him if she could be allowed to sleep in the room. The idea of the puppy in the room didn't appear to bother him, but he was still troubled by my reaction to her.

"Kara, have you been happy here with me?" he asked.

How else could I answer? "I'm very happy."

"Do you love me?"

"I love you."

# Chapter Thirteen

Autumn passed into winter.

Lord Trey told me they traveled a good deal in the spring and summer and were sometimes expected at court, but in late autumn and winter, he preferred to remain home at the Capello estate—as he appreciated a warm fire.

For my part, I appreciated our quiet days, and I'd even begun to find some measure of contentment in my new life. Adina and Trey were good company, and I delighted in Lily as she grew. She always came on walks about the estate with Royce and me. At first, he'd seemed put off by my overt affection for her, but this soon passed, and he began attempting to teach her to fetch a stick for him.

However, I never forgot my place or my duty here: to make Royce feel like a generous protector. For some reason, he needed this. I obeyed him in all things. I watched his face and his moods, and I adjusted our conversation or activities accordingly. As time drifted on though, one thought continued to nag me.

In many ways, my relationship to Royce bore similarities to my relationship with my lady.

Of course I had duties for him that I'd never had to perform for Lady Giselle, and in bed, he'd begun teaching me new ways to please him. I found some of the acts unpleasant or degrading, but I never let him know this. For the most part, as long as I made him feel like a kind and gentle man, he behaved like a kind and gentle man. I could simply never disagree with him or complain to him or show him my true feelings.

Still, as a family, he and I and Trey and Adina did well together inside the manor during those cold days, playing cards and sipping hot chocolate in the evening by a fire. I was almost beginning to accept my role and place in the household…and then everything changed.

One night, Royce walked into the dining room with a piece of paper in his hand. His expression was unreadable, but his jaw line was tense.

He looked to Trey.

"Loraine is arriving home," he said. "Tomorrow. Before lunch."

\* \* \* \*

In the night, Royce kissed me in desperation and with more pressure than usual, bruising one side of my mouth. He seemed to dread his wife's impending arrival. But he wouldn't talk to me. He wouldn't tell me anything, and I was left to wonder. Had he told her about me? Did she know he'd taken a mistress in her absence or was I to be an unwelcome surprise?

The next day, shortly before the lunch hour, we gathered in the dining hall to wait. Adina looked beautiful. Lord Trey looked resigned. Royce paced like a wolf.

I had no idea what to do or say.

We were not there long when a guard entered. "Lady Loraine's party is coming through the front gates, my lords."

"Thank you," Trey answered. He looked to the rest of us. "We must go to greet her."

Trey and Royce led the way, with Adina and me following.

As we walked down the hall, I grew nervous to the point of being frightened.

Before we reached the front doors, Adina took my hand. "It's all right, my dear. Royce wrote to her several weeks ago and informed her that he's taken a formal companion. This is common practice for men of his station, and he's well within his rights."

I cast her a grateful look. This was somewhat of a relief. At least Loraine had been informed.

But then we stepped out into the courtyard to a scene of chaos and activity. Fifteen of our own guards were dismounting their horses. There were two wagons, heavily laden with trunks and crates and casks. Servants climbed down from wagons and hurried toward a covered carriage with high wheels in the center of all this.

A thin girl with a frightened expression reached the door first, opening it.

"Might I get some assistance!" came a voice from inside the carriage.

Quickly, one of the guards strode to the open door and held out his hand. A woman took it and emerged into view, stepping onto the ground.

Her gaze flew to another guard who was attempting to unload a heavy trunk from a wagon.

"Be careful with that trunk!" she ordered. "There are porcelain plates in there. Break one, and it will come out of your pay."

This was my first sight of Loraine. As someone Royce would choose for a wife, she was not what I expected. She was perhaps ten years older than him, in her early forties, wearing a burgundy satin evening gown and a heavy ruby necklace during the day, as travel wear. Her bosom was large, as were her hips, and her waist was thick. Her eyes were prominent, and so was her nose—with a bump at the bridge. Her mouth was wide and full. A mass of reddish blond hair was her best feature, and this was piled elaborately on her head.

"I would have thought my family would have missed me enough to ride out and greet me along the road," she said somewhat petulantly to the thin, frightened girl.

"Welcome home, my lady," said Lord Trey.

Her head turned toward us in the doorway, first to Royce...and then down to me. For a moment, she wrinkled her brow until realization began to dawn. Taking a step closer, her eyes moved over my face in complete shock.

How could she be shocked? Adina had said she knew.

The shock turned to something more malevolent, and on instinct, I stepped up behind Royce.

With a cry, Loraine stumbled sideways.

"Royce!" she cried. "I am not well."

Like lightning, he ran forward and caught her arm. "My dear. Let me help you."

His voice was different than I'd ever heard it. He sounded...deferential. Putting one arm around her back, he supported her and led her past us through the front doors. He did not look at me.

"I'll get you upstairs and find a cold cloth for your head," he said to her.

Once they were gone, I turned to Adina.

What had just happened?

\* \* \* \*

Almost immediately, Adina grasped my hand and led me to the sitting room. Lord Trey remained in the courtyard to oversee the unpacking of the luggage.

Once in the sitting room, I sank down on a low couch by the fire, speechless.

Adina sat beside me, clearly distressed. "You see why I've never told you anything about her? I knew you'd need to meet her before I could try to explain."

Yes, Loraine was a force of nature, but my confusion lay in another direction. "But Royce was so…he was so…"

"I know," she answered. "He is always gently nurturing with her. He has to be."

Shaking my head, I didn't understand.

Adina sighed. "Has he told you anything about our finances?"

"No."

"Rents and taxes from the villages come in to Trey. But about fifteen years ago, before my time here, more of the tenants and farmers began moving to the cities, decreasing the Capello income. Trey found he could make his own tax payments to the king, but there wasn't much to spare. Soon…there was even less, and he began having to dismiss some of the servants."

"But we live so well now."

She nodded. "Eight years ago, Royce married Loraine. She'd become besotted with him and wanted the marriage. I don't know if he wanted it, but his mother was still alive then, and I had joined the household, and he worried for our comfort. Loraine's family is among the richest in all of Samourè, and she's first cousin to the king. Her dowry came in the form of a large yearly stipend, and from the stipend, she pays Royce an allowance. From that allowance, he pays for everything here: the servants' salaries, the fine meals we eat…our clothing. He's been generous to both me and his father."

I absorbed this slowly. Since my arrival, Royce had been buying me gowns and slippers. Had the money come from his allowance from Loraine?

"So you see," Adina went on. "He has to cater to her. The few times he's tried to curb her demands upon him, she's threatened to cut off his allowance."

"Her demands?"

Again, Adina sighed. "Loraine views herself as the sweetest of women, kind and loving to everyone. She sees herself as a victim, that people do not appreciate her. She is often ill and needs to lay upon a chaise lounge here in the sitting room so that we can attend to her. Royce has spent many nights in her room, mopping her head with a cloth and seeing to her needs because she wants no one but him…and yet she finds fault with nearly everything he does or accuses him of not doing enough."

"And he accepts this?"

"He has no choice. And if he ever needs to exceed his allowance, she exacts more of his attention. In early autumn, he lost a thousand silvers in a card game and knew he couldn't take that much from his allowance. That's why he sold the land to your de Marco lord. He needed the money. Loraine never needs know about the debt now."

I could hardly believe the things she was telling me. Why had I known none of this?

"But..." I began, "he believes she will accept my presence here?"

"Now she has no choice in *that*. As I told you before, he's well within his rights. But you are not what she expected. You look and behave nothing like the young women of court—and that is what she expected to find. Worse, Royce cares for you. He's come to need you in the same way some men need strong drink or opium." She paused. "I don't know what the next few days will bring, but we all must tread carefully."

\* \* \* \*

That night, when I walked into the dining hall, everyone else was already present. Royce was pale, but he stood talking politely to Loraine. She wore a gown of royal blue silk with yards and yards of fabric in the skirt.

Royce glanced over at me in the doorway, and in an unguarded moment, the longing on his face was unmistakable. Loraine saw this, and her features twisted. She looked at me in open hatred. And who could blame her? She leaves for a few months to visit the baths and comes home to find that her husband has installed a mistress.

Lord Trey smiled and walked to me, offering his arm and leading me to Loraine. "May I present the newest member of the household," he said to her. "I trust you will grow as fond of Kara as we have."

Loraine said nothing and glowered down at me. Standing next to her, I felt overly diminutive and wondered how I would possibly make it through dinner.

Once we were seated, Adina asked Loraine polite questions about her visit to the baths and any mutual friends Loraine might have seen. But Loraine answered the questions tightly and made it clear that she was distressed. I sat across from her and Royce, trying to focus on my plate, but halfway through the second course, I lifted my head to find him looking at me.

Loraine swayed in her chair and grasped hold of the table. "I am sorry!" she cried. "You all know how kind and accepting I am, but this is too much for my delicacy. I have tried, but I cannot sit at the same table as this...person."

"What do you mean, my dear?" Lord Trey asked, taking a bite of fish.

"I've had my maid make inquiries. This girl is the bastard daughter of no one, and should not be at the table in decent company. It is far beneath me to be forced to pretend otherwise."

Royce's body was rigid, but he said nothing.

"Kara is the daughter of Lady Giselle's brother," Lord Trey answered calmly, taking another bite, "and she was a ward of the de Marcos. She was most welcome at their table, my dear, and I'm sure you are sweet and loving enough to understand that we enjoy her company at ours."

But Loraine moaned and partially fell off her chair.

"Royce! I am not well."

He caught her as she swooned. Half lifting her, he said, "I'll get you upstairs, my love."

"And you'll stay with me. This has been too much for my fragile nature."

He helped her from the room.

Once they were gone, I couldn't take my eyes from my plate.

\* \* \* \*

As I prepared for bed that night, Royce did not come at his usual time— but I didn't expect him. However, as I had no idea what was expected, I left a candle lantern glowing on a table in case he arrived at some point and needed light. Then I crawled into bed with Lily. She was warm and wriggling and licked my face before curling up beside me. Exhausted from the day, I fell asleep.

At some point, hours later, I heard a noise and opened my eyes. Royce was beside the bed, pulling back the covers. He wore nothing but a pair of pants, and I saw no shirt or boots on the floor. Had he walked through the house like that? His hair was tousled, and his chest glistened with sweat, but I pulled Lily over so he could crawl into the bed.

"Are you all right?" I asked.

"No."

For once, I could not resist pressing him. "Royce, what is happening?"

"Loraine's finally asleep. I need some rest and some peace."

"No, I mean what is happening in the house? I don't understand any of this."

He'd not extinguished the candle lantern and looked at me in the low light. "She's insisted you be sent away. She has no objection to me taking a companion, only to your station. She believes you don't qualify as a formal mistress, and if I refuse to comply, she'll cut off my allowance."

My heart slowed. What would that mean for me? "How did you answer her?"

"I'm not sending you anywhere. You're the only thing keeping me sane."

My mind raced. What would happen to Adina and Trey if Royce had no allowance? Quickly, I climbed from the bed and went to my dressing table, taking the box with the diamond necklace from the top drawer. Then I hurried back to the bed.

"You could sell this. I do value it as you gave it to me, but I value your independence more. Please, Royce. Take it."

For an instant, I thought his eyes were wet as he touched my face. "I can't sell that. I didn't buy it. It was my mother's. But thank you for the offer." After taking the box and putting it aside, he pulled me back into the bed. "Just rest now and don't worry. I'll find some way to bargain with her."

\* \* \* \*

The next day, Royce and Trey rode out to visit a village that was late in paying its taxes—by their permission. They were going to discuss what might be arranged. After seeing them off, Adina and I went back into the house. Lily trotted at our heels. She accompanied me everywhere.

"We should probably go over the menus this morning," Adina said as we walked down the hall toward the sitting room. "Our cook told me we're already running low on apples and onions, so we may need to be sparse with dishes that call for either."

"Oh, that's a shame," I said. "Lord Trey loves apple tarts."

"He does."

But then we arrived at the sitting room to find servants running in and out. Stopping in the doorway, I looked inside to see Loraine lying on a chaise lounge near the fire, covered by a blanket. The thin, frightened girl from the day before was hovering about her head with a box of chocolates. There were numerous bowls and empty cups on the tables beside them.

"Oh, Adina, there you are," Loraine said. She wore a red velvet gown. "You know I'm not well after my journey, and you're just now coming to check on me? Royce cares nothing for my illness, and he's gone off somewhere. I would have hoped you'd be here sooner to comfort me."

"I'm here now, my dear," Adina said, walking in.

I began to follow, but Loraine sat up. "I will not have that *person* in the same room. She is too low and base."

Turning, Adina whispered, "Go to the library. I'll meet you later."

Only too glad to be excused from this scene, I hurried out and made my way to the library. There was no fire at this time of day, but I didn't care. Lily didn't seem affected by the cooler air, and I could use a blanket for a shawl. While I certainly didn't mind being banished from the sitting room, I was concerned about how the household would function now. With Loraine's arrival, the daily rhythms had been shattered.

A few hours later, Adina came through the library door, looking weary, and she raised an eyebrow at the sight of me wrapped in a warm shawl, curled up in a chair with a book in my hands and Lily in my lap.

"I've never once envied you before," she breathed, falling into a chair. "But I wish she couldn't stand to have me in the same room."

"Is she so awful?"

"Have you read stories about vampires?"

"Yes."

"She's like a type of vampire," Adina said. "She'll suck the life out of everyone around her and absorb it into herself. Then an hour later, she's hungry again and needs more people to suck dry."

Is spite of myself, I couldn't help smiling at her description, but then I sobered. "I do wish I could help." I wondered about something else. "Who is that thin girl who hovers around her?"

"Oh, that's her lady's maid, Giza. I don't think she's very good with hair, but Loraine can't seem to keep a proper maid no matter how much she pays."

Before I could respond, we heard a raised voice from down the hallway. Quietly, we both left the library to see what was happening.

Loraine's voice carried from the sitting room. "My first day back, and I'm not well, and you abandon me all day! I've been alone in here. Even Adina has abandoned me. You know I try to cause no trouble for anyone. I try to be as quiet as possible and keep of the way, but at least my husband could spare a few moments for my care!"

"I'm sorry, my love," Royce answered. "Father and I had business. I'll sit with you now."

He sounded so apologetic I barely recognized his voice.

"Oh..." Adina whispered. "The men are back. I'd better go and help Royce. I'll see you at dinner."

As the library had lost its call to me, I took a few moments to walk Lily near the house, out back. Then I slipped up to my room.

\* \* \* \*

That evening, as Abigail was dressing me for dinner, a knock sounded on my door.

"Kara, it's me," Adina said, opening the door and coming inside.

A servant followed her with a tray containing a plate of food and a goblet.

Shaking her head, Adina said. "I'm so sorry, but Royce has been striking bargains with Loraine, and they've both made some concessions. He'll not be forced to send you away, but you'll no longer join us at the dinner table. She says you aren't fit company for her delicate nature, but I think she just can't stand the way he looks at you." Her lower lip quivered. "You'll eat dinner in here."

Hurrying to her, I grasped her hands. "Please don't cry. It's fine. I would much rather hide in here than have to sit through another scene like last night." On impulse, I kissed her hands. "Truly."

"Well, I mind for you."

But there was nothing to be done, and she had to get downstairs. After she left, I excused the servant and Abigail.

Lily could smell dinner on the tray and wagged her tail. She'd already had her dinner, but I got her several good bites of chicken and then sat down to eat something myself. The thing was…I genuinely didn't mind eating in here, locked away from the eyes of everyone else. The only thought that troubled me was how similar this life was becoming to my previous life with my lady.

# Chapter Fourteen

Our days drifted onward.

Royce and Trey sometimes rode out for hours on some excuse, but the first snows had begun to fall, and Trey was in his fifties. He felt the cold in his bones and was more comfortable near a fire. As Loraine had claimed the sitting room, I hid in the library.

Adina snuck in with me as much as possible to sew or read aloud or play cards—and so did Lord Trey.

Royce always took his morning ride, even in the snow, but after that, his place was often with Loraine, finding ways to cajole and entertain her. Sometimes she napped, and he was able to join us for cards or a game of chess.

I brought books up to my room and never minded missing the formal dinners.

Royce nearly always came to join me in bed in the middle of the night. But he never kissed me or wanted me to pleasure him. He simply crawled in with me to sleep. He never minded Lily in the bed, and she slept up against his back. Sometimes when he arrived, he was fully clothed, but often, he was in the same state as that first late night, wearing nothing but his pants with his hair a mess and his chest beaded with sweat even in the cool winter air.

I began to wonder why, and one night, as he curled up against me, I whispered, "Do you join your body with Loraine's in bed as you do with me?"

He didn't answer at first and then bit off the word, "Yes."

From the tone of that single word, I could tell he did not care for the act, so I assumed she expected it. In that moment, I realized that his relationship to her was similar to my relationship to him, based on fear and domination—and I pitied him. I'd feared displeasing him for so long that it was a strange sensation to pity Royce Capello. But I did.

About two weeks after Loraine's return to the household, late morning, he found me in the library. I was alone with Lily.

He looked tired, and his face was drawn. "Loraine is asleep. Will you come out riding with me?"

I drew back into my chair, frightened. Riding? On a horse? I hadn't done that since the day I was taken by those raiders.

Instead of growing angry at my reaction, he said, "I know you're afraid. But you can ride behind and keep hold of me. Please."

I'd never refuse him anyway, but the word please tugged at my pity again. After settling Lily with Abigail and finding a warm cloak, I set off with Royce for the stable.

The afternoon proved a good deal more enjoyable than I expected. A light snow fell, turning the world white. But sitting behind Royce and holding his waist, I kept us both warm, and we rode for hours at a walk, exploring the estate farther than I'd ever gone. Through the day, I could feel his body relaxing as he pointed out trees he'd climbed as a child or a stream where he'd once fallen in. I kept my eyes down and off the sky, but the snow was helpful to me in this regard, and the sky did not seem so high or open.

The sun was nearly down by the time we got back. A groom took his horse, and we went in the front doors, walking down the main hall, speaking quietly of the ride and the sights we'd seen.

Then we stopped at the entrance to the sitting room.

Loraine and her maid, Giza, were inside looking out at us. There were half eaten plates of food on several tables. I was holding onto Royce's arm, and we were both still in our cloaks with our hair dusted in snow.

Loraine's face turned livid.

"This is where you've been all day?" she demanded of him. "I've been ill in my stomach, unable to eat a bite, sitting in here alone, trying to be a bother to no one, and you've been out in the snow with your whore?"

Royce flinched. I let go of his arm and fled down the hallway for the stairs.

But behind me, I could still hear her howling at him.

* * * *

The next day, I tried to be invisible, but Adina had asked me to check on a few supplies with our cook.

Taking Lily to the kitchens, I found the women baking bread and offered to help. The thought of hiding away in here and kneading bread sounded like paradise. The women chatted as they worked, and at some point, mid-morning, I noticed Lily was not in sight.

Leaving the table where I'd been working a portion of dough, I glanced about the kitchen and saw her near the doorway, wagging her tail. She trotted out of sight, and I followed.

In the passageway outside, I saw Loraine's maid, Giza, with a bowl in her hand. She was leaning down to set it in front of Lily. For some reason, terror flooded though me at the sight, and I rushed forward.

"Lily! No!"

The dog jumped, and I jerked the bowl from Giza's hand while looking at her face. Guilt washed over her features. Inside the bowl, I saw cuts of tender meat in gravy.

She had been about to poison my Lily—on the instructions of Loraine.

Something inside me snapped, and with a strength I would not have thought possible, I shoved her into the wall with my free hand, holding the bowl in front of her face.

"I have some skill in herbal arts," I whispered, "and I'll learn whatever poison is in this bowl. If you ever go near my dog again, you'll find it in your own breakfast one morning. Do you understand?"

Breathing quickly, she nodded.

I took a step back.

Seeing her chance, she ran.

To my surprise, I'd meant every word I'd just said.

* * * *

Several days later, in the afternoon, I learned from Abigail that there had been a bit of a fuss in the courtyard when Alexi had arrived unannounced with at least twenty guards who all needed to be fed and housed in the barracks—and Alexi needed dinner and a guest room.

Not long after, Adina came to find me.

"Goodness," she said. "It's odd enough for a man of his station to be traveling in winter, but for him to arrive unannounced is almost in bad taste. Apparently, he's been staying with friends and was due at the castle weeks ago. He's been officially called back and is on his way. Lord Trey has never been fond of unannounced guests."

And yet, Alexi was the king's brother and therefore allowed some eccentricities.

"He's specifically asked for you at dinner," she added.

"Oh, no," I said. "Loraine has forbidden that."

"Alexi outranks her, and it is his wish. But you'll need to brace yourself. I don't think he knew she was in residence yet, and those two have no love lost."

I remembered some mention of this from Alexi's first visit. "But aren't they first cousins?"

"Yes, and he was cruel to her when they were younger. He called her a draft horse because of her size. She never forgot this, and a few years back, his wife had an affair...and he didn't know. Loraine, Trey, and Royce were at court, and she exposed the scandal publicly. Alexi found out when everyone else did. It was humiliating for him. She pretended that she thought everyone already knew and that her slip was an accident, but he's never forgiven her." Adina sighed. "But he's asked for you at dinner, and so you must be there."

I spent the rest of the afternoon worrying, and this only increased when Adina arrived later with Abigail to dress me for dinner.

"I don't care what Royce says," Adina told me, "This color will suit you. I've had it hemmed, and I want you to try it on."

She carried a gown of the softest pale pink, like inside the shell of an oyster. I let them both dress me. It was a slim-fitting gown with a narrow skirt, and once I was laced in, I looked very slender. But the color did suit my pale skin, sliver-blond hair, and light blue eyes.

"Abigail?" Adina asked.

Abigail shook her head in wonder. "She's like something from another world."

"Yes, but is that what we want at dinner tonight?" I asked.

"Oh, I do think so," Adina answered.

* * * *

Adina walked down to the dining hall with me to meet the others, and I was glad for her presence.

When we passed through the archway, Royce, Alexi, Trey, and Loraine were standing by the table sipping wine. All heads turned. At the sight of me in the pink gown, Royce froze with his goblet halfway to his mouth. Loraine flushed red with anger, and I'd wondered if she'd been warned about my invitation.

But Alexi walked straight to me and kissed my hand. "Kara."

Somehow, his act felt more friendly and affectionate than flirtatious, and I did not mind him kissing my hand. "Alexi."

He smiled broadly back at Royce. "She speaks! I am honored. She is a vision tonight, is she not?"

"Yes," Royce answered.

Then I was angry with them both and drew my hand away. Loraine was Royce's wife, older than him, and these two men were openly fawning over his much younger mistress. I tried to imagine how this might feel, and I nearly felt sympathy for her. Had she not tried to poison my Lily, I would have felt sympathy.

"Shall we sit?" Adina asked.

As we gathered at the table, Trey took his place at the head. Adina, Alexi, and I sat on one side, and Loraine and Royce sat across from us.

The soup course was served.

"So, Amandine has called you home?" Loraine asked Alexi. "What duties could he possibly require from you?"

"Nothing to concern you," he answered, "as you've never undertaken a duty in your life."

I dropped my eyes to my plate, fearing their verbal sparing might worsen.

"True," she answered him, her voice brittle, "but we women tend to find other ways to pass the time. How is your dear wife, Eleesa? Is she waiting for you at court...or perhaps, she is elsewhere?"

Glancing at Alexi, I saw his face harden, and he looked at me. With my eyes, I begged him to stop, but he turned back to Loraine.

"I still cannot get over how Royce just stumbled upon this beauty of a girl," he said. "And he is so fond of her. Did you know on my last visit, I offered him five thousand silver pieces for her and he refused me? Can you imagine? Someone in his financial position, willing to take truly desperate measures, and he turns down five thousand?"

From across the table, Royce shook his head once, and Loraine's eyes were like daggers. Adina and Trey both appeared at a loss. I half expected Loraine to swoon and order Royce to take her upstairs, but she didn't.

Perhaps she did not want Alexi to witness this type of display.

"Please," I whispered to him.

"Oh, all right," he said to me. Then he smiled at Loraine, but it was cold. "Shall we stop flinging blades at each other?" Turning to Adina, he said, "I do hope your cook made her roast pheasant tonight. She has just the right touch with the herbs."

"Yes," Adina answered, visibly relieved. "By luck, we had a pheasant, and I know how you enjoy her preparation."

Somehow, from there, we made it through the rest of dinner.

When dessert was finished, Loraine stood up to signal the ladies would be leaving for the sitting room.

"We will leave you gentlemen to your port," she said.

Rising, I breathed more easily. Once out of this dining room, I'd be expected to vanish—and relished the thought.

"I think not," Alexi said, standing. "I fear that by the time we join you, Kara will have been sent off to the dungeon, and I've a mind to play chess."

Across the table, Royce's face darkened. For some reason, tonight he seemed bothered by Alexi's attention to me. At the last dinner, he'd been flattered.

Offering me his arm, Alexi said, "My dear?"

I glanced to Royce. His expression grew darker, but he nodded. What else could he do? He would need to escort Loraine. Alexi swept me through the archway and down the hall. But once we were out of earshot, he leaned close to my ear.

"You don't really want to disappear off by yourself, do you?"

As his question sounded genuine, I answered, "Would you blame me?"

He laughed. "No, I suppose not. My gods though, would I love to drag you off alone for no other reason than to have you tell me how you've been surviving Hurricane Loraine these past weeks. But I fear Royce would not approve." Patting my hand, he added. "Just come and play a few games of chess with me."

"If you promise to stop baiting her."

"Do you pity her?"

"Sometimes...almost. She's very unhappy, and I don't think she's capable of feeling happiness. That would be a terrible way to live."

"You are an unusual creature."

As we all entered the sitting room, Adina said, "If Alexi and Kara are going to play chess, that still leaves us with a quartet. Perhaps we could play a game of Spades in teams?"

"Yes, my dear," Loraine answered her. "That sounds—"

But Royce interrupted, "Alexi, perhaps you would prefer the game of Spades? I would rather play chess with Kara."

A moment of awkward silence followed, and I found Royce's suggestion a mistake on several levels. Of course I understood that this was my first time down to dinner in weeks, and he felt Alexi was monopolizing me, but Alexi was a royal guest, and Loraine's mouth went tight with anger.

"No," Alexi answered slowly. "You have the pleasure of Kara's company at your leisure, and I've been longing for a rematch. She'll not beat me again."

After that, there was nothing more to be said, but I didn't mind sitting in the corner with Alexi, playing chess. I was out of Loraine's way, and thankfully, Alexi ignored her.

Tonight, he was a different player though, far more careful and far less aggressive. The game took well over an hour. He watched every move I made, and he took more of my pieces than I took of his. In the end, he wore me down and cornered my king.

"Checkmate," he said.

I smiled.

"Did he just win?" Trey asked from the card table.

"He did," I answered. "But he took the game more seriously. Last time, he thought me an easy victory."

"Ah, my lady," Alexi said. "I would never make the mistake of thinking you an easy victory."

At this, Royce glared at him, and Loraine said, "She is not a lady, and you do both Adina and myself a disservice by using the term."

Her voice was brittle again, and as Alexi opened his mouth to offer a returning barb, I shook my head at him. He sighed.

Leaning forward over the chessboard, I whispered. "Might I please be excused, my lord? Please."

A flicker of sadness crossed his eyes. "You really want to go?"

I nodded.

"Go on then. Of course."

I fled.

＊ ＊ ＊ ＊

That night, I thought Royce would come late and dreaded his arrival. He'd appeared almost jealous of Alexi, and I had no idea what type of mood that might bring on. But I left a candle lantern glowing and crawled into bed with Lily.

Royce never came.

The next morning, once Abigail had dressed me, I went downstairs to see Alexi off. Trey and Adina were already downstairs, in the main hallway, walking toward the front doors with Alexi. Neither Royce nor Loraine were present.

"There you are," Alexi said, offering me his arm. "I hoped you'd come to say good-bye."

Footsteps sounded behind us, and Royce came walking from the direction of the stairway. His face was haggard, and he still wore the same clothing from last night.

"You look terrible, my friend," Alexi said. "Don't tell me Loraine kept you up all night with her antics? But I suppose you should have expected some hysteria. I'm probably to blame."

Royce's eyes dropped to my hand on Alexi's arm, but he didn't speak.

Lord Trey led us out into courtyard, where the royal guards had gathered in preparation for departure.

"Come and see this horse, my dear," Alexi said to me, leading me away from everyone else. "I've just purchased him."

But when we reached the horse, his voice dropped low and lost any hint of frivolity. "Kara, I want you to look to your right at the Capello guard with the shorn head."

I glanced over and saw one of our own men helping to load luggage.

"I've paid that man twenty silvers and promised him my protection," Alexi said, barely loud enough to be heard. "If you ever need anything, give him a message, and he'll get it to me. I swear to you, I will come."

Startled, I took a step back.

"I mean it," he rushed on. "I know I play the fool, but there's something building in this house, something…more than family drama. If you need help, send a message."

Turning away, he mounted his horse and smiled to Lord Trey, Adina, and Royce. "Farewell my friends, and thank you again. I hope to see you at court in the spring."

With that, his entire party was off, trotting toward the front gates. Trey and Adina walked back for the front doors to the manor, but Royce came to me. He did look terrible, with dark circles under his eyes.

"You need to rest," I said.

"What Alexi did just say to you?"

He sounded manic, and I needed to defuse this quickly.

"Oh, he was just being Alexi," I said lightly. "I never know how to respond to him. You know I'm not good at word play."

Royce stood close enough that I could feel his stale breath on my cheek. "I want you at dinner tonight."

"With just the family? I can't. Loraine has forbidden that."

He grabbed my wrist. "I want you dressed and in the dining room before dinner. Do you understand?"

"Yes."

* * * *

The night, I let Abigail dress me for dinner, but I was in dread of what might follow.

When I arrived in the dining room, Trey, Adina, and Loraine were there, but Royce had not arrived yet.

Loraine colored at the sight of me walking in. "What are you doing in here? Get out."

"No," Royce said, walking in behind me. He'd bathed and now wore his black, sleeveless tunic. "I want her here. From now on, she dines with us every night."

Trey and Adina both watched this exchange in alarm, and I wanted to disappear into the wall.

"She will not!" Loraine answered. "And you will send her out of here at once."

"No," Royce said again, and I had the distinct feeling that tonight was the first time he'd ever told her no.

"This was our agreement," she said, walking toward him with a rustle of silk.

His eyes glittered, and I nearly cried out to her to stay out of his reach. Could she not see he was on the edge?

"If you don't hold to our bargain," she said, "I will cut off your allowance, and I will not reinstate it."

"Good!" Royce shouted into her face, causing her to stumble backward. "Cut it off tonight! I don't care. I'll sell family paintings and jewels if need be. I can set us up for years if we change some ways and let half the servants go." He pointed at me. "But I would rather eat day-old bread and scrambled eggs for dinner with her than eat a six-course meal with you!"

She stared at him, speechless.

"And I'm sending you to the cottage in Chèlan," he went on. "As your husband, I'm ordering you to go. I will be free of you."

Fear passed through her eyes as she began to understand what was happening. The only thing she had to hold over him was money. If he cared nothing for the money, she had no way to control him, and in all other aspects, he was her lord. He could do as he liked with her.

However, even amid this breaking of chains, Royce looked to Trey and Adina. This affected them as well.

"Father?"

Trey met his eyes and nodded. "Yes. You cannot go on like this. There are some debts I can call in, and we can economize. We'll find a way to manage."

Loraine moaned and grabbed the back of a chair for support, but Royce whirled and took hold of my arm.

"Come with me."

I had little choice as he dragged me down the hallway toward the stairs.

"What are you doing?" I asked, trying to pull away.

He didn't notice my struggles and kept going, taking me up the stairs three floors and then to my room. Pulling me inside, he closed the door behind us.

Something inside of him had broken, and pent up emotions were pouring out. Turning me around, he began rapidly unlacing the back of my gown. He'd never done anything like this before. He'd always waited for Abigail to prepare me for bed. He wasn't hurting me. He was simply moving too fast.

Within moments, he had my gown unlaced and tugged it off my shoulders, along with my shift. Then he kissed me so hard I couldn't help trying to push him away.

"Royce!"

My feet came off the ground as he lifted me with one arm and walked to the bed.

Once there, he grasped my face. "I want you."

The sound of him speaking filled me with relief, as perhaps he'd partially come back to himself.

"Yes," I said quickly. "But you go too fast. I'm frightened."

My admission that I was afraid had an effect, and he nodded. Then he kissed me more gently.

Dutifully, I kissed him back.

\* \* \* \*

The following day, I hid in my room with no idea what was happening in the house. I wasn't sure I wanted to know. Had Loraine officially cut Royce off from her income? Had he packed her up and sent her away?

Whatever was happening, I didn't want to see it.

In the evening though, when Abigail came to dress me, I couldn't refuse. Royce had ordered me to join the family for dinners. She laced me into a white silk, but I told her not to bother curling my hair or applying make-up, and for once, she listened.

Downstairs, when I entered the dining room, only Royce and Trey were waiting.

"Where have you been all day, my dear?" Trey asked.

"Hiding. What has happened?"

"Nothing," Royce answered. "Loraine has hidden in her room as well, and I've not pressed the matter...yet. A short while ago, she asked to see Adina."

As if bidden, Adina came hurrying into the dining hall. She went straight to Royce.

"Oh, Royce," she said. "I have good news. I've been with Loraine, and I think your outburst last night caused her to see things in a new light. She's sorry for some of her behavior and sees now that she's asked too much of you. She's agreed not to alter your finances if you agree to no more than allowing her to remain here at the manor. She's even reconciled to your attachment to Kara."

Royce shook his head. "No. She doesn't mean it. She'll wait until she thinks we can't do without her wealth again, and this will start all over. I want our life here to go back to the way it was in the autumn, with just the four of us. To get that back, I'm willing to live without the money."

Adina's expression grew wistful. "You say that now, and you may still say it in a year. But in two years...three years' time, when there are no more paintings to sell and you've been eating potatoes from the garden for a week and the leaking roof needs repair, you may feel differently."

She spoke of these things as if she had knowledge of them, and I realized how little I knew of her past.

But Royce was listening to her.

"Just hear what she has to say," Adina urged.

A voice came from the archway. "I assure you, you'll be pleased with my terms."

Loraine stood there dressed in a velvet gown of forest green with her hair piled high. She carried a small bottle of wine in her hand.

Royce walked over to meet her, and I hung back with Adina and Trey to let them speak.

Loraine touched Royce's hand, and the gesture was conciliatory. Her voice was low, but I could hear her apologizing to him.

"And you'll treat Kara as part of the family," he asked, "as my chosen companion, while I have no other obligations to you?"

"Of course. I only wish to remain here, in my home."

They spoke a few moments longer, with him making requests and her agreeing. He was surprised by her answers, but his face filled with hope.

Opening the bottle of wine, she asked, "Are we agreed then? I've brought your favorite dark port."

She poured two goblets and handed him one. After raising hers, she drank deeply. Without warning, a memory flashed into my mind of Giza setting down the bowl of food for Lily.

"Royce!"

But it was too late. He'd already taken a swallow.

As I never shouted, Royce, Adina, and Trey all turned to me in surprise, but when Loraine smiled at me, I saw only triumph. She'd wanted me to witness this.

The first sign was a trickle of blood running from her nose.

"No," I breathed.

Trey saw it too, and in horror, his gaze flew to Royce's goblet.

Royce touched his nose. His hand came away with blood on his fingers. "Loraine, what have you done?"

She laughed. "Did you really think I was going to stand by and watch you leave me for your little mouse of a girl? To quietly accept being married to you in name only? You belong to me. You always have, and now, you always will."

Wavering on her feet, she grabbed for a side table.

I ran forward, taking the goblet from Royce's hand. "You have to retch! Put your fingers down your throat. You must bring it back up!"

Loraine fell, dropping to the floor, with blood running from her nose and ears. Her eyes were open.

Adina cried out, and Trey was at my side, shouting at Royce. "Do what Kara says! Bring it back up."

But I could see Loraine was already dead. Whatever she had given them acted quickly. Royce fell to his knees, and Trey grabbed hold of him. "No!"

Royce looked to me. "Kara."

Then he fell and his father could not hold him up and all I could hear was the sound of Trey sobbing.

* * * *

Over the next few days, Trey seemed to age ten years. He had lost his son.

But I kept my head. The situation needed to be both exposed and put to rest, as this was a murder suicide involving a member of the royal family. So I sent for Alexi.

For myself, I was almost numb. Though I felt regret over Royce's death, I was not in mourning for someone I'd loved. I'd feared him too much, and perhaps it was impossible for me to love someone I feared.

When Alexi learned what happened, he brought Francis—who was apparently educated and skilled in the practice of law.

We gathered in the sitting room, and Adina held Trey's hand.

"I've located several documents from among Royce's things," Francis began. "On my last visit, I helped him make a new will."

Royce had said nothing to me of this, but then why would he? However, this was not the line of discussion I'd expected. Why were we speaking of wills? I wanted Francis to pronounce that no one in the house besides Loraine would be held accountable.

Francis shifted uncomfortably. "The sequence of events here matters greatly. Trey, you've told us that Loraine died first, and you have several witnesses who can swear to this. Upon her death, all her money went to Royce." He paused. "Upon Royce's death, the money then went to you and Kara. Two-thirds to you and one-third to Kara."

Trey's brow furrowed as if he didn't understand. "Loraine's money?"

"Yes," Francis said. "It all belongs to you and Kara now."

I dropped my eyes to my hands in my lap, but when I glanced up, Alexi was watching me.

\* \* \* \*

That evening, a knock sounded on my bedroom door.

"Kara?" Adina asked.

Opening the door, I found her and Trey on the other side. Poor Trey. His close-trimmed beard was turning white. I stepped back to invite them inside.

"Are you both well?" I asked.

Trey said. "My dear…I am aware you did not come to live here of your own accord, but you are a woman of independent means now. You can go anywhere you like and do anything you like."

"I've no interest in travel," I answered.

"No, but if you wish, you could go back to Lady Giselle and live on de Marco lands."

Adina took my hand. "Or you could stay here with us. The three of us have become a family, don't you think?"

Her voice was thick with hope.

Suddenly, I had choices.

But I had no wish to return to Lady Giselle now. I had no wish to spend my days pleasing someone else. Adina and Trey accepted me for exactly who I was, and they expected nothing more.

"Of course I'll stay," I said. "You are my family."

\* \* \* \*

The next morning, we said our good-byes and gave our thanks to Alexi and Francis in the courtyard.

Alexi did not kiss my hand, but he said, "Now you'll not ever need to send for me, will you?"

I tried to smile at him. "No. I am content and safe here."

Nodding, he mounted his horse.

Adina took my arm, and together, with Lily trotting at our heels, we walked back toward the front doors.

I was home.

\* \* \* \*

The courtyard around me disappeared, and I found myself once again inside the small shack, kneeling by the hearth and staring into the center panel of the three-tiered mirror.

Fighting to take in air, I thought on all that I had just lived through.

The faces of Royce…Adina…Trey…and Loraine swam around me.

But the dark-haired woman was now looking out from the left panel.

"That would be the outcome of the second choice," she said. "Now you'll go back to the beginning again, to live out the third choice."

"Wait!" I begged. "Give me a moment."

I needed to think.

"To the beginning once more," she said. "To live out the third choice."

My mind went blank, and the interior of the shack vanished.

# The Third Choice
# The Settlement

# Chapter Fifteen

I stood in the darkness just outside the door of the shack, feeling dizzy and disoriented, as if I'd forgotten something and needed to remember. What was I doing out here? Then I remembered that Raven had just left me—with the door unlocked—and I had to a decision to make.

He'd given me the option of leaving with his troupe in the morning or staying here and taking my chances—or I could escape the settlement and try to get back to my lady. Looking to the left, I saw the long tree line stretching along the backs of several dwellings. I could make my way along these trees far enough to slip down into the chute.

But instead, I just stood there, knowing I couldn't force myself to take such an act.

Ashamed, I went back inside and crouched down by the fire. I stayed like that all night, even after the logs had burned to ashes.

Outside, once the sky had begun turning gray, I heard footsteps approaching, and I watched the door. Caine entered first, with Raven behind him. Both men appeared tense, but Caine didn't react to the door having been unlocked. Perhaps he already knew.

He wasted no time. "Raven's just asked that you be given a choice to go on the road with his group. I'm asking you to stay."

Before he finished speaking, I'd made up my mind. I didn't know either one of them, but I couldn't risk leaving this place with a group of strangers and traveling further from my lady and my home.

Caine stood there looking down at me with his dark eyes locked into mine, and I suddenly wished that I were not crouched on the floor. Standing, I tried to straighten my wrinkled and mud-spattered gown.

"I've decided to remain in the settlement," I answered.

Caine closed his eyes and exhaled. With visible relief, he turned to Raven. "She's staying here with me."

Startled, I wondered if I should correct him. I'd not offered to remain with him, only to remain in the settlement.

Raven spoke up. "You're certain, Kara? You want to stay?"

I *wanted* someone here to take me home, but that choice had not been offered. "Yes."

He shrugged, perhaps believing his part here was done. "All right then." Touching Caine's arm, he said to his brother, "I need to go and help with the packing, and then we're rolling out, but I'll see you after the first snow."

Caine nodded. "Be safe. Take care of Jade and Sean."

Raven was already walking out the door. "I will."

Then I was alone with Caine, and I wavered. His features were narrow, and his cheekbones were high. He wore his black hair quite short, not even an inch in length, and even I could see that most women would find him handsome. But he was so tall. Raven had promised Caine wouldn't hurt me or sell me. I hoped this promise could be trusted.

"Come with me," he said.

"Where are we going?"

"Just come."

With little choice, I followed him out the door of the shack. He led me around the front and headed deeper into the settlement, down a center path.

Walking through the settlement in daylight, I could see that it was indeed larger than my first view in the night. At least forty dwellings were scattered about in no apparent pattern. Several constructions were larger than the others, such as the stable and barn and what appeared to be a smithy.

Beyond the farthest dwelling, I could see more cleared land now growing apple trees. Each dwelling we passed sported its own kitchen garden, but at this time of the year, only potatoes, carrots, turnips, and onions remained in the ground. Chickens pecked in the dirt, and goats wandered loose, eating grass and weeds. There were pigs inside fenced areas. Even at the crack of dawn, a number of people were up and about, feeding chickens, gathering eggs, and milking goats.

As Caine and I continued on, people nodded to him and cast surprised glances at me.

He said nothing and led me onward all the way through the settlement to the side farthest from the chute. There, he approached the largest house I'd seen here. It was one-level, but built entirely from logs, with a wrap-around porch.

Opening the front door, he motioned me inside.

Stepping in, I found myself in an open room. The floors were hard wood, but there were a few rugs placed beneath polished wooden furniture. One entire side appeared to be the sitting room, with a stone hearth, while the other side contained a wood stove, counter, and a dining table with chairs. The walls held numerous shelves filled with cups, plates, and jars of spices. It seemed a comfortable arrangement to have the kitchen, dining area, and living room all in the same large room.

But I wasn't there long.

Caine led me to an archway in the back of the room and down a hall. He opened the first door on his right.

"In here."

Following him inside, I found myself in a bedroom. The four-poster bed was good-sized and covered in a red and blue quilt. There was a wardrobe, several side tables, and a wooden couch with a long pad on the seat. There was a pitcher and basin on one table. Another table contained a plate of bread, apples, and cheese.

I stopped not far inside the doorway, wondering why he'd brought me here.

"This place is my home," he said from the doorway. "And this is my room. There's water in that pitcher and food on the table. I have a number of things to attend to today, so I need to leave you in here. You're welcome to wash and eat."

"You want me to stay in here?"

"I don't want you to leave this room. I'd like your agreement to stay in here, but I'll order you if need be."

Confused, I shook my head. "Order me?"

"You're my property. You'll do what I say."

A knot began growing in my stomach. "Raven said I had choices."

"No. Raven *gave* you a few choices, and you chose to stay with me. I took you as property from those noblemen. You belong to me."

My breaths came faster. This was not what I'd agreed to...or what I thought I'd agreed to. "Where is Raven? I'll go with him and his troupe."

Caine pulled the door halfway closed. "He's rolling toward the chute by now, and you already made your decision. You'll be safe in here, but do not leave this room. I mean it."

Closing the door, he shut me inside.

Alone, I was even more frightened—as I had time to think. I'd made a terrible mistake. I'd made the wrong choice.

* * * *

In autumn, sunset came early, and by late afternoon, dusk was approaching. I'd not disobeyed Caine and had remained in the bedroom all day without even going near the door. I'd washed my face and hands, but I needed clean clothing, and all the clothes in the wardrobe were his—mainly a collection of wool shirts, vests, and a long coat.

There was no flint in sight, and I wondered what I might do for light once darkness set in. Perhaps there was a flint in one of the table drawers. I'd just started looking when the bedroom door opened.

I whirled.

Caine stood on the other side. Leaning down, he lifted something heavy from beside him. It was my trunk.

"Your things are in here," he said. "I thought you'd like some clean clothes. But I want you to change and then come with me."

"Where are we going?"

"Just do it."

After setting down my trunk, he closed the door, leaving me alone again. I'd not packed the trunk myself and had no idea what was inside. Kneeling down, I opened it, finding a white silk gown, an ice blue silk gown, and two muslin day-dresses, one white and one of ice blue. There were clean slippers, stockings, undergarments, and a fresh shift. My silver hairbrush and mirror lay at the bottom, along with a few silver hair clips that had been gifts from my lady.

The silk gowns laced up the back, so I'd need help with one of those. Both of the day-dresses laced up the front. After removing my mud-spattered dress, I chose some clean undergarments, the white muslin, and the clean slippers. After this, I dressed quickly, fearing Caine might walk in to check on me.

I'd just finished lacing the dress up when he knocked. "Are you ready?"

"Almost."

My hair was in snarls, so I brushed it out.

He knocked again.

"I'm ready," I said through the door.

Opening the door, he entered, starting slightly at the sight of me all in white. He seemed so affected it took him a moment to recover, and then he said, "We're going to the common house for dinner, but my grandfather will be there, and before we eat, I'd like him to marry us."

I shook my head, uncertain I'd heard him correctly.

"I'm in earnest," he said. "I want you to marry me now. I know it sounds mad, but I can't risk losing you to some other…choice someone might offer. Raven caught me off guard this morning, and I won't risk anything like that happening again." He stepped closer. "Will you?"

"No," I answered, moving away. No matter what he claimed, he sounded mad to me. "I can't marry you."

He sighed. "I didn't think you would." Closing the distance between us, he took hold of my wrist. "What's about to happen may seem harsh, but you haven't given me another choice."

Dragging me from the room, he walked back to the main sitting room and let me go. I looked at the door leading outside and considered trying to flee, but knew I'd never outrun him. Kneeling down, he opened a chest and began digging through it. Then he drew out a thin, leather-bound book.

In spite of my fear, I asked, "What is that?"

"A book of laws. Can you read?"

"Yes."

"Good. So can I."

Grabbing my wrist again, he pulled me out the front door of the house and halfway back through the settlement, stopping at the door of the second largest building—the largest being the barn.

"This is our common house," he said, still carrying the book.

He let go of my wrist long enough to open the door and then took me inside. The vast room was filled with long tables and benches…and people. Scents of warm food filled the air, fresh bread and something savory.

All heads turned when we entered, and everyone stared at my silver-blond hair and white muslin dress, but their faces expressed more trepidation than anything else. They all wore shades of dark wool. They all had dark hair, dark eyes, and dusky skin. I must have looked beyond foreign in this setting.

Caine wasted no time and drew me to a group of three people standing near the hearth. I recognized some of them from my arrival. Logan was as tall as Caine. His shoulders were broader, but his features were not so defined. Beside him stood the woman with the thick braid who'd first noticed me up on the horse last night. They both watched us approach with expressions somewhere between shock and disapproval.

But the third member was Caine's grandfather. As we drew closer, I noticed how much he looked like Raven, of medium height, with a solid build and strong jaw. His long gray hair hung loose down his back. He watched me with an expression of concern, and when Caine stopped only a few paces away, the elder man came to me.

"I am Tristan," he said, holding out his hand. "These people with me are Logan and Brida."

His voice was kind and so were his eyes, and I badly wanted to take his hand, but I was frozen in place with no idea what was about to happen.

"Grandfather," Caine said with a bow of respect.

"Has the girl agreed to marry you?" Tristan asked. Apparently, he knew some of Caine's plans.

"No."

"Then you'll have to wait. "

"No," Caine said again, holding up the book. "I'm invoking the fourteenth law, and I choose to take her as wife instead of servant."

I felt dizzy, and the room began to spin. What was he saying?

Brida gasped. "You can't! That law hasn't been used in over a hundred years, before our people settled here, back when they were still barbaric travelers making up rules to accommodate anything they took."

Caine opened the book and read aloud. "If a woman is taken in a raid as property, she can be claimed as either servant or wife." He looked up.

"But she's not willing!" Brida argued. "Look at her!"

"She was property," Caine answered. "I took her as property, and now, I'm claiming her as wife. That is the end of it."

Tristan listened to all this carefully and asked Caine. "And she will live in the house with you and me?"

"Of course. She's my wife."

As of yet, Logan hadn't spoken, but his face was a mask of anger. "Grandfather, we cannot allow him to use an old law to bring an outsider into our midst, into our family."

When Tristan didn't answer, Caine turned to his brother. "I think you'll find that Grandfather would be hesitant to let you question any of the laws. Because if you question the fourteenth law, I may question the first one."

Everyone in the small group went still, and although I had no idea what the first law might be, Caine's threat caused Logan to fall silent.

Brida wrung her hands as if distressed. "So, is there to be some travesty of a hand-fasting ceremony, where you force her to make vows?"

"No," Caine answered. "Nothing is needed. It's done. I've claimed her as my wife." He looked down at me. "Are you hungry? I think dinner is ready."

Unable to answer, I swayed on my feet.

I was Caine's wife?

When he caught me, a flash of regret crossed his features, but he did not relent.

"Come and sit down," he said. "Try to eat something."

\* \* \* \*

The rest of the evening at the common house was a blur. At Caine's bidding, I'd tried to eat some bread but couldn't manage. When he and Tristan finished their own suppers and were ready to leave, they took me home.

Upon entering the house, Tristan vanished into a side room off the kitchen, and Caine took me down the hallway to the bedroom. Only when he followed me inside and closed the door did a bolt of fear strike through me.

I was his wife.

Fear turned to panic as I looked from the bed to him.

At the sight of my expression, he stepped away in alarm. "I'm not going to…" Then he grew insulted. "What do you take me for?"

What did I take him for? I took him for a man who'd forcibly stolen me and then married me without my consent. At this point, I would not have put anything past him.

Still watching me, he seemed to come to the same conclusion and turned away. "I just needed to make a claim. I don't expect anything else from you." He walked to the door. "Logan will make this difficult, so I need to sleep in here for the sake of appearance. You get ready for bed and under the blankets. I'll be back in a few minutes, but I'll sleep on that couch."

\* \* \* \*

The next morning, when I woke up, I was alone in the room, but the door was slightly ajar. Rising, I dressed quickly—back into my white muslin—and left the room slowly, walking to the edge of the hallway where I could peer into the large living area.

Caine was nowhere in sight, but Tristan limped around near the cooking stove, setting a teakettle onto the top. I must have made some kind of sound with my steps because he looked over and smiled.

"You look like a little winter bird to me," he said. "Come have tea, and then we'll go out and find eggs and potatoes to cook for breakfast."

Something about him reminded me of Raven. There was a kindness in his manner. And I was hungry now. All I'd eaten the day before was a bit of bread, apple, and cheese mid-morning.

Walking to join him in the kitchen, I asked, "Where is Caine?"

"Gone out for the day. He's never idle. Some of the men are bringing in the last of the apples. He may be helping them. Some are repairing the roof of the barn. He may be with them. Some went hunting." Tristan nodded. "He could be with them."

I found this an odd response that Tristan had no idea where Caine might have gone. But what about me? I must do something here to earn my keep.

"What are my duties?"

"Duties?" he repeated. "To spend the day with me."

He finished making the tea and poured two mugs, adding sugar and goat's milk. Sipping it, I sighed.

"This is delicious."

He smiled again, but took in my dress. "Do you have anything darker and warmer to wear? That won't do for gathering eggs or digging in the garden."

"I don't. I have only one other day-dress clean, but it's light blue and made from the same fabric."

I found him easy to talk to and didn't mind telling him anything he asked.

"Bring your tea," he said. "Has Caine showed you much of the house?"

"No."

Pointing to a small open doorway off the kitchen, he said, "That's my work room. You'll see that by and by." But he led me down the hallway, past Caine's bedroom. "This second room is mine, and this is our storage room."

He opened a door and brought me into a room stacked with crates. There were bags of oats, cornmeal, lentils, and rice. But he went to a trunk in the back and opened it. "Come and look, Little Bird. You may find some things here. Caine's mother was not as small as you, but these might fit."

Kneeling beside him, I saw several folded wool gowns, one of deep red, one of tan, and another of midnight blue. All three laced up the front. Tristan lifted them out and handed them to me.

"Here is a pair of soft boots too," he said. "I haven't seen these in years. Caine was only fourteen when she died. "

I sank down beside him. "Caine's mother is dead?"

"Yes, long ago."

"Was she your daughter?"

"No. She married my son."

"And where is he?"

Tristan blinked and looked down into the trunk. "Dead too. Killed in a raid gone wrong."

"Oh, I am sorry."

"I have my grandsons."

The blue gown felt soft in my hands. "Are you sure about the clothes? Caine won't mind me wearing them?"

"No, no. He would be glad. He has a good heart."

While I was not sure about this last statement, I was beginning to believe that Tristan had a good heart.

"Go and put one on," Tristan urged.

After bringing the gowns to the room I shared with Caine, I donned the midnight blue dress and laced it up. It was too long, but otherwise fit me—warm and comfortable. The boots were a little too big, but would work. Tristan nodded when I reappeared into the large living area.

"Better," he said, picking up an empty bowl. "Let's go find breakfast."

Uncertain what he meant, I followed him down the hall again and out a back door. Only then did I look up and feel an unwanted rush of fear. This was the first time I'd been outside in the settlement without Caine dragging me someplace, but now with time to think, time to look up, the endless sky pressed down.

Tristan frowned. "What is it?"

"Nothing."

I kept my eyes down and tried to breathe. Just ahead, I saw a hen house and a kitchen garden. There were potatoes, onions, carrots, and herbs. A few tomatoes still hung from their vines. Tristan went to the hen house and opened the door. Eight chickens came out to greet us, clucking and pecking at the ground.

"I put them inside at night or the foxes get them," he said. "I'll feed them while you gather eggs."

Although I was well practiced at cooking, I'd never once gone outside to collect the ingredients in this manner. Curious, I entered the hen house and saw a collection of nests. Most of the nests contained an egg, and I gathered them into the bowl. When I emerged, I purposefully kept my eyes down. Tristan was tossing grain onto the ground for the hens.

"How many eggs?" he asked.

"Seven."

"One of the hens has stopped laying."

After this, he fetched a trowel from the hen house, and we went to the garden. Handing me the trowel, he said, "Dig us some potatoes."

I knew what the potato plants looked like, but I'd never dug for them myself. Still, I plowed the trowel into the rather hard dirt, looking for a potato.

"Deeper," he said.

Continuing, I dug downward until I saw a reddish skin. To my surprise, I was enjoying myself and smiled. "I found one." But then I made the mistake of looking up, and the open sky pressed down, and I curled inward.

"Little Bird," Tristan said. "Tell me what is wrong." His voice was different now, less gentle and more commanding.

"It's the sky," I whispered.

"The sky?"

"Until a few days ago, I'd never been outside like this in a strange place. I didn't understand how big everything is." I closed my eyes. "It's all so big."

Taking the trowel from my hand, he said, "Tell me. Tell me where you come from."

Without looking up, I began to speak quietly. I told him of my life with my lady at the manor as her and Lord Jean's ward. I told him how Royce had bought me. I told him of being lifted onto a horse and then led down the road away from my home.

He listened.

When I finished, he said. "You lived your whole life in a manor with a lady you attended, and then your lord, this Lord Jean, traded you to another nobleman for a piece of land, and that man took you away?"

I nodded.

"When did Caine and Raven take you from him?"

"The same day, near dusk."

Without speaking, Tristan finished digging the potatoes. When he'd found three, we both stood and went back into to the house. Neither of us spoke much after that, but the silence was not uncomfortable. He'd asked me what he needed to know, and I'd told him.

We washed and sliced the potatoes. Then he fried the pieces with a bit of bacon fat. I scrambled four of the eggs. By the time we'd dished up, I was famished and ate most of a plateful.

"I like red potatoes," I said.

"Me too."

After breakfast he went into the side room off the kitchen and returned carrying a fishing pole and a bucket in the same hand. "Come, Little Bird."

But I hesitated, realizing he wanted me to go outside again.

"It's all right," he said. "Just come."

I followed him down the hall.

Once we were outside, he took my hand. "Just hold onto me and don't look up. Soon, the sky won't seem so big."

We walked into the forest. His limp did not slow him down much, but my dress dragged the ground, and I had to hold it up at times. He led me to a wide, rushing stream, and there, the trees made a canopy, so I felt somewhat more at ease. We spent the entire day out there, fishing and speaking of small things—of the squirrels, rabbits, and birds that came near to us.

Tristan caught three trout, and the last one was over a foot long.

"Well done!" I said, clapping.

He smiled.

Before leaving the stream, he filled the bucket with fresh water.

When we returned home and laid our trout on the counter, I thought on all the food I'd seen in the storage room.

"Could I make us dinner for tonight or do you normally go to the common house?"

"We stay home sometimes, and I need to do some things in my workroom. Can you cook in here by yourself?"

"Of course."

Following him to the door of the workroom, I finally had a look inside. It was larger than I'd expected and quite a chaotic mess, filled with tables, arrows, pieces of leather, feathers, thread, and a variety of tools.

"I'm working on a sheath," he said, pointing to the nearest table. There, I saw pieces of cut leather and thread. He entered the room and went to sit at the table.

Turning, I set about planning dinner. Dusk had not yet set in, and I had time. The first thing I did took courage. I went out back into the garden, by myself, and gathered three tomatoes and an onion. Then in the storeroom, I found rice.

The kitchen was well set up with a stout counter and sharp knives.

I diced the onion and tomatoes. Then I cooked a pot of rice. By this point, dusk was setting in, so I lit a few candle lanterns. After sautéing the onions, I mixed them and the fresh tomatoes with the rice. Going through the herb rack, I found dried basil and oregano, and I mixed these herbs into the rice dish. Once this was done, I covered the pot and turned to preparing the trout, cleaning and boning the fish. When the trout were ready, I fried them with a tablespoon of bacon fat in a cast iron pan, but once they were done, I thought fresh parsley would help bring out their flavor.

There were herbs out in the garden.

Again, I braved the outdoors, even in the fading light, and then I came through the back door into the house with handful of parsley. But up ahead, I heard voices. Quietly, I walked up the hallway just far enough to see out into the sitting room.

Caine stood near a wooden couch, looking down at his grandfather. "What do you mean it was the same day?"

"As I told you, she'd lived her whole life inside a manor as companion to a lady. One day, her lord traded her away to another nobleman in the morning, and you raided their traveling party that night. She didn't even know the man who had bought her." Tristan's voice was firm. "She knows nothing of the world and is afraid of the sky. She could be easily broken. You had best tread carefully."

Caine didn't answer at first, but when he did, his voice was thick with discomfort. "I will."

Pretending I'd not overheard, I walked from the hallway carrying the parsley. Caine watched me enter, his gaze dropping to the wool dress, which was so long it covered my feet.

I stopped. "Oh…I had nothing suitable. This was your mother's. I hope you don't mind."

"No. I don't mind." He turned his head toward the kitchen area. "What is all this? Are we eating here?"

"Yes," Tristan answered. "She cooked."

Caine nodded, but he still appeared uncomfortable, almost awkward, and a thought struck me. He had little idea what to say to me. For some reason, he'd gone to desperate lengths to claim me as his wife and now seemed at a complete loss that there was a woman living in his house.

As I went to set the table, Tristan made more tea. I expected Caine to get a pitcher and go to the storeroom for ale or wine, but he didn't. He sat down and accepted a cup of tea. Something about this pleased me, but I didn't know why. In all my life, I'd never sat down to dinner where the men and women didn't drink wine.

I dished everyone portions of the trout and rice dish and set the plates on the table.

"Thank you," Tristan said.

As I sat, Caine took a bite of the rice. "This is good."

It bothered me a little that his praise pleased me, and I tried to push the feeling down.

"I'd not have expected you to know how to cook," he added, "or do much of anything, really."

Offended, I asked, "And why is that?"

"Oh…I didn't mean anything by…just the way you were dressed and traveling with nobles, and Grandfather told me you'd grown up in a manor."

"I had many duties," I informed him sharply, "and I can assure you I'm neither idle nor useless." Only then did I hear the tone of my own voice.

I'd never spoken to anyone like that. But somehow, I'd not been afraid to call Caine on his insult.

Tristan raised his fork as if amused. "Well. The little bird can speak up when she needs to. That's a good sign."

At a loss, Caine turned back to his dinner.

"What did you work on today?" Tristan asked him.

"The roof on the barn. I'd hoped we could mend it, but the whole thing needs replacing."

The two men began discussing work to be done in the settlement, and I listened. I'd had a pleasant day with Tristan, but I'd not lost sight of the reason for my choice to remain here: to get a message to my lady. I needed to know how the settlement functioned—and who arrived and who left.

By the end of dinner, I'd learned nothing of use, so I filled a basin with water from the bucket in the kitchen and washed the dishes.

"What shall we do now?" I asked. "Play cards?"

Tristan perked. "You like to play cards?"

"I do. Most of the games I know are for two people, but there is one that any number of people can play called 'Lose the Jack'. The object is to get rid of all your cards and make sure you aren't stuck with a Jack in your hand."

Caine appeared dubious, but Tristan found a deck immediately, and I explained the rules. It was a lively game, and in the initial round, Tristan went out first while Caine had two Jacks in his hand, thus dubbing him the loser.

With a wry smile, Caine told me, "Deal a new hand."

We played until long after dark, and Tristan seemed disappointed when Caine announced it was time we all got some sleep.

"Good-night," I told Tristan, and on impulse, I kissed his cheek. Then I was embarrassed, not knowing why I'd done such a thing.

"Good-night, Little Bird," he said, going to his room.

Tonight, Caine came in with me, carrying a candle, and he simply turned his back while I got undressed and crawled into the bed. The couch hardly looked long enough for him.

"Perhaps I should sleep on the couch," I suggested. "You're too tall."

But he was already pulling his shirt over his head, exposing his back and shoulders. Startled, I glanced away, never having seen a man in that state of undress.

"No. You keep the bed," he answered. Then he blew out the candle. But as he got settled, he said through the darkness. "Thank you for tonight. I've not seen Grandfather laugh like that in a long time. We usually go to the common room so he can visit with others or play a few games of dice, but he misses a time when more of the family lived here, and we spent some evenings at home."

"Who all lived here?"

"Everyone. Mother, Father, Logan, and Raven. When we were young, Father had us on the road some of the year, but Logan hated it so much that we started to spend more and more time here. Even after Mother died, and this became a house of men, we stayed home some nights. Then Logan married, and Brida wanted her own house—and who could blame her? And Raven is…he built his own house as soon as possible, and he's traveling much of the time. He never lets anyone get too close." Caine paused. "Then four years ago, Father was killed, and since then, it's been just Grandfather and me. I fear I'm not good company for him."

"What of Tristan's wife?" I asked. "Your grandmother."

"I never knew her. She died giving birth to my father. Grandfather doesn't talk about her, but he must have loved her. He never re-married."

It felt strange to be lying here, speaking softly with Caine in a dark room. This was the first time he'd spoken to me so openly. I liked the sound of his voice.

"Get some sleep," he said.

# Chapter Sixteen

The following day was similar.

I woke up to find Caine gone. Tristan and I cared for the hens, gathered eggs, and made breakfast. Then he took me walking in the orchards, having me hold his hand and practice not looking up at the sky—at least not yet.

But I noticed he walked a little slower today, and his limp seemed more pronounced.

"Is your leg bothering you?"

"I'm old," he answered. "My bones don't work the way they used to. I was handsome once. You should have seen me when I was young."

"You're handsome still. You look a good deal like Raven."

In the early afternoon, I sensed he might do better indoors today and suggested we go home. He worked on his sheath, and I hemmed the red wool dress, so that I might wear it without having it drag the ground.

In the later afternoon, Tristan killed one of hens—the one that had stopped laying. He plucked it and brought it to me. I boiled the meat off the bone and made a thick stew. Then I mixed cornmeal with water, eggs, and parsley, and I fried up some corncakes in bacon fat.

By the time Caine got home, dinner was ready.

He was especially fond of the corncakes and ate three of them. He thanked me for dinner and made no comments about being surprised that I wasn't completely useless. After washing the dishes though, I thought Tristan still looked a little tired and wondered if I might suggest something besides cards for entertainment.

"Do you have any books with stories?" I asked. "I could read aloud."

Tristan grew wistful. "I like stories, but we have only the law book here. I taught Caine to read, but his brothers had no interest. We have never been a people for books."

"That's all right," I answered. "I'll tell you some stories. I know dozens. Would you like a comedy, adventure, or romance?"

"An adventure."

So, as I settled Tristan in the sitting room, Caine took a chair, but I remained standing.

"There was once a young man who grew tired of his parents and his home and his life," I began. "He decided to become a sailor and run away to sea."

With one hand under his chin, Caine watched me.

* * * *

The next morning, I wore the hemmed red dress. Tristan and I made breakfast as usual, but as I began to clean up he said, "Little Bird, come and sit with me."

"Let me just finish washing."

"Come here now."

I went to him and sat at the table. "What's wrong?"

"These past two days have been good days, but today, it's time you take your place among the women."

Fear rose inside me. "With the women?"

"The women here work on many things as a group. You need to take your place with them."

I had no wish to be thrown into a crowd of unfamiliar women who viewed me as a foreigner. "No, please. Can't I stay here with you? Just a few more days. Please."

With sad eyes, he shook his head. "I would keep you with me. But it would be selfish and do you no service." His gaze drifted. "I won't live forever, and when I'm gone, either Logan or Caine will follow me as leader here, as tórnya. Brida is a good woman, and she has many skills. The women respect her. You must earn their respect as well."

Still frightened, I tried to absorb his words. "When you pass away, either Caine or Logan will succeed you?"

"Yes."

"And how is that decided?"

"By me. It is the first law. A tórnya chooses who will follow."

Caine's words to Logan on that night in the common house came back.

*I think you'll find that Grandfather would be hesitant to let you question*
*any of the laws. Because if you question the fourteenth law, I may question*
*the first one.*

"Logan believes you'll choose him," I said.

Tristan didn't answer. "You need to take your place with the women,"
he said, "but don't be afraid. Caine has asked Doris to come here this
morning. She will take you."

"Who is Doris?"

As if to answer, a knock sounded on the door. "Tristan? It's me."

"Come in," Tristan called.

I stood.

The door opened, and a lithe, wiry woman of about forty came through
the door on quick steps. Her chin was pointed, and her black hair very
straight.

Looking me up and down she said, "Goodness me. She is an odd little
thing. Is she not? At least she's not dressed all in white today. That's an
improvement. People still haven't stopped talking about Caine dragging
her into the common room in that white gown. She looked like something
from beyond the veil."

She said all of this in a rush, and I had a feeling she normally spoke
quickly, but her blunt opinions took me aback.

"Kara, this is Doris," Tristan said.

It was the first time he'd used my name, and I sensed my world had
just shifted again. I looked at him helplessly, pleading he let me remain
here with him.

"We should do something with that hair," Doris said. "It's not just that it's
nearly white...but there is so much of it. Tristan, do you have a leather tie?"

"Yes."

As Tristan limped to his workroom, Doris quick-stepped to me. "Sit
down, my girl."

I obeyed, and as rapidly as she did everything else, she began to plait
my hair into one long braid. Tristan returned with a thin string of leather,
and Doris tied off my braid.

"Well," she said, assessing me. "That's not much better, but it's the
best we can do. All right, my girl. Gather up anything to be washed. It's
laundry day."

I was at a loss, and Tristan said, "I'll get the wash."

He left us and returned carrying a large basket with my light blue muslin
dress, several shirts, and two pairs of pants.

"This is all we have," he said.

Taking the basket from him, Doris ushered me for the door. "I'll look out for her, Tristan, and make sure Brida doesn't swallow her whole, but I don't know what in the world Caine was thinking by bringing her here, and I don't mind a bit if you tell him I said so."

Then suddenly, I was outside the front door with this abrupt woman and she was leading me down the main settlement path.

"I've a daughter just about your age," she chatted on, "named Jemma. She travels with Raven and loves her life on the road, dancing in his show. I miss her, but I've not the heart to keep her here if she wants to go."

She went on talking the entire way to the common house, but she stopped walking and faced me before opening the door. "Now, you'll need to brace yourself. There are a few of the younger women who aren't happy about any of this business. Caine may not be the most interesting of men, with almost nothing to say, but he's in line to be our next tórnya and therefore seen as a catch, and you've stolen him right out from under the girls here."

"I didn't steal him," I said quietly. "He took me."

This was first thing I'd said, or rather the first thing she'd allowed me to say, and at the sound of my voice, she actually fell quiet for a moment.

"Yes...well," she said finally. "So long as you know what's waiting on the other side of that door. But I'll handle Brida for you. She was beginning to hope Caine might never marry."

This confused me. "Why?"

Doris rolled her eyes. "Because Tristan wants a family man to follow him. Everyone knows that."

Here, I was so lost that I couldn't even form a question, and Doris somehow managed to open the door while carrying a large basket that required two hands. Then she used the basket to half push me inside.

The tables had been moved near walls and replaced by tubs. About twenty-five women bustled about, boiling pots of water on the cook stove and pouring them into the tubs. There were several babies in wooden cradles set up on the tables. Children between the ages of two and perhaps ten ran about the room.

Brida walked between the tubs, supervising.

"Not so much, Treena!" she said sharply. "You'll fill it too full."

Several heads turned in our direction...and then several more. But Doris headed farther into the room, and I followed.

"I've brought Caine's wife," Doris said to Brida, "and I promised Tristan I'd look out for her. Would you like us washing or hanging?"

Brida looked at me as if she'd have liked to drop me off a cliff. "She's probably better suited for hanging. Look at her hands. They're too soft for the soap."

There were three young women in the group, around my age, listening. The girl Brida had called Treena was quite pretty, with dark waving hair, a tiny nose, and smooth skin. She watched me coldly.

But Doris didn't react to Brida's cutting comments and simply nodded. "Good enough. We'll go help hang."

After setting the basket on the floor, she led me out the back door.

Outside, eight women were hanging lines. A heavyset, older woman with thick gray hair put her hands on her hips as we emerged. Her eyes widened at the sight of me.

"Is that Caine's girl? People have been talking, but I've not seen her." Stepping closer, she squinted to examine me. "Good gods. She'll take some getting used to, won't she?"

Nodding in agreement, Doris answered, "I don't know what Caine was thinking. Poor girl. I heard he stole her from two noblemen in a raid." Turning, she said to me, "Kara, this is Charlotte. She's a good sort, and you can trust her."

I was rapidly becoming overwhelmed, but I saw a woman struggling to fasten a line and hurried to help.

Soon, women from inside began carrying out baskets of wet clothing and sheets. Outside, I helped Doris and Charlotte to wring out and then straighten the clothing as much as possible, and we hung the pieces to dry.

"Do the women here always do laundry together?" I asked.

"We gather once a week," Doris answered. "This is the best way."

The work was straightforward, and I liked to keep busy. We hung clothing until we needed to string more lines…and then we hung more clothing. Hours passed quickly.

By early afternoon, all the laundry was clean and hanging to dry, and we emptied the tubs and stowed them. After a light meal of cheese and ham, Doris informed me, "Now, we'll move the tables back in place and start on the bread."

As we were back inside now, a few dark glances were cast my way, but I stayed close to Doris and Charlotte. The common house boasted both a cook stove and a wood-fired oven. Flour, yeast, and salt appeared from several cupboards. Other women hauled in buckets of fresh water, and we went to work making dough.

I was skilled at making bread and required no instruction. Brida watched me carefully but made no comment on my work. By the time the loaves of bread were baking, it was late afternoon, and after bringing in the laundry, we started on supper—large pots of goat stew. I was set to chopping onions with Charlotte.

"How many are we feeding?" I asked Charlotte.

"Never can tell. There are just over a hundred and fifty people here, but not everyone comes to the common room every night."

The pretty girl called Treena glowered at me a few times, but she was not otherwise unkind.

Though I didn't mind the work, I missed my quiet two days with Tristan. He liked me for who I was and never made me feel like an outsider. By the time dinner was ready, we were working by the light of candle lanterns, and then the men began arriving, and the common room began to fill.

Though I tried not to, I found myself continually glancing toward the door and breathed in relief when Tristan came through. He scanned the room with concerned eyes until he spotted me. Caine was right behind him.

I went to them quickly.

Tristan asked, "Little Bird, how was your day?"

Both men waited for my answer, and I sensed it was an important question, but I wasn't sure why.

"It was good," I answered. "We did laundry, baked bread, and then made dinner."

"And the women...You spoke with some of the women?"

In truth, I'd only spoken to two of them, so I answered, "Yes. Doris and Charlotte were kind."

My answers pleased both men, and Tristan patted my arm. Caine had dark smudges on one side of his face and the back of one hand. He looked weary, and I wondered what he'd been doing—probably working on the barn's roof.

"Let's sit," he said, leading the way across the room to a table by a window.

Logan and Brida had already gathered there, standing beside two small boys, the eldest of whom looked about seven. Both boys lit up at the sight of Tristan.

"Grandfather!" the younger one called.

Technically, he was their great-grandfather, but this hardly mattered.

As Tristan greeted both boys and tousled their hair, Logan stared down with a hard expression.

"Where have you been? We've not seen you in two days."

"Where have I been?" Tristan responded. "Home. Kara has been making dinner. She's a fine cook."

This answer didn't please Logan or Brida, and I said to Caine, "I'll get your supper."

Though I'd been working hard all day, so had he. I could tell that from looking at him.

Turning away, I went to a long table near the stove where we had set out bowls, spoons, mugs, bread, and pots of stew. There was both water and ale to drink.

Suddenly, Brida was beside me. "I always get Tristan's supper," she said. "Always."

With no intention of gainsaying her, I asked, "Would Caine prefer ale or water to drink?"

"You don't know?"

"No, he's been drinking tea at home."

She winced at the word "home" as if it bothered her to even think of me residing in Tristan and Caine's house. "Just bring him water."

In the end, she and I made several trips to make sure everyone had stew, bread, and something to drink, but she made a point of serving Tristan, and I did not get in her way. Then, she and I sat, and everyone began to eat.

"How was the hunt?" Caine asked Logan.

His brother didn't appear inclined to speak to him, but answered, "No deer. We brought back a few rabbits."

Tristan glanced into his mug of water. "I think I will have some ale tonight." Brida began to stand, but he waved her back down. "I'll get it."

As he walked away, I noticed his limp seemed worse. But when I turned back, Logan's eyes were fixed on me. I'd had men look at me in shock, hunger, and discomfort, but I'd never had one look at me the way he did: with revulsion.

Looking to Caine, he said, "I don't know what you're doing, but you cannot truly mean to call this foreigner your wife? To bring her into our family? Do you wish for sons who grow up looking like her? Undersized creatures, barely larger than children, with pale hair and pale eyes and wrists that would snap like twigs?"

I dropped my eyes to my bowl.

"Leave it alone," Caine said. "It's not your business."

"Not my business?" Logan was incredulous now. "It is my business if you choose to poison our line."

He spoke of me as if I were barely human, as if he could snuff out my life and not give it a moment's thought.

Tristan returned with a cup of ale, and Brida asked him how the new sheath was coming along. Logan spoke no more of me, but I had a difficult time eating.

I was afraid of him.

* * * *

That night in bed, though I was tired, I had trouble falling asleep.

"I'm sorry about Logan," Caine said through the darkness.

I'd thought he'd been sleeping but was glad for the sound of his voice. "He hates me."

"He doesn't like outsiders. That's all."

"Then why did you bring me here?"

"I had to."

That wasn't an answer.

"But I will protect you," Caine added. "I will. You just need to stay away from Logan. Stay out of his way."

I had no response to that and wondered if Caine would say more.

He didn't.

* * * *

The next day, mid-morning, Doris stopped by for me again, and we set off for the common hall. About halfway there, a commotion up ahead caught our attention. People were hurrying for the west end of the settlement— toward the chute.

"What is it?" Doris called out to Treena.

Treena smiled back at us. "Didn't you hear the whistles? It's Aiden's group. They've returned."

"Oh, good," Doris said. "Well and safe, I hope." She looked to me. "Let us go greet them and see what they've brought back."

Confused, I followed her to the gathering of the people near the mouth of the chute, and then the first of four riders emerged on a sweating horse. One by one, they appeared, all leading extra horses with bags tied to their backs. Then I understood. This was another raiding party, like Raven and Caine's.

Treena ran toward the leader, who jumped off his horse at the sight of her. He was in his early twenties with thick arms and black hair to his shoulders. His eyes warmed as he looked at her.

"Treena," he said.

Logan and Caine came striding up. Caine carried a hammer as if he'd been pounding nails.

"Aiden, are you well?" Logan asked. "Is anyone hurt?"

"We're well," Aiden answered, "but we had to run from some of the king's men. We managed to lose them."

"What?" Logan asked. "You didn't try to steal from the king's soldiers?"

"No. What do you take us for? We know to avoid anyone in a purple and orange tabard. We were on our way back home, and they came across us in the forest. They seemed to be searching for something, spotted us, and gave chase."

Logan turned on Caine and pointed to me. "They were searching for her! Royal soldiers gave chase to our men."

Caine was about to respond when one of the men on watch over the top of the chute called out, "Logan."

Caine, Logan, and Aiden strode to the top of the cliff looking down. Caine's face went pale, and he whirled around. "Get more quivers and bows. Now!"

People began scrambling, hurrying into a nearby shack and emerging again with long bows and quivers. I had no wish to get in anyone's way, but I needed to know what was happening, so I walked further down the cliff where I might peer over the side. At the sight below me, I drew in a sharp breath. Riders in armor, wearing orange and purple tabards were coming around the curve of the chute. I counted at least twenty.

Logan, Caine, and six other men now stood on the edge of the cliff with loaded longbows. Caine's arm was drawn back, ready to fire, and he'd slung a quiver over his shoulder.

"Wait until they're all around the curve," Logan said. His voice was low, but it carried down the line to the armed men. "Aiden and Bretten, you drop the two rear horses to cut off escape. Everyone else take the soldiers, aim for heads and eyes."

Horror flooded through me as I realized what was about to happen.

Moments ticked past.

"Fire," Logan said.

Arrows rained down into the chute. Two horses at the rear screamed as they were struck at the tops of their throats. One stumbled and fell. The other struggled to stay on its feet. Caine shot that horse's rider through the eye, and the man fell.

Panic and shouting erupted in the chute below.

"Retreat!" called the man in the lead.

When his men tried to turn in the narrow space, they were partially blocked by injured horses, and more arrows rained down. I watched Caine. His face was tense. He drew his bow again without effort and fired, striking the leader through the temple.

Logan used his bow with equal skill, but his face was impassive, as if he felt nothing.

I tried not to look at him, but when my gaze shifted back to Caine, he fired again, striking another soldier through the eye. Men below were screaming. They had no defense. One jumped off his horse to try and run on foot.

Logan shot him.

There were only eight men above and twenty below, but this brutal display did not last long, and within a matter of moments, the only things moving in the chute were panicked horses. The soldiers all lay on the ground.

Caine stepped away from the edge and looked around as if lost. At the sight of me, a short ways down the cliff, he froze. Then he started toward me.

My body began to shake, and I couldn't stop it.

"Did you just see all that?" he cried in anguish.

Yes. I'd watched him kill three men. Or had he killed them? No. I'd killed them.

"It's my fault," I said.

His eyes widened. "No."

"It was not her fault!" Logan closed in on Caine. "It's your fault! You brought this down on us, and *you* killed those men. Do think soldiers from the king's army would be out searching for stolen horses or silver?" He pointed to me. "They were looking for her!"

Caine stared at him, breathing hard, but he had no response.

"You brought royal soldiers hunting us!" Logan shouted.

Aiden and a few of the other archers walked up, watching this exchange in discomfort. Perhaps it was unlike Tristan's grandsons to shout at each other like this. Logan turned away from Caine and walked back to the edge, looking down.

"We need to clean that up," Logan said, "to kill anyone still alive and bring the bodies up here to bury them." But he said this with no emotion at all, as if the men below were merely a mess to be cleared away.

Caine looked to me. "Run to the house and send Tristan. We need him for this next part. You stay at home."

Yes. This got through to me. Tristan was needed here, and I could hide at home.

Turning, I ran.

# Chapter Seventeen

The next few days passed quickly. At first I wondered what the repercussions of the massacre would be, but the only people who seemed affected by the event were Caine and Logan…and me.

Almost everyone else, including Tristan, appeared to view the incident as an unfortunate necessity. To them, soldiers had somehow managed to follow Aiden's group home and then located the chute, and as a result, they'd had to be killed. Should they have reached us and discovered our existence, the number of stolen goods and horses here would have been grounds for arrest and hanging.

It was a risk these people lived with.

"We have to fight like everyone else," Doris said to me. "We must defend ourselves."

But I saw it differently. Though I'd never say it aloud, in essence, Logan was right. Had Caine not stolen me, Royce would not have requested royal assistance in a search, and none of those men would have died. The problem was that Caine understood this too, and it weighed on him. He was a brooder by nature, but he'd been more quiet than usual.

More and more, my thoughts turned to my lady, to how lonely and sad she must be, to how I might get a message out to her, to how I might leave this place and go back to her.

I spent my days with the women here, washing clothes, sewing, baking, and cooking. One day when the women were trying to sew and the children were restless, shouting and running between the tables, I took all the children outside and organized a game of Blind Man's Bluff. We played through much of the afternoon, and when we'd exhausted the game, I acted out several stories for their entertainment.

Instead of thinking me lazy for not helping with the sewing, several women—even one of the younger ones—thanked me.

"Bless you, girl," Charlotte said. "We may put you in charge of the children full time."

I managed a smile, but my mind was on my lady. The problem was that except for Raven's group and the small parties of raiders, no one ever came to or left this place. How could I possibly get a message out under these conditions?

On the afternoon of the third day following the tragedy at the chute, I was in the common house with the women, working with Doris, Charlotte, and Brida on a quilt. My stitches were tiny and neat, and I normally enjoyed quilting, but today, despair had begun to set in that I would never find a way to get word to my lady.

Excusing myself, I walked out back, near the tree line, needing a few moments of solitude to try and push away the despair.

"You are not happy here," someone said.

Turning, I saw that Brida had followed me out. Instantly, I was on my guard. She'd made no secret of her dislike for me. But when she walked up, studying my face, her eyes held no hostility. Did she want an answer?

"It's not that," I said. "I've not been unhappy here. I simply belong someplace else."

Her brow knitted. "And where is that?"

Except for Tristan, no one here had asked where I'd come from. I didn't think Caine wanted to know too much. Brida motioned toward a fallen log, and we both sat.

"Tell me," she said.

I began to speak. I didn't tell her as much as I'd told Tristan, but she listened carefully as I told her about my life at the de Marco manor, about my lady, and about why I needed to go back.

"But I can't go back," I finished. "She doesn't even know where I am."

"Have you tried to get a message out?" Brida asked.

This caused me to sit straight. I was cautious, but also desperate. "And how would I do that? Almost no one ever comes or leaves."

"Do you want to leave?" she asked. "Do you want to go home?"

When I didn't answer, she spoke again.

"Caine was wrong to bring you here," she said. "I don't say this so much out of concern for you as concern for our people. You don't belong here."

"And you hate me enough that'd you'd help me?"

"I don't hate you at all. I just want you gone. If you can trust in anything, you can trust in that."

My mind raced. Taking a great risk, I asked. "Could you help me get a message to my lady?"

She sat quietly for a while, thinking. "Tristan says you can read and write. If you write a message, I can have one of our men ride out on the excuse of selling some of the recent stolen goods or horses."

"One of the men would do this, in secret?"

"There are a few here who feel as Logan and I do, that you don't belong." She tilted her head. "You say this de Marco estate is about a two-day ride to the west and then north?"

My heart pounded. "Yes. But no one could come up here to the settlement to fetch me."

"No, but there's village called Tuloose about a half day's walk south of here. It's easy to find. In your message, you could direct your lady to send someone to fetch you in Tuloose. Once the message has been sent, we wait a few days. Then during dinner, when nearly everyone is at the common hall, I'll help get you to the mouth of the chute. If you stay pressed to the near wall in the darkness, you'll not be seen from the cliffs by our night watchmen. You can walk to Tuloose and someone from your lady's guard can collect you."

I sat in hope. Could this work? I didn't trust Brida, but I trusted her desire to want me gone.

"Will you help me gather paper, quill, and ink?" I asked.

* * * *

That night, as I helped the women to finish dinner, I tried not to show the shining light of my hope. Events over the course of the afternoon had moved swiftly. Brida located writing materials from some of the stores taken in raids.

I'd written a detailed letter to Lady Giselle, explaining what had happened to me. I gave no information regarding the settlement, but Brida helped me to provide clear directions to Tuloose, and I told my lady she could send guards to fetch me there. I knew she would, and by this point, Lord Jean would have seen and begun to regret her sadness. He would allow me to stay with her.

After folding the letter carefully, I'd given it to Brida, and she promised to find a messenger.

After this, we slipped back into the common house and began helping with dinner. I almost couldn't believe the weight lifted from my shoulders now that a plan had been set into motion, and soon, my lady would have me back.

My only pang of guilt hit when Tristan and Caine came through the common house to join the family for dinner. I cared for Caine's feelings, and I'd come to love Tristan. But my lady needed me.

"Did you have a good day, Little Bird?" Tristan asked, limping up.

The common hall was so crowded tonight that I had to speak up to answer. "I did."

Caine put a hand on my back and steered me toward our usual table. Tristan followed. Logan and the boys were already there, but no one had taken a seat yet. I didn't see Brida at first, and then I saw her coming through the crowd with a determined expression. She carried no bowls or cups.

Instead, she stopped at the table and looked to Tristan. "I have something to say."

He raised an eyebrow. "Yes?"

Reaching into the pocket of her dress, she drew out the letter I'd written to Lady Giselle. My heart slowed.

Holding up the letter, Brida said, "This is a message from Kara to her lady on de Marco lands. Kara asked me to find a messenger to deliver this letter so that de Marco guards might be sent after her."

"What?" Caine turned to me and then shook his head at Brida. "No, that can't be."

I wanted to slip under the floor.

She'd betrayed me.

Brida slapped the letter on the table and pushed it toward Caine. "Read it. She came to me for help, so I knew that I needed to take control. She'd have brought guards to fetch her and bring her home."

I had not gone to her for help. She had come and offered, but that meant nothing here.

Before Caine could pick up the letter, Tristan reached out and opened it, reading the contents.

"It says here she's asked to be picked up in Tuloose, and there are clear directions written out." He looked at Brida. "How could she have known about Tuloose or where to find it?"

"Does that matter?" Brida demanded. "Even if they had picked her up in Tuloose, she knows the way to the entrance to the chute. Once she told them where she'd been, they could send an entire regiment of the king's army."

Around us, people had gone quiet and were listening. Caine's expression shifted to anger and disbelief as he stared at me.

"I don't blame her," Brida went on. "She's an outsider who cares nothing for us. It's Caine's judgment I question. He brought her here, and she's the cause of those royal soldiers coming up the chute. Now, she would place us in danger of discovery yet again! What kind of tórnya would Caine make if his decisions are so poor they put the entire settlement at risk not once, but twice?"

And then I realized what she'd done, and how I'd played right into her hands. Rather than getting rid of me, she'd opted to use my desperation to make Caine appear an irresponsible leader who was still saddled with me as a wife—and now I could not be trusted.

Logan had been listening to all this in surprise, so she must not have told him her plans. But when she finished speaking, he glanced at me in disgust and then looked to Tristan.

"Brida's right," he said. "You know she's right."

Tristan shook his head sadly. "You do yourself no service by this act," he said to Brida. "And you do yourself no honor." Then he said. "Caine and Kara, come with me."

Still carrying the letter, he started for the door. Caine was so angry with me that his dark eyes seemed to burn. Turning, I hurried after Tristan, and a few moments later, the three of us were outside in the night air.

"No one speak until we get home," Tristan ordered.

Within a few paces, Caine was out in front, walking swiftly on his long legs. His entire body was like a coiled spring of tension. I came behind with Tristan, who walked more slowly, and when the two of us entered the house, Caine stood in the middle of the sitting room.

As soon as Tristan closed the front door, Caine exploded.

Closing on me, he shouted into my face. "Why?"

I'd seen Caine angry before but never with me, and I couldn't help shrinking away from him. He didn't stop.

"Haven't we tried to make you feel welcome?" he shouted. "To give you a safe home?

The walls shook from the volume of his voice, and everything pressed down on me. Images flashed through my mind…the sad face of Lady Giselle…Royce Capello lifting me onto a horse…Caine locking me in the shack in the darkness…men down in the chute screaming as arrows pierced their eyes…Brida slapping my message on the table.

Caine was still shouting into my face. "And the only thing you care about is returning to your lady? Why?"

"Because she is alone!" I cried back. "Lord Jean is no companion to her, and she has no daughters. She spends her days alone now! I was her only comfort, and I am gone."

Caine blinked and his anger faded. "You worry for her? This isn't about yourself?"

The sorrow racking me was so heavy I couldn't try to answer.

Tristan limped to me. "Kara..." he began gently, speaking to me as if I were a child. "Do you understand what would happen if you did get a message to your lady and she sent guards to bring you home?"

"Yes," I managed to answer. "I would be with her again."

"Only for a few days. Your de Marco lord would send word to the man who bought you. He would have no choice."

I shook my head. "No. Lord Jean will have seen my lady's sorrow. He'd not take me from her again. He'd let me to stay with her."

"He could not. For him to keep you would be the same as theft. Surely, you can see this?"

The room began to spin as I absorbed Tristan's words. "He would give me back to Royce?"

"Yes."

Wrapping my arms around myself, I could not contain a sob. "Then she is lost to me! And I am lost to her!"

After the first sob, more followed. Stumbling sideways, I grasped the back of a couch to stay on my feet, weeping with loud sounds of pain.

"Kara!" Caine caught me and swept an arm beneath my knees, lifting me off the ground.

In a sea of loss, I clung to his neck and buried my face in his shoulder.

"She's tired," he said, "and overwrought. I'm putting her to bed."

Tristan didn't answer, and Caine carried me down the hallway to our room. Once there, he laid me on the bed and then rushed to the washbasin, wetting a cloth and hurrying back to me. Sitting on the bed, he wiped the cloth over my eyes and cheeks. I was still weeping.

"It's all right," he said. "Try to relax."

With my lady forever lost to me, I didn't want to be alone.

"Don't leave," I begged, grasping the back of his hand. "Don't leave me in here."

"I won't, but you need to rest. You need to let yourself relax."

After dropping the cloth on the floor, he pulled off his boots. "Roll over onto your side."

Without thinking, I did as he asked, and he laid down behind me, wrapping his body around mine, with his chest against my back and his chin over the top of my head, enveloping me with his right arm.

"Try to close your eyes," he said.

"You won't leave?"

"I won't."

\* \* \* \*

The next morning, when I woke, Caine was still wrapped around me. I'd not woken up with him in the room before, much less in the bed.

"Are you awake?" he whispered.

I sat up and looked down at him. He'd stayed with me all night.

"I didn't want to leave this morning until I knew you were better," he said.

Was I better? I was calm now, but the revelations of last night were still raw.

"Are you hungry?" he asked.

"Yes."

"So am I. We didn't eat dinner."

He was right. We hadn't. But this seemed unimportant, and I wished he would ask me about things that mattered. My actions in trying to send that message had hurt him in more ways than one.

After climbing from the bed, we left the room, walking down the hallway together.

In the kitchen, Tristan was boiling eggs. The message I'd written to Lady Giselle was lying open on the table.

"I should eat and then get to work on the barn," Caine said.

"No," Tristan answered. "The barn can wait. Sit down. Both of you."

Caine frowned, but Tristan's tone brooked no refusal so we both sat at the table. Soon, Tristan brought mugs of tea and boiled eggs.

"Last night was a night for tears," he said. "But today we need to speak."

Shifting in his chair, Caine took a sip of tea. "About what?"

Tristan offered him a measured look. "I understand why Kara did what she did. She was taken twice against her will, once by this nobleman, Royce, and then once by you. Of course she would take action to control her own path. No one could blame her for that." He turned to me. "I may not give many orders here, but I am the tórnya of this settlement. Fourteenth law or not, if you wish to go back to de Marco lands, I will order Caine to take you back."

Caine went stiff, but didn't speak.

Though Tristan's offer moved me, he must have known it was no offer at all.

"So that I might be given back to Royce?" I asked. "No. I've no wish for that."

"Then is there is somewhere else you wish to go?"

I pondered the question. Where else would I go? I couldn't return to the manor, and I'd never been anyplace else. "No."

Perhaps he'd simply wanted me to see the truth.

"Good then," he said. "So you accept that this is now your home, that Caine and I are your family?"

Gripping the warm mug, I allowed this reality to sink in. For better or worse, I was home. "Yes."

Caine must have begun to understand this discussion as well, and cast his grandfather a look of gratitude.

"All right then," Tristan said, cracking an egg and peeling it. "We must repair the damage done by Brida. Caine is a good deal more respected here than she realizes. He's in no danger of losing his status among the people. But Kara is another matter."

"I won't be trusted at all now," I said.

Tristan pushed my letter toward Caine. "Look at this."

Caine scowled. "Why would I want to look at that?"

"To see the words, to see the handwriting."

Puzzled, Caine picked up the letter.

While he was reading it, Tristan said. "Logan has suggested that next year, we stop the raids, and I am inclined to agree with him."

This conversation was jumping around so quickly I couldn't guess where it was going.

But Caine glanced up and nodded. "So am I. He's wrong in some things, but not this. The raids are a leftover tradition from the old days, and they pose too much risk."

"So, if we end the raids," Tristan said, "the only contact we'll have with the outside world is via Raven's group of travelers. They will become more important."

"Why?" Caine asked.

"Because our people, our children, need contact with the outside. I may not agree with *how* you brought Kara here, but the fact that you did proves our people do not always have enough choices. We have a number of fine young women here, and yet you wanted someone else. You had access to the outside. Our other young people deserve choices. They need to know there is something beyond this settlement."

"And how do we do this?" Caine asked.

"First by preparing them. Kara knows many things we do not. You see that letter? I thought myself a fair writer, but I cannot write anything like that." He turned to me. "Can you write numbers? Can you add written numbers and subtract them?"

"Yes, of course."

I still had no idea where he was going with this.

"You know the old abandoned house near the stream?" Tristan asked Caine.

"Yes."

"I want you to help Kara turn it into a school. I want her to teach the children skills they'll need to know and about the people outside of this place. Then…next year, if some of our young people wish to see more of the world, we'll send them with Raven and allow them travel."

"But you founded the settlement so that most of us might stop traveling," Caine answered, "so we might have a safe place all our own."

"I know. But in some things, I may have been wrong." Tristan's eyes rested on me. "I see that now, and I need to adjust our path before it's too late." Reaching out, he touched my hand. "There are others here who feel as I do. If the people can see that you'll use your skills to help our children, they will begin to trust you again."

I had no experience being a teacher, but I trusted Tristan, and if he wanted me to try, I would.

"Show me this abandoned house."

# Chapter Eighteen

Caine and I spent the next two days working on the old house, but we worked in secret.

"Logan will fight this idea," Caine said. "So we must keep it quiet until Grandfather is ready to tell the people."

From what I'd seen of Logan, I agreed.

I cleaned the inside while Caine mended the roof. The chimney of the hearth was blocked, and he used a long pole to break through and try to clean out the residue so that we might have a heat source. Then he brought tables, benches, and chairs, and we arranged them so they faced the front of the room.

Lady Giselle had been my tutor, and she'd taught me well, but our lessons had been one-on-one. I wondered about teaching a larger group.

"I'll need to teach the children the alphabet," I said. "I'll need to show them the written letters. The settlement has some paper in the stores, but it's not enough, and using it up wouldn't be efficient."

"How did you learn to write?"

"When I was young, I had a slate and chalk." Walking to the front of the room, I said, "But with so many students, at first it would be better to have a large piece that could be seen by everyone at the same time."

He put a hand to his chin.

The next day, he carried in a large, slender piece of dark shale—about the size of a door—and he built a stand for it.

"It's perfect," I said when he'd finished. "Where did you get it?"

"There's a quarry not far into the forest. Come out with me and we'll see about chalk."

Together, we walked through the trees.

Over the past few days, Caine had rarely spoken of anything other than the tasks upon which we worked, but I couldn't help asking, "Do you approve of this idea of Tristan's? To educate the children and let them travel with Raven if they wish?"

"I do. He's right that too many of us have become too cut off, too set in the idea that nothing exists below that chute. It's not a healthy way to live."

I smiled. "You'll make a good leader."

At that, he stopped and put one hand in front of me. "You think so?"

"Of course I do. You think beyond only what you want. You care for the needs of others."

As he studied me, my response seemed to shame him, and he began walking again. "There's a short cliff not far from here with a chalk face. I can cut out some pieces."

* * * *

That evening, we let Tristan know we were ready.

I'd not been among any of the women to help with the work in the past few days, and the three of us had eaten dinner at home, but that night, I accompanied Caine and Tristan to the common house. When we walked in, a number of people glanced in our direction. Logan, Brida, and their boys were at our usual family table.

Tristan wasted no time and walked to the hearth of the vast room.

"I have something to say," he called.

Silence fell. Instinctively, I moved closer to Caine, but we remained in place near the front door.

"I have spoken at length with Kara," Tristan continued, "and I understand that she meant no harm by trying to send out a message. She sought to bring no one here, only to reach out to someone who had been left behind, as any of you might have done."

Unable to stop myself, I glanced at Brida. Her eyes were like glass as she listened.

"We are fortunate that Kara possesses skills many of us do not," Tristan continued. "She reads and writes much better than myself, and to show her desire to be useful here, she has agreed to teach our children to read and write as well as she does. She's offered to teach them to write numbers. Caine has repaired the old house by the stream to create a school."

Murmurs broke out all around the common house, and Caine observed reactions. Some people were appalled, but many appeared interested.

"This will be a choice for each family." Tristan said. "But tomorrow morning, if it is your wish, send your children to the schoolhouse."

With that, he limped toward our table, leaving everyone else buzzing at this news.

"I'll get dinner," I told Caine.

"You get the food," he said, "and I'll get drinks. I know you want only water."

Somehow, I had a feeling he wished to avoid the family table as long as possible. But moments later, we were dished up and had no choice but to sit with Logan and Brida. Tristan seemed determined to pretend that nothing was amiss, but Logan had not touched his stew.

"A school, Grandfather?" he asked.

"Yes," Tristan answered. "A school."

"My boys will not be there."

"Then Kara won't expect them in the morning."

\* \* \* \*

The next morning, I stood in the schoolroom with nerves in my stomach. What if no one arrived? Worse, what if they did? Since last night, I'd been calling on the memories of myself as a child, and the methods Lady Giselle had used to teach me.

The tables, chairs, and benches were in place. The dark slate was positioned on its stand in the front of the room. I had numerous pieces of chalk ready, and yet I hoped I'd be able to do this. Tristan had suggested that I hold school for only about two hours in the beginning, as that would be enough time for the young students to absorb information without becoming frustrated or bored. Plus, some of the older children had duties and chores to perform elsewhere.

The door opened, and several children entered. I knew a few of the younger ones from the common house, but then a girl of about eleven entered the room. I'd never spoken to her but had seen her in the common house, as she was just becoming old enough to take her part with the women in their work. As opposed to black, her hair was a shade of chocolate brown. Then a boy of about fifteen walked in. This did take me aback slightly, as he was a head taller than me with arms that showed the developing muscles of a man.

He looked just as nervous as I felt.

"Welcome," I said. "Please sit anywhere you like."

Once everyone was settled, and it seemed that no more students would come through the door, I counted fourteen children. The youngest was about seven, and the oldest was the tall boy.

"Some of you already know me," I said, "but I don't know everyone here. Perhaps you could tell me your names?"

The tall boy was sitting up front, and my gaze dropped to him.

"Trace," he said quietly.

I nodded. One by one they gave me their names. The brown-haired girl was Isabella. Something about her kept my attention. As opposed to nervous, she appeared eager. But after everyone had completed an introduction, it was time for me to begin.

"Sometimes, people refer to writing as 'drawing sounds' but this only means that certain symbols can represent a sound."

At their puzzled expressions, I realized I was already talking over their heads, so I turned to the slate and wrote out the alphabet, sounding out each letter as I wrote it. Then I taught the children the names of the letters and had them practice with different sounds each letter might make.

This took a while, but they remained engaged, and when we had exhausted this, I used a cloth to wipe the slate clean and then called them all up to join me—as there were only fourteen of them. I gave everyone a piece of chalk and helped them to write letters. This was an active exercise, and they enjoyed it.

Isabella caught on quickly, and I soon had her helping the smaller children. This pleased her. Our time nearly flew by and near the end, Trace wrote the word "dog" on the slate and sounded it out.

Looking down at me, he asked, "This means I know how to write?"

"Yes. You know how to write."

His face broke into a smile.

\* \* \* \*

After the children left, I straightened the classroom and headed off to the common house to help with the baking. I felt I'd been lax in my work with the other women.

As I arrived, I saw Trace speaking with Charlotte, and his face was animated. She patted his back and sent him on his way down the path toward the barn, but at the sight of me, she put her hands on her hips.

"Well, young Kara," she said. "You've won over my grandson, Trace. He just told me he knows how to write. I'd no idea he longed for such things."

"Perhaps he didn't know such things existed," I answered.

"Perhaps."

We walked into the common house, and inside, Isabella was speaking to a thin, middle-aged woman in the same animated manner. Of course I'd seen this woman before, but few of the women here actually spoke to me. As I took my place at a table to begin making dough, the thin woman approached.

"That's my girl, Isabella," she said.

"She's very bright," I answered, "the best student in the class."

"Is she?" The woman glanced away. "My name is Martene...and I thank you."

Nodding, I reached for the flour, and several other women who'd never spoken to me before came to join us.

Only Brida pretended I did not exist.

\* \* \* \*

The next morning, as the students practiced writing letters and words on the slate, I wondered about the possibility of acquiring smaller, individual slates. Caine had said there was a quarry nearby. I would speak with him about this.

Our time for the morning was nearly over when I had Isabella write the word "king" on the slate.

A younger girl, named Zoë pulled at my sleeve. "Kara, what is a king?"

All the children turned to hear my answer. Nonplussed, I said, "The king rules the nation." Upon seeing their confused expressions, I added. "He is a leader."

"Oh," Isabella said, "like Tristan."

"Well...yes, but not quite like Tristan. King Amandine rules all of Samourè."

"What is Samourè?" Trace asked.

*Oh, dear*, I thought. Then I made a mental note to plan a few careful lessons on both geography and the functions of the national government. I had no maps, but I could draw one. This would be a worthwhile use of paper and ink.

"Samourè is the nation in which we live," I explained. "And the king normally lives in a castle in the city of Lascaùx."

"What's a castle?" Isabella asked.

"What's a city?" Zoë asked.

Suddenly, I understood why Tristan wanted them to receive some education before attempting any travels with Raven.

"A city is a large place where many people live," I answered.

"What does it look like?"

Now there, Zoë had me. I might have been educated in some areas, but like all of the children here, I had been raised in one limited place and never even visited a village.

But then a movement in the doorway caught my eye, and I looked over to see Caine and Logan standing there, watching us. Logan's entire body was tense, but Caine wore a wry smile as he observed me floundering.

Some retribution seemed fair.

"I myself have never visited a city," I said, "but Caine has certainly seen a few, and he would be glad to explain them. Caine, come in and tell us about cities."

All the children turned to him expectantly. Startled, he flashed me an annoyed glance and said, "Another time maybe. But it's past lunch, and we've come to fetch you. We need Trace up on the barn roof."

"Oh," I answered. "Is it that late? I am sorry."

Quickly, I ushered the children toward the door. Logan stared at me as if I were an insect he longed to step on. Then he turned and walked off by himself, not waiting for Caine.

I sighed.

"Don't mind him," Caine said. "He has a hard time with change. But he respects Grandfather's wishes. He'll come around."

I wasn't so sure about that, but as today was laundry day, I needed to straighten up the schoolroom and get to the common house.

"I'll see you tonight," I told Caine.

He stood close, and for just an instant, I thought he was going to kiss the side of my face. Instead, he straightened.

"Yes, I'll see you tonight."

He left.

\* \* \* \*

Once I had the schoolroom back in order and ready for the next day, I hurried toward the common house. But one of my normal laundry duties was to help hang the clothing out back, so I walked up the back side of the settlement, near to the tree line. My mind was busy with thoughts on how I might present new ideas and concepts to the children.

While distracted, I didn't notice a shadow near a tree until I was almost on top of it, and then someone large stepped out to block my path.

It was Logan.

Glancing around, I realized the two of us were alone, and this made me anxious.

"Excuse me," I said quietly, moving to step around him.

He moved with me, not allowing me to pass.

"I want you to close the school," he said.

This was the first time he'd ever spoken directly to me. He'd often spoken about me to others while in my presence, but never *to* me, and from the strain in his voice now, I sensed it was difficult for him.

However, I had no intention of speaking with him on this matter. "You'll need to speak to your grandfather of this, not to me. I'm only following his request." Again, I tried to move past him.

This time, he stopped me by holding out his arm. "No. I'm speaking to you. You will tell Grandfather that you've no wish to continue with the school, that it's too much for you. He won't force you to continue."

What a coward he was, and a bully. I'd sometimes seen Lord Jean bully my lady. I hadn't liked it then, and I didn't like it now.

"No," I said. "If you want the school closed, you talk to Tristan yourself."

"Can't you see what you're doing?" he asked angrily. "I was there today! I saw you. You are poisoning our children's minds, making them see false visions of the world outside, making it look desirable as opposed to the dark, filthy place it is."

His eyes were manic, with a kind of madness in their depths. Stepping in, he towered over me.

"Tell my grandfather you want to close down the school."

"No."

Without warning, his right hand snaked out, and he grabbed my throat with his thumb on my windpipe. Then he began to tighten his fingers, cutting off my air. Clutching his solid wrist, I fought to pull his hand away. Then wildly, I clawed at his hand, trying to make him let go.

But his face was calm now, as if he felt nothing, as if I were a rabbit he'd caught in his garden, and he needed to wring my neck. The pain of his fingers pressing into my throat grew blinding, and I fought to breathe as terror coursed through me.

"Logan!" someone shouted.

Through a haze of pain, I saw Brida pulling on his arm.

"Let her go!" Brida shouted, hitting him several times and pulling at his arm again. "Logan, let go!"

Suddenly, I was free and falling to my knees, fighting to take in air.

"You can't kill her!" Brida cried. "Whether you accept it or not, she is viewed as Caine's wife. She is seen as one of us! If you kill her and anyone finds out, you'll be banished. Is that what you want? You, who should be tórnya, to be banished for murder?"

My throat was on fire, and almost no air was coming in.

Brida dropped beside me. "Try to be calm," she said. "Don't fight it. Take slow breaths."

With effort, I stopped struggling to breathe and tried to take smaller breaths. My throat opened slightly, and in a moment, I was breathing.

Logan looked down at me, but he appeared shaken now. Perhaps Brida's image of what could have happened affected him. A few more seconds, and I would have been dead at his hands.

"Kara, listen," Brida said. "You cannot tell Tristan or Caine of this. Logan acted without thinking…almost as an accident. As things stand, the love between two brothers has been strained, and you don't want it broken. You don't want Logan and Caine to become enemies. Can you imagine life here should one of them become tórnya while the other is an enemy? What harm might that do our people?"

Through the haze in my mind and the pain in my throat, I understood what she meant. If Caine learned of this, he might not forgive Logan, and the repercussions of that could harm the entire settlement.

"Logan will never lay hands on you again," she said. "I swear. Will you be silent on this?"

"Yes," I managed to say.

She rocked back in relief. "Let me help you home."

"No." I drew away and struggled to my feet. "Just tell the women I'm not well, that I won't be coming today."

Turning, I left them and made my way home.

Upon opening the front door of our house and entering the sitting room, I heard Tristan call from the workroom. "Caine, is that you?"

"No, it's me." But my voice was strained, and he emerged into the kitchen. "Little Bird? Are you not well?"

"I'm just tired. I think I need to rest. Could we stay in tonight?"

His brow furrowed. "Yes, of course. But you don't look well. What's wrong?"

"I just need to some rest."

He seemed about to press the matter but only said, "Go and lie down. I'll send to word to Caine to come when he finishes his work."

\* \* \* \*

I rested through the afternoon, but felt well enough to help Tristan with dinner. He insisted on making the main dish—scrambled eggs with potatoes—but he let me fry up some corncakes. My throat still hurt, but now it felt sore as opposed to on fire.

When Caine came home, darkness had fallen. He wanted to know if I was all right. I assured him that I was and had only been a little tired. He accepted this and never minded eating at home. We ate by the light of a candle lantern.

Afterward, Tristan entertained us by telling stories of his youth, including a time he'd brought a fox cub home and tried to raise it as a pet, and it ended up killing his mother's chickens.

When it was time to go to bed, Caine carried a candle lantern to our room.

Since that night when I'd been so overwrought, he'd not slept in the bed again, and there were times when I wished he would. I had liked waking up with my back pressed into his chest. But of course I could never suggest such a thing.

Still, something had changed, and neither of us bothered turning around while the other got ready to sleep. I tended to just take off my dress and sleep in my shift. Tonight, as I removed my dress and laid it over a chair, he pulled his shirt over his head.

But when I started for the bed, he said, "Kara, wait. There's something all over your neck. Did you splatter something on yourself?"

Before I could think, he lifted a candle lantern with one hand and reached out toward my neck with the other, as if to wipe something away. Then his eyes narrowed, and he looked closer.

"What is all this?"

"I…I…"

"Are those bruises?" He leaned closer. "These are bad. Your windpipe is bruised and these on the side look like…" He trailed off.

I knew what they must have looked like: finger imprints. Earlier, in the daylight, no marks had been visible or Tristan would have noticed. The bruises must have begun to appear after sunset.

"Is this why you came home ill today?" he asked. "Someone grabbed you by the throat?"

My mind went blank, and I couldn't think of a plausible lie to explain bruises in the shapes of fingers.

His voice turned angry. "Was it Logan?"

"It was an accident!" I blurted out. "He didn't mean to. He asked me to close down the school, and I wouldn't agree and when I tried to walk off, he tried to stop me. That's all that happened."

Caine looked down at my throat for a few more seconds. Then he started for the door.

"Where are you going?" I cried.

"To leave a few bruises on Logan. I'll say it was an accident."

"No!" I ran to the door, cutting him off. "Please don't. There's been enough trouble on my account, and I don't want you and Logan falling out. Please don't do anything. I'm asking you."

We were speaking loudly enough that Tristan could probably hear us.

Caine wavered. "I'll leave it alone on one condition."

"What?" I'd have promised him anything.

"If he comes near you again, you don't try to hide it. You tell me right away. Do you swear?"

"Yes, I swear."

To my gratitude, he relented and stayed with me in the room.

* * * *

The next day, I found a scarf in the same trunk from where Tristan had taken my wool dresses, and I tied it around my neck. For the following few days, I made sure to finish my lessons with the children on time, and I walked with Trace all the way back to the common house.

A week passed and the bruises faded.

I continued teaching the children in the mornings and then working with the women in the afternoons, becoming more and more a part of this community. At night, in our room, Caine now watched me undress, and when he thought I wasn't looking, I saw longing in his eyes. One night, I almost asked him to sleep in the bed with me again, but couldn't manage to say the words.

Then one day, before lunch, I arrived at the common house to help with the quilting. The women would stretch the quilts out so that four or five of us could sit around and work on one together.

Upon slipping inside the front door, I spotted a few of the younger women, including Treena, sitting with Brida. Doris was with them as well.

"Oh, Kara, come and sit with us," Treena called. "You have the neatest stitches."

Of late, Treena had been friendlier to me. I wasn't sure why, but somehow I didn't think this change had anything to do with the school.

Going over, I sat down and picked up a needle.

"What were you saying about Aiden?" Doris asked Treena. "Your parents have given their permission?"

"Yes." Treena beamed. "Now that Kara's finally taken Caine off the market, they've stopped pressing me to marry him. Last night, Father agreed to let Aiden and me hand-fast. Mother and I are planning a ceremony for the winter solstice."

One of the younger women sighed. "To marry Aiden. You're so lucky. Have you kissed him yet?"

Treena laughed. "More than that."

"Really? What was it like?"

"Swoon worthy," Treena answered.

The other women, including Brida, all laughed, but I felt myself turning pink. It appeared I'd walked into a rather frank discussion.

But it got worse.

"Kara," Treena asked. "Caine is always so serious. And he never talks of anything besides horses or crops or the roof on the barn. I've always wanted to ask you, what's he like?"

"What's he like?" I repeated uncomfortably.

"What's he like in bed?"

Most of the other women burst into laughter again, but as I stuttered to come up with some semblance of an answer, Brida sat at full attention, fixating on my face.

"What is he like?" she asked, only she wasn't teasing. "Do you know?"

"Stop this," Doris said, still laughing. "Can't you see you've made Kara blush? Perhaps she'd prefer not to share such secrets with the rest of us."

The discussion moved back to Aiden and Treena's hand-fasting ceremony.

But Brida sat in her chair with her eyes shifting back and forth in thought.

I focused on my quilting.

In the early afternoon, some of the men came in to see what might be available for lunch. Sometimes, the men brought food with them when they worked, and sometimes they came in here, seeking cheese, ham, or bread.

Today, Caine, Logan, Trace, and Aiden all came through the front door discussing the possibility of adding more stalls to the stable. They gathered near the stove to warm their hands. Leaving my small group of quilters, I went to see if I could help slice bread or make tea. Brida followed.

Going to the stove, I filled the kettle with water.

Brida picked up a knife and sliced a piece of bread. Handing it to Caine, she asked him, "Have you and Kara consummated your marriage?"

This caught him so unawares he dropped the bread.

"What?"

Trace turned away in embarrassment and pretended to focus on the quilting.

"It's a simple question," Brida said. "Have you?"

"That is none of your concern," Caine snapped.

"It is my concern if you don't have a true marriage, and I certainly think it would be Tristan's concern."

This was too much for me. First, I'd endured teasing by the women, and now Brida was asking Caine if he'd bedded me—and she was doing this right in front of one of my students.

Leaving the stove, I walked out the back door of the common house and down the tree line, stepping into the forest and leaving everyone else behind. I burned with shame and had no intention of going back in there until the men were gone.

"Kara!"

Caine's voice sounded behind me. He ran through the trees and caught up to me.

"I'm sorry," he said. "I don't know what gave her the idea to ask me that. She's just trying to make it appear that you and I aren't truly married."

"Why would she care?"

With a sigh, Caine pointed to a clear spot on the ground and drew me down beside him. "Because Grandfather won't name me tórnya unless I'm married with a family. He wants a family man to lead the settlement…and I understand why."

I remembered Doris's words from the day we met.

*Because Tristan wants a family man to follow him. Everyone knows that.*

I hadn't thought on this at the time as that was my first day among the women, and I'd had other concerns.

"If Tristan believes we're not living as husband and wife," I asked, "will that affect his decision?"

When Caine didn't answer, I thought on what this would mean. Logan would be named as the next leader. I couldn't imagine what the settlement would be like with Logan in charge. He was not fit to make decisions for other people.

Caine would make a fine leader. He was strong but could bend in the wind.

I saw only one way around this.

Though I didn't know much about what happened between men and women, I knew it normally started with a kiss. Leaning in, I touched my lips to Caine's. Startled, he sat back, and ran his eyes over my face. Then he grasped the back of my head and pressed his mouth down on mine.

The act felt foreign and slightly invasive, and when he opened his mouth, I had to force myself not to resist. I wanted to do this. I wanted to do it for him. His breaths quickened, and he kissed me deeper.

But then he wrenched himself away.

"No," he said raggedly. "Not like this."

"Not in the forest? Do you want to go home?"

"No, I mean not like this. We're not married. Not really. I called on that old law because I was desperate, but you never consented to marry me. We never hand-fasted."

"Then ask me."

"Ask you what?"

"To marry you."

He sat up on knees. "Would you?"

"Yes."

"Would you marry me tonight?"

"Yes."

\* \* \* \*

I spent the rest of the afternoon quilting with the women and once we'd put the quilts away, I helped to start dinner. But when everyone was busy, I slipped out the front door of the common house and went home. Tristan wasn't there, and I had the place to myself.

First, I went to my trunk and looked at my own gowns. Neither of the silks seemed right to me. This was not a world for silk. Instead, I drew out the ice blue muslin that I'd not yet worn. After putting it on and lacing it up, I undid my braid, brushed out my hair, and let it fall in waves around my shoulders and down my back.

I knew that Treena and Aiden wanted a well-planned ceremony, with holly berries for decorations and two days worth of food preparation. I did not need any of that, and neither did Caine. When the time was right, I left the house and walked back to the common house, knowing that by this point it would be crowded, and Tristan and Caine would already be there.

When I entered, heads began to turn and people began to fall silent. I knew they didn't find me beautiful when I was dressed like this with my mass of silver-blond hair down. They found me too otherworldly.

But Caine crossed the room and took my hand. Looking back at Tristan, he said, "Grandfather, will you hand-fast us? We want to have the ceremony."

Tristan spoke to me. "You wish for this?"

"Yes."

Logan had been seated, and he jumped to his feet, but he said nothing. I ignored him as several other people in the room flew into action. Doris was at my side, kissing my face, and Charlotte hurried to Tristan, carrying a white ribbon.

Other people made way for Caine and me as we walked to Tristan.

With the ribbon, Tristan bound our right hands together. "Do you, Caine, swear to love Kara and to protect her heart and to place her above all others for the rest of your life?"

"I swear."

Tristan turned to me. "Do you, Kara, swear to love Caine and to protect his heart and to place him above all others for the rest of your life?"

In front of everyone, I said, "I swear."

No one could doubt that Caine and I were married.

\* \* \* \*

Our wedding night was not exactly awful.

Caine was worried about hurting me, which I appreciated. But the act itself was more physically uncomfortable than I'd expected, and I'm not sure he received any pleasure.

The next night, he worried that I still needed to recover from the previous night. I could see that he wanted me, that he'd been waiting for this, but he only kissed me and then wrapped himself around me again, like that first night he'd slept in the bed.

On the third night, we tried again. The problem was the difference in our sizes. He was so much larger, and he feared putting his weight on me.

"Kara, move on top of me," he whispered.

Although this seemed odd, I did as he asked, and his suggestion became clearer. With me on top, he was able to relax, and I slowly took him inside me, moving my body in rhythm with his.

This was better.

It was easier.

A warm feeling had begun to build in my stomach when his body convulsed, and he made a sound from the back of throat as he held me with both arms. He convulsed several times and whispered in my ear.

"I love you. I've never loved anyone as I love you."

I respected and admired him. He was kind, and I cared for him. In a marriage, this must be love.

"I love you," I told him.

He held me tighter, pushing his face into the crook of my neck.

At least we were finding our way here in the bedroom. I wondered if other new couples struggled to find their path down this side of things.

But I suspected they did.

# Chapter Nineteen

As late autumn moved toward winter, Brida announced one morning that the supply of flour was running low and we would need to ration. I don't know why I'd never questioned the source of some of our food supplies here, but the people did not grow wheat.

"From where does the flour, sugar, and other dry foods come?" I asked Doris.

"Raven and Jade bring it in the early autumn, and then again in winter. They'll be home in a few weeks, and they normally buy enough to get us through winter and spring. By late spring, the gardens are bursting, and we have plenty of other food."

I'd not realized how dependent we were on Raven's group of travelers. Asking Doris a few more questions, I also came to learn that Tristan was the only person in the settlement with bags of flour, rice, cornmeal, and lentils at home.

"Those are private gifts from Raven," she explained. "Everything else he brings back goes into the communal stores."

Apparently, while other members of the settlement kept chickens and had kitchen gardens, they often had little choice besides eating dinner in the common house. This reality turned my concerns in another direction within the week.

Brida was viewed as leader among the women. She decided what we made for dinner each night in the common house, and she normally chose goat stew. Sometimes she chose rabbit stew or venison stew, depending on what the men had brought back after hunting. Most of the people didn't mind eating stew nearly every night so long as there was plenty of bread to go with it.

But once we began rationing flour and the bread was limited, I began to see looks of disappointment at the prospect of another stew for dinner. Wondering about other choices for our menu, I looked through the cookware in the cupboards of the common house and found a number of long baking pans. The next morning, I asked Caine if he could put off other work and take a few of the men fishing for trout.

Mid-morning, Trace and Aiden arrived at the common house with four large buckets filled with trout, and I asked Brida if I might pose something different for dinner. As I purposefully asked her in front of the other women—who could see all the trout—she had little choice but to agree. Quickly, I went home and asked Tristan if I might use some of our own cornmeal stores.

"Of course," he said. "You never need ask. I don't wish to hurt Raven by refusing his gifts, but you are always welcome to take anything in our storeroom for the people."

Grateful, I took a bag of cornmeal, along with a good-sized helping of parsley, back to the women at the common house.

That afternoon, we worked to clean and bone all the trout, and we laid the pieces of fish in the long pans. I boiled the cornmeal into a thick mixture, adding goat cheese and parsley, and we spread this on top of the fish. Then we began baking the pans in the wood-fired oven, creating a kind of fish pie.

We were baking the last of the pans when our men began arriving. At the prospect of something different for dinner, their pleasure was clear. A number of people declared the pies delicious, but I think they appreciated the variety more than anything else.

The next night we had goat stew.

The following morning, I went into the storage room of communal supplies and took stock. We still had onions, potatoes, lentils, oats, ham, bacon fat, goat cheese, and several large bags of rice.

That afternoon, I had the women slice potatoes thinly. Again, we laid these in the long pans, adding cheese and pieces of ham. We baked the pans until the potatoes were soft and the cheese had melted.

The children liked this dish, and I don't think Logan knew that I had started planning meals, because when he took a bite, he looked up at Brida and said, "This is good."

She didn't respond.

The next day, I asked the women to gather any remaining tomatoes. Before the first frost, most of us had brought our still-green tomatoes inside to let them ripen. I gathered dried herbs from home, and I taught the women how to make the rice dish with onions, herbs, and diced tomatoes. Then we gathered eggs and parsley, and I mixed these with cornmeal to make up the batter for fried corncakes. Even though the meal contained no meat, no one seemed to notice, and every bite of food vanished.

The next day, in the early afternoon, Treena asked me, "Kara, what are we making for dinner tonight? Do you need us to gather anything?"

"Yes. See if anyone still has carrots in their gardens. I thought we'd do pots of lentils with ham and vegetables."

"That sounds good," Charlotte said. "We still have oats. Perhaps we could fry up some oat cakes."

Only then did I notice that Brida had gone pale as she listened. Always before, the women had asked her what needed to be readied for dinner. Now they came to me. I neither apologized to her nor corrected the other women.

Not long after this, the first snow fell.

Though it was bitterly cold outside, we had plenty of firewood, and I was always warm at home or in the school or in the common house. I spent my nights under the blankets with Caine, and we continued learning more about how to please each other. He often whispered that he loved me, and I knew that he did.

I was loved, and I was content.

Supplies of rice and oats began to run low. The sugar was long gone, and the flour was nearly gone, but no one seemed concerned.

Then one afternoon, when the women were gathered at the common house, working on quilts, Trace stuck his head in the front door.

"Grandmother!" he called to Charlotte. "Raven and Jade are back. They're coming up the chute now."

Smiles broke out all around me. Everyone left their sewing and hurried to grab their cloaks. I followed suit and was soon swept down the path with a group of chattering women.

"I hope they brought some bolts of red wool," Treena said. "My red dress is worn thin."

Up ahead, I could see a small crowd had gathered in the open area near the mouth of the chute. Caine and Tristan were already there. Just as I arrived, a white wagon emerged. Raven was driving, but a woman and a boy sat on the bench beside him. The next wagon emerged with Badger driving. Four more followed. The feeling all around me was one of celebration. Even in the frigid air, everyone was smiling as people began jumping off wagons.

A pretty girl about my age ran to Doris and hugged her.

"Oh, Mama," she said. "We've brought so much food back, and some beautiful green wool for gowns and shirts. Wait until you see."

Raven climbed down from the bench of the wagon and embraced Caine. I stood back uncertainly. These two were close. Anyone could see that. But then the woman and boy who'd been sitting beside Raven climbed down.

Caine looked around until spotting me. "Kara, there you are. Come here and meet Jade and Sean."

Cautiously, I approached. The boy hovered near Raven. I didn't know Raven well, and the woman was a stranger. I'd never liked meeting new people. In her late twenties, she was tall, about the height of Raven. Her skin was flawless. Like Isabella, her hair was a rich shade of chocolate brown—and so were her eyes. Though her waist was small, her body showed more curves than mine.

She was lovely, but she took in my hair and eyes with some surprise. Then she said, "Oh, Caine. This is your girl? The one you stole from those noblemen?"

"Jade," Caine answered, "she is my wife."

"Wife?" Raven repeated, and his expression shifted to concern as he glanced between us. "For how long?"

"Since late autumn," Caine answered, sounding less than pleased by his brother's response.

But Tristan limped up and grasped my hand. "Kara has chosen to live with us at the house, and we are blessed to have her there."

I gripped his hand.

"Oh..." Raven said, and he smiled at Caine. "Well, then congratulations. I can't believe you're married."

"Me either," Caine answered, and he smiled back. From him, a smile was a rare event.

Logan came through the crowd, striding straight for Raven.

"Did you make sure you weren't followed?" he demanded.

Raven blinked. "Followed? No, we weren't followed." He looked to Caine. "What is this?"

Jade frowned, listening.

"It's nothing," Caine answered, but his voice caught and I knew well how this topic distressed him. "We had some trouble not long after you left. Soldiers from the king's army followed one of our raiding parties home, and they found the chute. We let them get them get halfway up, and killed them. The bodies are long buried. We've had no trouble since."

But I shivered inside my cloak, remembering that awful day. Men had died because of me.

"It was *not* nothing!" Logan nearly spat, turning on Caine. "We cannot risk outsiders finding this place."

Tristan held up his free hand. "Raven and his people have just returned. They are most likely tired, cold, and hungry. Logan, you can see they were not followed. Let them eat and rest, and we will speak of these things tomorrow."

Though Raven appeared somewhat put off by this welcome, he nodded and grasped Jade's hand. "We'll see you all at dinner."

\* \* \* \*

In the late afternoon, the women of the settlement began putting together a feast to recognize the return of Raven's group. We put the lard, flour, and sugar they'd brought to good use, making sweet rolls and apple tarts. Brida supervised the creation of an herbed chicken stew that was quite good.

When people gathered in the common room that evening, the mood was one of celebration, and cheers sounded when Raven had a large cask of wine rolled in. With a broad smile, Tristan went to help him open it.

As soon as they finished, Raven jumped up onto a bench.

Jade stood about twenty paces away, watching him.

"My friends!" he called, and his voice carried. "I have an announcement that will help us celebrate far into the night." He smiled at Jade. "I've asked Jade to hand-fast with me, and she's agreed. Grandfather has given his permission, and he'll marry us before dinner."

Cheers exploded. Charlotte put her hands to her mouth and called, "Well, it's about time, you rogue."

People laughed. I wasn't sure what to think, but apparently, Raven and Jade's announcement to hand-fast was long-awaited news. Like Caine and me, the two of them did not need a well-planned ceremony. They wished only to be wed. Treena pulled a ribbon from her hair and ran over to Tristan.

Quietly, I made my way to Caine, and he drew me up against him as we watched his brother and Jade swear their vows to each other. Jade's face glowed. The sight made me happy.

"She loves him," I whispered.

"He loves her too," Caine whispered back. "But he's made her wait a long time."

When the ceremony was over, everyone ate and drank wine. Even Logan and Brida seemed to enjoy this night of Raven's wedding.

"Jade is a good woman," Brida said, loudly enough for Caine and me to hear. "She has spirit and is not timid like a mouse."

Though I ignored this slight upon myself, I did notice that only an hour after the ceremony, Raven and Jade had squared off. She had her hands on her hips, and he looked angry.

"What do you mean we'll live in your house?" she demanded. "That's ridiculous. The three of us will live in my house. It's larger and has actual bedrooms."

"I never agreed to that," he answered, biting off the words.

Puzzled, I looked up at Caine. "Are they fighting?"

Caine shrugged and smiled for the second time in one day. "They've been fighting since they were six years old. It's what they do."

I did not understand.

But later, near the mid of night, when people were still celebrating, I longed to go home and asked Caine if I might fetch my cloak.

"Of course."

As I went to get it, Raven approached me, catching me alone. "You consented to marry Caine?" he asked. "It was your choice?"

I liked his face. It reminded me of Tristan's, but his questions threw me. "Yes."

"And you're happy?" he pressed.

No one had ever asked me that, and I thought on the question.

"Yes," I answered honestly. "I am happy."

\* \* \* \*

Winter passed into spring. The air began to warm, the ground thawed, and the trees began budding with leaves. Yellow and purple flowers came up from the ground, and I rejoiced in being able to walk outside without my cloak.

The people of the settlement began inspecting both their gardens and the cleared lands near the orchards in preparation to till and plant new crops. Caine was busy from dawn to dark every day.

One afternoon, I sat with Treena in the common house, helping her to make a new dress from some of the wool Raven and Jade had brought back.

Watching me sew, she sighed. "I wish my stitches were as invisible as yours. I don't know how you do that."

Leaning close, I tried to show her, but instead of looking down, she said. "Kara, I'm so sorry that I wasn't kind to you when you first arrived. When I think of how I treated you, I'm ashamed."

"It's all right. You didn't know me."

"No, it wasn't that. My parents were pressing me to marry Caine. Every girl here had parents pressing her to marry Caine. None of us wanted to, but winning became so important. Then one day, he arrived with you and announced he was claiming you as his wife without a hand-fasting. My parents were angry with me, blaming me for having failed...and so I was angry with you."

Poor Treena. I'd had no idea. "I am sorry."

"But it all worked out so well. Once they could see that Caine loved you, my parents gave up and agreed to let me marry Aiden. I was so relieved. I couldn't imagine an entire lifetime being tied to Caine." She shuddered.

My sympathy faded.

Offended, I asked, "And what exactly do you find so distasteful about Caine?"

"Oh, Kara." Her eyes widened. "I didn't mean anything by that. Everyone respects Caine. No one works harder than he does. We all see him as the finest and best of men."

Not wishing to continue this discussion, I nodded.

Caine was the finest and best of men.

* * * *

With the coming of spring, a new worry began to plague me.

Tristan was not well. He hid it from everyone else, but I closed down the school for the tilling season—as the children were needed—and began spending my mornings at home with him.

His limp was worse, and several times, his face had begun to twitch in a manner he could not control, and once, this caused him to bite his tongue. I had no knowledge of this ailment or idea of how to help him. I begged him to let me tell Caine, as someone here might have more knowledge than me. But he swore me to secrecy. He said as tórnya, he had to appear strong. I hated keeping anything from Caine, but I was loyal to Tristan as well, and he expected me to obey his wishes.

This silence was painful. I loved Tristan like a father, and my worry for him began taking a toll. I couldn't imagine life without him, and I had no one with whom to share my fear.

Raven and Jade had let it be known they would soon be back on the road, and this time, they would be gone until early autumn. I would be sorry to see them go. I liked Jade's open manner, and Raven's good humor was much needed in the family. He somehow helped temper the bond between

Caine and Logan. It was hard for them to be angry at each other with Raven teasing them and making jokes. He was like a breath of warm air.

One morning, I was home with Tristan. He was in his workroom, and I used the time to give the house a good cleaning. Upon hearing footsteps outside, I looked toward the front door. Raven walked in without knocking, carrying a heavy bag of cornmeal.

"Hello, Kara," he said. "We'll be leaving in a week or two, and I wanted to make sure you were well stocked."

As Tristan had told me to accept anything Raven brought, I answered. "Thank you. Can you bring it to the store room?"

As he moved to follow me, a loud thumping sounded from the workroom. I bolted, running through the doorway, with Raven right behind me. At the sight inside, I cried out. Tristan was on the floor, and his entire body was jerking and twitching. Running to him, I tried to hold his mouth, so he would not bite his tongue.

"Get a piece of leather!" I called to Raven.

He flew into action, grabbing a piece of leather off a table. Quickly, I got it between Tristan's teeth until his body calmed. Then I removed the leather from his mouth. This was by far the worst episode I'd seen. Still on the floor, he gripped my arms.

"My girl," he whispered, and I could see he was in pain.

"Oh, Tristan. Let us get you to bed."

Raven hadn't spoken, but he looked down at me. "You knew what to do." Then his voice turned accusing. "You knew *exactly* what to do! Have you seen this before?"

"Please, Raven. Help me get him to bed."

Relenting, Raven leaned down and gently helped Tristan to his feet. Together, we half carried Tristan to his room and got him settled.

By then, he seemed more himself, and he grabbed Raven's arm. "You won't say a word of this, not to anyone. That is an order. Do you understand?"

"Grandfather…"

"It's an order. Kara's sworn to silence, and she won't speak. I expect the same from you."

"Why?"

"You know why."

Apparently, Raven did know why, because he slowly pulled his arm from Tristan's grip and stopped arguing.

"Both of you leave me now," Tristan said.

"Can I get you anything?" I asked. "A cup of water?"

"No. Just let me rest."

Turning, I walked from the room, down the hall, and into the sitting room. There, I sank onto a couch. Raven came out and stood in front of me.

"How long has this been going on?" he asked.

"Weeks," I whispered. "He won't let me tell Caine. He won't let me do anything. I've been all alone in this."

Tears began running down my face from all the pent up worry and the memory of the sight of Tristan on the floor. I hated to cry, and rarely did, but I couldn't stop.

"Oh, Kara."

Suddenly, Raven was on the couch beside me, reaching out to pull me close. I needed the comfort and allowed him to draw me up into his shoulder. But then...the strangest thing happened. The instant he touched me, the feel of his body was like coming home, as if physically blending with him was the most natural thing in the world. His arms were around me, and he gasped softly as if he felt the sensation too.

Drawing his head back, he stared at me. Leaning down, he touched his mouth to mine. His kiss was light at first, just a brush of his lips. I seemed to melt into him, again as if this were natural, requiring no thought at all. When he opened his mouth, I opened mine in answer. My body responded to his.

Then I came back to myself and pushed on his shoulders.

He jumped up as if I was on fire and moved away. "Kara, I'm so sorry. I don't know why I...I would never do anything to..."

But I was shaken and still felt the soft, welcome pressure of his mouth on mine. This brought shame. I did not love Raven as a man. I didn't desire him. He was my husband's brother.

"Please go," I begged.

After breathing hard for a moment to gather himself, he left.

* * * *

That afternoon was among the worst in my life. I was tortured over keeping Tristan's secret and now I had one of my own—which I intended to take to my grave. By this point, I'd reasoned well enough that Raven and I had both been distraught about Tristan. What happened had been some kind of reaction. That didn't explain the feelings when he touched me, but it explained the action.

That evening at dinner in the common house, I could see Raven was troubled. He and I could barely look at each other.

I would need to fix this.

Not long after dinner, he and Jade began fighting about arrangements for the wagons. She wanted him to move into hers and give his to Tannen and Badger. I didn't follow all of this, but it ended with him storming out the back door.

Seeing my chance, I slipped away from the family table and followed him out back, spotting him walking along the tree line.

"Raven."

At the sound of my voice, he turned and winced. I was probably the last person he wanted to see.

"I'm sorry about this morning," I said instantly. "We were both upset about Tristan. That's all. I needed comfort, and we were both distraught."

Somehow, I'd said the exact right thing. Relaxing visibly, he nodded. "Of course you're right. It didn't mean anything. I love Jade."

"I love Caine. You are his brother, and we must always be good friends."

With a sigh, he smiled. "You may not say much, but you're fair-minded when you do."

"Will you come back inside?"

"Yes."

He fell into step beside me. Before this was over, I needed to know something.

"We'll never speak of this again," I said, "but could I ask you one thing about this morning?"

"What's that?"

"When most men and women…touch like we did, does it normally feel like that?"

At first, he didn't speak, and then he said, "No. I've never felt anything like that in my life."

Somehow, this was the answer I had expected.

* * * *

A few days later, my secret about Raven seemed to lose any importance as I became certain about something else. My courses had not come in two months, and I could not keep down my breakfast.

Tristan was home that morning, in his workroom, and I went in to see him. For some reason, though I wasn't ready to tell Caine yet, I wanted to tell Tristan.

"Little Bird," he said. "Do you need me?"

"No, I wanted to talk to you about something."

"If it's about my health, you can save your breath."

"It's something else. Something I think will please you." I touched my stomach. "You will have another great-grandchild."

He stood up and came to me. "Oh, Kara. You have made me so glad."

\* \* \* \*

Not long before Raven's group was scheduled to leave, Caine brought down a large buck deer with his bow. The men built a fire outside and set up a spit, and they roasted the venison. The flour supply Raven had brought was beginning to run low, so Brida had ordered a rationing of bread, but there was plenty of roasted meat.

Everyone gathered in the common room that night.

Caine and I sat at our family table with Tristan, Logan, Brida, their two sons, Raven, and Jade.

Tristan took a bite of meat and raised his cup to Caine. "Fine venison," he said. "Rich and tender."

But he didn't take another bite. Instead, one side of his face twitched, and then his entire body jerked as he fell off his chair. Raven was on his feet first.

"Grandfather!"

Everyone was up, but Tristan lay on the floor with the side of his face still twitching. I wanted to run to him, but he was surrounded.

"Raven, help me," Caine said. "We have to get him home."

\* \* \* \*

That night, the family held vigil around Tristan's bed.

Near the mid of night, he awoke and looked around.

"Grandfather," Raven said, kneeling to grasp his hand.

"Where am I?" Tristan asked, but speaking was difficult for him.

"In your room. You collapsed."

Neither Raven or I gave away that we had seen this before. I got Tristan a cup of water, but Brida took it from me and moved to the other side of the bed to help him to sip. "You are ill," she said to him. "I know it seems unfeeling to speak of such things, but what if you do not recover? You must name a successor."

Aghast, Raven stood up and stepped away from the bed. "Brida!"

Neither Caine nor Logan reacted. Instead, they both looked to Tristan.

Raising his hand, Tristan pointed to Caine.

"Caine."

This was the only word he managed to say. Then his body jerked again, the side of his face twitching more fiercely. He went stiff from the force of it, and then he went still. My heart was breaking.

"No!" Raven cried, rushing back to his side.

But Tristan's eyes were closed, and he did not breathe. He was dead.

The room was silent but for the sounds of Raven's sorrow. I was too numb to weep, and Raven wept for me.

\* \* \* \*

We prepared the body, and the people of the settlement came to say their goodbyes. Once this was done, the men built a pyre, and Tristan's body was burned. Caine's form of mourning was more internal than most people's. He took the ashes and let them drift in the air from the top of the cliffs as a symbol of the safe place that Tristan had found for us all.

A number of us stood beside Caine, and when the last of the ashes were gone, I asked him quietly, "Now that it's happened, do you wish to be leader?"

He looked down at me. "Yes. I was never certain before you came. But I want it. I want to do what's best for our people."

That night, he called a meeting in the common room. When everyone had gathered, he stood near the hearth. Logan and Brida stood near him. Raven was having trouble accepting Tristan's death. He sat in a chair with Jade on one side and me on the other.

Caine addressed the room, and his voice carried.

"Tristan has passed over to the other side, and we all mourn him. He was tórnya for as long as most of us remember. Before he died, he named me to succeed him, but at first, I hope to simply carry on with his wishes. It was his wish that there be no more autumn raids. We don't need the luxuries those raids provide, and it will be safer to us to live within the laws of those on the outside."

No one appeared surprised by this announcement. Even in their sorrow at the loss of Tristan, many nodded their agreement.

"This will place an extra burden on Raven's group in purchasing supplies," Caine continued. "But I've spoken with him. We still have silver from the raids I can give to him and Jade. They will do their best to help us through the winters." Stepping away from the hearth, he said, "For now, that is all."

"It is not all," Logan said. He walked up to the hearth and addressed the room. "In addition to ending the raids, I propose there be no more of us traveling through any part of the year. Everyone should remain in the settlement. We'll dismantle the homes on the wagons and use the wagons for other needs."

"No," Raven said, rising from his chair.

Caine turned around to face Logan. "As a member of our people, you are always welcome to voice a proposal. I hear your proposal now and reject it. You have no other authority here."

Logan had been nearly silent since Tristan's death, probably filled with pent up disappointment. His face twisted into rage. "Then you are no leader! You care nothing for the safety of our people, and I call upon the sixth law!"

Brida started in alarm.

But Caine strode toward Logan, closing the distance rapidly. "Is that what you want? Trial by combat?"

People all around were becoming frightened, and I wanted to stop this. "Caine, please..." I said, stepping forward.

But Raven caught me around the waist, holding me tightly. With his other arm, he caught Jade, pulling us both away from the conflict. "Keep back," he said.

"I invoke the sixth law!" Logan shouted.

Caine answered, "And how do you interpret the sixth law when you can't even read it?"

Logan aimed a punch, hitting Caine in the jaw and sending him stumbling backward. Then he grabbed a fire poker from the hearth. As Caine gained his balance, Logan swung the poker at his head. But Caine leaned back swiftly, and as the poker flew past, he swung with his fist, smashing it into Logan's nose and dazing him.

Then Caine swept Logan's leg, using a move I'd seen before, and Logan's large body hit the floor. Caine kicked him in the head hard enough to make a thudding sound that resounded around the common room, rendering Logan unconscious.

It all happened in a blink, but the result was critical.

Whirling on Brida, Caine said, "Logan cannot invoke the sixth law twice!" He paused. "I am tórnya."

Tightly, she nodded.

Caine looked around. "Am I recognized?"

People all across the room nodded, and Doris said aloud. "Yes."

Pulling at Raven's arm, I said, "Let me go. Please."

He released me, and I went to Caine. His mouth was bleeding and the side of his face was already turning black.

But he was the settlement's new leader.

* * * *

A few days later Raven and Jade and their group of travelers packed the wagons to leave for the rest of spring and the summer. Jade's larger wagon was now in the lead. She, Raven, and Sean would live there, and Raven had given his smaller wagon to Tannen and Badger.

Though I'd still not told Caine I was pregnant, I planned to tell him tonight.

For now, we had farewells to make, and I was sorry to see Jade and Raven go.

"We'll miss you," I told her.

She embraced me. "We'll be back in the autumn. I'll try to find you some blue wool material for a new dress."

But she was happy to be rolling off with Raven. I could see this. Jade must have the blood of a traveler.

Caine hugged Raven. Everyone who would remain in the settlement said their good-byes. After climbing up onto the bench of the lead wagon, Raven settled in beside Sean and Jade and picked up the reins. Clucking to his horses, he started the caravan, and one by one, the wagons disappeared down the chute.

Turning back toward the settlement, Caine offered me his arm. I took it.

"Do you ever think back to that first day here," he asked, "when Raven gave you the choice to go with him? Do you ever wish you'd gone?"

I laughed. "Traveling on the road from place to place with no home? I think not."

"So you're glad you stayed with me?"

"Very glad."

Perhaps Caine was overly serious, and perhaps he did spend much of his time focused on the good of the settlement, but I didn't mind.

He was the finest and best of men.

# The Choice

# Chapter Twenty

The settlement around me vanished, and I found myself inside the shack, kneeling by the hearth, staring into the three-tiered mirror. The memories of all three experiences I'd just lived swirled around in my head at the same time.

Now, there were three reflections of the dark-haired woman as she gazed out at me from all three panels.

"Which path?" the woman asked. "You must choose."

Images and emotions surged through me until I couldn't think clearly.

"Which of the paths will you follow?" she asked. "The road...or flight... or the settlement?" she paused. "Raven...or Royce...or Caine?"

Her statement of the choices let me focus, and my mind flowed backward to the life I'd lived with Raven. I ached for him. I could still feel his mouth on mine and the natural act of touching him. I saw myself on the stage telling stories, in open-air markets shopping for bread, and scenes of cooking by a fire with Jemma. I felt a sense of freedom. I felt my connection to the rest of the troupe.

I felt the warmth of joining my body with Raven's under a blanket in our wagon.

But then I saw Jade's face on the night he and I were married.

I saw the pain in Caine's eyes.

I saw the frightened faces of the people in the settlement when Logan was named leader and he cut them off from outside contact.

I saw myself leaving all this behind, leaving Jade behind, and rolling out into the world with Raven.

*Raven.*

The images rolled forward to my life as Royce's mistress, to the night he'd forced himself on me to the following morning when I'd begged his forgiveness for resisting him. I saw myself living in fear.

But I also saw the gentle comforts of living in the Capello manor, the library and the chessboard. I saw the faces of Adina and Trey, and I could still feel my love for them. I could feel Lily wriggling in my arms.

I saw Royce dead on the floor with blood running from his nose. I heard Francis telling me I'd inherited a third of Loraine's fortune. I heard Trey's kind voice as he asked me to stay and be a family with him and Adina.

Images rolled forward to the third life, to Caine. I saw my fear and loneliness in the early days. I heard Tristan's kind voice. I saw myself taking my place among the women. I saw myself at the front of the school.

I saw Caine through my eyes as my feelings for him began to change and deepen. How I admired him, how I wanted him to become leader, how content I had been in my life with him.

My mind raced. Did I now know the future? There were acts I regretted. If I chose Raven, could I find a way to convince Jade to bring Scan and come with us? In the third life, if I broke my word to Tristan and told Caine of his growing illness, might someone in the settlement know of a way to help Tristan?

The dark-haired woman in the mirror watched me.

"Once I choose," I asked, "will I still remember what I've seen? Can I alter events via what I've seen here?"

She shook her head. "These are the possible paths, and you have been given the gift to see and to choose. But once you have chosen, all the memories you have seen will be gone."

I closed my eyes. I'd remember nothing.

"Choose for yourself," she said. "This is a gift, and there is nothing more I can tell you. Which of the paths will you follow? The road…flight…the settlement? Raven…Royce…Caine?"

But I could not choose.

I understood now that although I did love Caine, my feelings for him were starkly different from my feelings for Raven. If I chose Caine, I would never experience sweeping, encompassing, passionate love. But what would become of Caine should I opt for the first choice, for a life on the road? Would he never marry and live his life alone? With Logan as leader, would Caine's voice of reason be silenced? What would become of the people in the settlement?

What of the child I'd carried?

And yet, what would become of Adina and Trey should I not choose Royce? Would they be fated to live their entire lives under Loraine's oppression?

In the end, it was Jade's voice I heard from when she'd spoken to Raven on the night he married me.

*You and your talk of choices. You cling to your preaching of choices like a religion, but in truth, it's just an excuse for you to do what you please instead of doing what is right.*

I would do what was right.

"I choose Caine," I whispered and opened my eyes.

The dark-haired woman nodded, standing now only in the left panel. "The third choice."

The air before me wavered, and the mirror vanished

\* \* \* \*

I stood in the darkness just outside the door of the shack, feeling dizzy and disoriented, as if I'd forgotten something and needed to remember. What was I doing out here? Then I remembered that Raven had just left me—with the door unlocked—and I had to a decision to make.

He'd given me the option of leaving with his troupe in the morning or staying here and taking my chances—or I could escape the settlement and try to get back to my lady. Looking to the left, I saw the long tree line stretching along the backs of several dwellings. I could make my way along these trees far enough to slip down into the chute.

But instead, I just stood there, knowing I couldn't force myself to take such an act.

Ashamed, I went back inside and crouched down by the fire. I stayed like that all night, even after the logs had burned to ashes.

Outside, once the sky had begun turning gray, I heard footsteps approaching, and I watched the door. Caine entered first, with Raven behind him.

Caine wasted no time. "Raven's just asked that you be given a choice to go on the road with his troupe. I'm asking you to stay."

Before he'd finished speaking, I'd made up my mind. I didn't know either one of them, but I couldn't risk leaving this place with a group of strangers and traveling further from my lady and my home.

Caine stood there looking down at me with his dark eyes locked into mine, and I suddenly wished that I were not crouched on the floor. Standing, I tried to straighten my wrinkled and mud-spattered gown.

"I've decided to remain in the settlement," I answered.

He closed his eyes and exhaled. With visible relief, he turned to Raven. "She's staying here with me."

Read on for a preview of the next Dark Glass novel
from New York Times bestselling author
Barb Hendee…

**A CHOICE OF SECRETS**

**Available in November 2018**

# Chapter One

At the age of seventeen, I had no real understanding of the danger of secrets...of keeping them, of sharing them, of telling the wrong person for the right reasons.

But I was soon to learn the depths of my own ignorance.

One afternoon, in midsummer, I was in the vast kitchen of my family home, with six other women, rolling dough for peach and strawberry tarts. One of our housemaids, Jenny, stuck her head in the back door.

"Lady Nicole," she said to me. "Lord Erik and Lord Christophe have arrived. They're in the hunting hall."

This news made me smile. "Does Lady Chloe know? Or my mother and father?"

"Not, yet. I'll go and find them."

"Thank you."

Not bothering to even take off my apron or shake the flour from my hair, I hurried out the door and into the open-air center of what was known as White Deer Lodge. All around me, ten large log buildings had been constructed in a circle. Small paths connected each building to the next. Two of the constructions functioned as our family's residence. Others housed guests or servants or our guards. One was designated for storage. The largest construction was our gathering hall for communal events. Outside of this circle, a village thrived, with dwellings, shops, stables, and a smithy.

A stone wall surrounded the village, and heavy forests surrounded three sides of the wall, but not far beyond the west side, the ocean stretched down the coast of the nation of Samourè. This lodge was my home, and my father, Gideon Montagna, was lord of these lands.

In that moment, though, I gave little thought to my home or my father, and instead, I continued in my quick pace to the smallest of the log buildings—known as the hunting hall. In truth, I didn't care for this hall, as it was decorated with spears, longbows, and the heads of animals. But nonetheless, once inside the front door, I looked toward the unlit great hearth with a flood of happiness rising inside me.

My elder brother Erik and Lord Christophe de Fiore stood in conversation. Both men wore chain armor and swords. Several servants bustled about, pouring mugs of ale.

As I came through the door, Erik's face broke into a smile, and he called out, "Nicole!"

I ran to him. Well over a head taller, he swept me up in both arms, lifting my feet off the ground. Our father was a tall man with solid bones, straight red-blond hair, pale skin, and blue eyes. Our mother was tiny, like a bird, with light brown eyes and a mass of wavy brown hair. Erik looked like my father. I looked like my mother. We had a sister between us in age, Chloe, who resembled a mix of both our parents.

I let Erik hold me for a while.

Then I struggled. "Put me down." Once he'd set me back on my feet, I grasped both his hands, inspecting his fingers and wrists. "You are all right, not injured?"

He and Christophe had been on patrol for nearly three weeks.

"I'm fine," Erik answered, "but look at you. What *have* you been doing? You're covered in flour."

"Making tarts, strawberry for you and peach for Christophe."

With that, I turned to Christophe, grasping his hands in turn. "And you? You're not injured? You're well."

He didn't embrace me, but his eyes moved over my face. "I am well."

Though both men were tall, Christophe de Fiore was a sharp contrast to my brother. While Erik normally overflowed with laughter and affection, Christophe was stoic and kept his thoughts to himself. He wore his dark hair cut short. His eyes were gray, and his skin was tan. I'd heard once that he had to shave twice a day to keep his jaw line from becoming stubbled. He and Erik were the same age, both having turned twenty-six the previous winter, but I'd known Christophe my whole life. The de Fiore lands bordered ours on the north. They were our closest noble neighbors and good friends to my family.

Turning back to Erik, I said, "We received your message that you'd be back today. Mother and I are planning a buffet banquet tonight, with dancing. While you were away she made you a new tunic of red silk with gold thread, and I made Christophe a blue one, with silver thread. Do either of you want a bath ordered?"

"I do," Erik answered. "And something stronger to drink than ale. We rode hard to get home today."

"For goodness sake," I said. "Don't start drinking spirits until after dinner. You know Mother doesn't approve."

Flashing a grin, he was about to answer when the door opened again, held by one of our guards, and our sister, Chloe, walked in with the regal grace of a princess. I smiled at her, but she merely nodded in return—which is what I expected.

Chloe was the loveliest young woman I'd ever seen. She'd inherited our father's height and coloring, but our mother's small features and slender bone structure. Her long, blond hair—with just a hint of red—hung down her back, and she tended to dress in narrow silk gowns of green or amber.

Erik did not call out to her, and she did not run to him.

Instead, she walked slowly, with her head high, to join us, nodding first to Erik, "Brother," and to Christophe, "My lord."

"My lady," Christophe answered, but his voice held no warmth, and I wanted to sigh.

Though he and Chloe had been betrothed for several months, they hardly behaved like two people on the verge of marriage.

When she looked down at me, Chloe's features shifted to an expression of affection. "Look at the state of you. Have you been baking? You realize we do employ perfectly capable kitchen maids? You'll need to wash your hair before dressing for the banquet."

I drew in a quick breath and gripped her hand. "The banquet? Has Father...?" I trailed off.

She nodded. "Yes. I've spoken to him, and he's agreed to let you attend. I'll help you choose a gown."

At this news, Christophe's eyes moved over my face again, and a flicker of relief crossed his features. Was he glad for me? How kind of him.

"You're certain?" Erik asked in surprise. "Father agreed?"

"Yes," Chloe answered. "But it did take a little convincing. The way he treats her is absurd. Nicole is hardly a child."

"I'm well aware of that," Erik said.

Both happiness and nervousness rose up in my chest. This would be my first buffet banquet with dancing. As I was the youngest of my father's children, and I looked like a copy of my mother, my father had not bothered to hide his favor of me. Unfortunately, this favor had also caused him to perpetually view me as a little girl—and to treat me as one. I was included at formal sit-down dinners, but he'd never allowed me to attend more potentially raucous events.

Looking up at Chloe in gratitude, I said, "Thank you. But I do need to finish the tarts. You know Cook always makes too many of the strawberry this time of year, and Christophe prefers peach. Afterwards, I'll come to our rooms to dress. Please see what you can find for me to wear."

She and I had slept in adjoining rooms all our lives, and as a result, we had little sense of privacy when it came to each other.

After nodding regally to both Erik and Christophe, she said, "I am glad to see you both returned to us safely. Now, if you will excuse me, I must go and choose my own gown for this evening."

With that, she turned and walked toward the door. The same guard who had opened it for her still stood on the other side. Once she passed through, he closed it. Chloe rarely had to touch a door.

When Erik glanced at Christophe, I couldn't help noting a flash of concern...as Christophe hardly seemed to even notice Chloe had left the room. However would those two navigate a marriage?

"How long will you be staying with us?" I asked Christophe.

"Only until tomorrow." His voice was low and quiet. "Then I need to get home to Whale's Keep. My sister, Mildreth, has been managing in my absence."

"All right then." I headed for the door. "I'll see you this evening. Mother has you in your usual guest room, and you'll find the new tunic on your bed. I'll order baths for you both."

"You'd best order one for yourself," Erik called after me. "And don't forget to wash your hair." He was always teasing me, but I liked it.

Stepping out into the warm afternoon air, I looked around at the great circle of log buildings. Along with connecting paths, the grounds between each construction sported a mix of rose, herb, and kitchen gardens. Though I could not see the ocean, over the west side of the wall, I could hear waves crashing into the shore. We were safe here, protected. This place was a haven, and I wondered how Chloe could bear the thought of leaving it and going to live with Christophe. Was this the reason for her coolness to him? Perhaps I could ask her? In this regard, I wasn't sure. Even between sisters as close as us, some things were private.

But her betrothal was of great importance to our family, and she knew it.

Our property spread inland and down the coast for miles, and the people in the villages under my father's protection, who lived outside our wall, had come under a new threat over the past few years—one of which none of us could have foreseen.

The nation of Samourè was bordered on the south by the kingdom of Partheney, named for its capitol city. The western coastline of the continent ran all along both nations. Under the rule of Queen Ashton de Blaise, Partheney enjoyed a strong border patrol. Few who were unwelcome would dare attempt a landing on their coastline.

My father's lands, Montagna lands, were at the southwestern most point of Samourè, reaching the border between nations. King Amandine, who ruled Samourè, lived in the northwest, but our standing army was small, and soldiers could not be spared to patrol the Montagna coastline.

Until recently, this had never been an issue. My grandfather, followed by my father, had no argument with the few smugglers who landed now and then, so long as they went about their business and troubled none of our own people.

For the most part, our shores were safe.

My family required only enough trained guards to protect White Deer Lodge and to accompany my father or Erik when they went to check on harvests or collect taxes. We had never needed more. My father invested our money back into our lands, into improving our crops, the upkeep of villages, and the replanting of trees for future timber.

Christophe's family, the de Fiores, lived on their estate on an island called Whale's Keep, just off the coast. But their lands spread inland a good distance and up the coast. Partly because of the geographical separation of the estate and partly because of his nature, Christophe's father had long invested in a large, well-trained retinue of guards…soldiers. This was where a good deal of the family money went—payment, housing, and training for a standing private military. Christophe's mother had long been dead, and his father had died three years ago, leaving him in charge of the family.

Then, two years ago, the first wave of savage raiders landed upon de Fiore shores. We still had no idea from where they came, but they were large men, dressed in furs and plate armor. They would land in groups of about forty men, and then raid villages, burning, looting, killing, and taking people as slaves. After one or two raids, they would return to their boats and leave as suddenly as they'd arrived.

Christophe responded swiftly and with force, ordering his men along the de Fiore coastline, where they were able to kill or send back any of these raiders before they ever reached the tree line.

All too soon, the raiders began landing on the unprotected Montagna shoreline, burning our villages, killing and taking our people. My family was safe inside our stone wall, but our people were suffering. We did not employ anything like the de Fiore's well-trained, private military, and to create one of our own would take years and far more wealth than was available. My father had good connections at court, and he was respected among the nobles, so he appealed to the king, but not enough soldiers could be spared to indefinitely guard our coastline.

Christophe sent help during the worst of the raids, but only after the fact, to try to chase down escaping raiders and recover any stolen people. Even so, due to distance, the soldiers rarely made it in time, and sending these men was clearly a favor on his part. My father did not care to be indebted, even to Christophe.

Over the previous spring, a solution occurred to my father, and he approached Christophe with a proposal to join our families in marriage. My father offered a thousand acres of prime timberland as dowry for Chloe, along with a yearly stipend. In exchange, some of Christophe's men would patrol our shoreline and expel any raiders attempting to land.

The de Fiores needed good timber.

Even more, Father knew that Christophe cared a great deal for bloodlines, and he would accept a bride only from an ancient noble family. Ours was such a bloodline. The deal was struck.

For the past weeks, Erik and Christophe had been riding from one Montagna village to the next, with a de Fiore contingent, assessing any damage, hunting for raiders, and promising our people they would be safe.

Soon Chloe and Christophe would be wed, and our lands would be protected. This seemed a perfect solution but for the fact that the soon-to-be bride and groom barely seemed to notice one another's existence.

I hoped that perhaps at tonight's banquet they might have the chance to dance together. This thought filled me with both hope and excitement that I would be there to witness such an event.

A part of me still couldn't believe Father had agreed to let me attend. What gown would Chloe choose for me? She knew best in such matters. But first I hurried back to the kitchen, as I needed to finish making Christophe's peach tarts.

He had never cared for strawberries.

\* \* \* \*

That night, the banquet started off well enough.

I was somewhat late in arriving, as it took longer than expected for my hair to dry, and I sent Chloe on ahead, not wishing to make her wait. There was nothing she loved more than a party with dancing. She loved to be admired, and who could blame her? She was so graceful and beautiful.

Still, as I hurried down the path toward the gathering hall, I felt rather pretty myself. Chloe had gifted me with a gown of lavender muslin. All her talk of "choosing a gown" had been a ruse. This gown had once been hers, and she'd had it hemmed as a surprise. The color brought out my light brown eyes and set off my brown hair. Jenny, our maid, had used her hands to scrunch my hair as it dried, so that it fell all around my shoulders in even more waves than usual. I wore silver earrings and a small diamond pendant.

Tonight, my father would see that I was a woman now—no longer a child. I knew for a fact that some noblewomen my age were married and running their own households, not that I had any desire to marry. I loved my home and my family and never wished to leave White Deer Lodge. But I *did* wish to be seen as a grown woman.

Though darkness had fallen, I knew these paths by heart.

Finally, I arrived at the door of the gathering hall and slipped inside, where the sights and sounds almost overwhelmed me. A loud mix of voices and music filled the crowded hall. Guests had been arriving all afternoon, mainly merchants and their wives who lived close enough to make the journey. But there were also a few military officers in Christophe's employ and a few nobles who were currently in residence at the lodge.

The walls of the hall had been strung with garlands, and the sconces above them glowed with light provided by fat candles. The tables were laden with food, and musicians played a lively tune.

My eyes scanned the room until I spotted my parents, and my mother smiled and held out one hand toward me. I hurried over to her. She wore a red velvet gown that accented her small waist. In her late forties, her face was nearly unlined and her hair still a rich shade of brown.

"How lovely you are," she said to me.

My father stood beside her, staring down at me with a frown. "Where did you get that dress?"

"Chloe had it hemmed for me. Do you like it?" I asked, worried. The square neckline was a bit low, and I hoped he would not tell me to go and change. I had nothing so pretty in my own closet.

My mother glanced up at him with a challenging gaze.

"Of course I like it," he answered quickly. "It's fine…for tonight."

With that, I turned my attention to the festivities. Erik was out dancing with a merchant's daughter. I hoped to see Chloe dancing with Christophe, but she was not. When I saw her partner, mild distaste rose in my mouth.

She was dancing with Julian Belledini, a man to whom she paid far too much attention in my opinion. Julian was handsome and he knew it, with dark blue eyes and blond hair that curled down around his ears to the top of his collar. He was slender and well built at the same time, and I had to admit he cut a dashing figure in a black, sleeveless tunic. But he was also the third son of a minor baron. He had no real prospects and yet never failed to mention the old bloodlines of his family.

Not knowing what else to do with him, his own father had sent him to mine.

Julian had lived with us since the spring. The idea was that my father and Erik would teach Julian archery and skill with a sword, and then my father—who had solid connections—would help him arrange for a commission in the royal military as an officer. Julian's father had no qualms about paying for the commission. He simply required assistance with Julian's training and introductions.

My father was always glad to help someone help himself.

I had my doubts, however. From what I could see, Julian had little interest in either archery or the military. He preferred playing cards with our house guards and drinking wine from our stores and talking to my sister.

I didn't care for him, and as a result, he didn't care for me. Julian was a man who liked to be admired.

And now, at Erik and Christophe's welcome party, he was once again monopolizing Chloe's time…and she was letting him. Wearing a gown of emerald green silk, she clung to his shoulder and hand, allowing him to spin her around the dance floor as if there was no place she would rather be.

No wonder my father was frowning.

"Nicole," someone said.

Turning, I saw Christophe coming toward us, looking fine in his new blue tunic. The silver thread had been a good choice, if I did say so myself. His eyes were on me as he crossed the room, taking in my lavender dress and the waves in my hair.

After greeting my parents politely, he said to my mother, "I thank you for this fine banquet."

As the evening meal was buffet, a number of people were already dished up and eating while watching the dancing. The food did look enticing, and I hoped to sample the roasted pheasant with plum sauce soon.

"Your safe return was a good excuse for a gathering," she answered.

"I've heard you encountered no raiders," my father said. "But were you and Erik able to reassure most of the villagers?"

"Yes," Christophe answered. "They understand my soldiers will soon be patrolling your coast."

This seemed to please my father, and his tight body relaxed slightly.

But then Christophe held one hand out to me. "Would you dance?"

I knew a number of dances—as Chloe and Erik had taught me—but I'd never danced in public before, and although I'd been allowed to *attend* this event, I wasn't sure how far Father was willing to let me participate.

Still, he could have little objection to me dancing with Christophe, who would soon be part of our family—and my brother-in-law.

Looking up at my father, I asked, "May I dance with Christophe?"

Father's expression tightened again. He glanced over at Chloe dancing with Julian Belledini. But he answered, "Yes. Of course."

Though he hardly sounded enthusiastic, I wasn't about to waste this chance, and I grasped Christophe's hand.

Without hesitation, he led me onto the dance floor.

"Do you often dance?" I asked him.

"No. Almost never."

A new song had begun. This dance, the "Evalda," was somewhat challenging. The tempo was quick, the turns were fast, and after every ten steps the man gripped his partner by the waist and lifted her above his head.

Still, as Christophe and I quick-stepped with the other dancers, I was not daunted. Erik had taught me the "Evalada," and in his typical playful moods, he'd often lifted me higher than necessary. Because of this, I was accustomed to the strength in a man's arms and hands, so now, I simply clung to Christophe and let him lead. As we rounded a turn, he gripped my waist and lifted me above his head as if I weighed nothing. With my hands on his shoulders, I laughed. I trusted him completely and knew he'd never drop me.

Once my feet touched the floor, we were off again. He was a skilled dancer, and I needed to do little more than follow his steps as fast as I could. It was exhilarating. On the tenth step, he lifted me again, and I could see that he was having fun. It was good to see him smile. Christophe seldom smiled.

When last note ended, we both laughed and clapped.

Chloe had been dancing with Julian, and although she was smiling, she looked a bit pale and breathless to me. I wondered why. Normally, Chloe could dance all night. But my worries for her vanished when I saw Erik staring at Christophe and me. His normally jovial expression was gone, and as he approached us through the crowd, he seemed almost displeased.

"Did you see me?" I asked him. "I didn't miss a step."

He tried to smile. "Yes, you did well...but perhaps Christophe might dance with Chloe next?"

"Of course," I answered and then turned to Christophe. "You should ask her before the next song begins."

"Ask me what?" Chloe said, suddenly upon us.

"To dance," I answered.

"Perhaps later," Christophe said. "I was hoping to continue dancing with Nicole for a while."

"Please do," Chloe answered. "Julian is asking the musician to play the 'Ruodlieb,' and I'm promised to him for the song." She still seemed pale to me, and I wondered if she'd eaten yet.

Erik frowned, but Christophe ignored him and took my hand again. I could see that Erik thought it might be best for Christophe to dance with Chloe, but if neither of them was inclined to dance with the other, what could be done? And in truth, at least Christophe wasn't dancing with some flirty merchant's daughter.

He was only dancing with me. What harm could there be?

Chloe joined Julian as the first note struck.

This dance was not quite so fast, and more couples joined us on the floor. Once again, I just held Christophe's strong hand and let him sweep me around. It was great fun, and I loved the flowing movements and the joy of dancing in unison with others all around us. One song soon blended into the next…and the next.

After the fifth song, he asked me, "Are you thirsty."

I nodded. "Yes, and perhaps hungry too. Have you eaten?"

"Not much."

He offered me his arm, and I took it with both hands so he could lead me through the crowded room for a table laden with food. With his free hand, he reached down and pinched off a bite of roasted pheasant.

"Here," he said, feeding it to me.

He took a bite for himself, and then fed me part of a peach tart. After this, he poured a goblet of wine.

When he held it to my mouth, though, I hesitated. Normally, I did not drink wine, and I wasn't sure what Father would think, so I glanced over to where my parents had been standing.

My father stood staring at us with eyes as hard as ice, and I realized among the crowd near the table, I was still clinging to Christophe's arm. With heat rising to my face, I felt that somehow, I'd done something wrong. My father strode toward us with the same hard expression, and I took my hands from Christophe's arm.

"Nicole," my father said as soon as he was close enough to be heard. "It's getting late. It's time you went to bed."

Christophe had not seen him coming and turned quickly, his features tensing with anger. "It's early yet," he said carefully.

My father ignored him. "To bed, Nicole. Now."

"Yes, Father."

Christophe's jaw muscle twitched, but he said nothing.

Feeling like a chastised child, I hurried for the door.

\* \* \* \*

Long after our maid, Jenny, had unlaced my gown, seen me into bed, and then left the room, I lay awake, covered by a quilt, wondering what I had done to anger my father so.

What harm could there be in my dancing with Christophe and eating a bit of pheasant and peach tart? And yet, Father had treated me as if I'd behaved badly, as if I'd behaved disgracefully. Chloe might love a party with dancing, but I loved my family, and I'd never attend a dance again if such an event would cause Father to see me as a disgrace.

Unbidden, two tears slipped down my cheeks. Perhaps tomorrow, I might speak to my mother and see if she could enlighten me about my father's censure. This thought gave me some comfort, and I finally closed my eyes, drifting off to sleep.

I don't remember any dreams, but at what seemed much later, I was awakened by a strange sound, like that of someone gagging.

Sitting up, I realized the sound was coming from the adjoining room. The gagging was accompanied by the sound of choking, and I jumped from my bed, running across my room and jerking open the door that separated my room from Chloe's.

There, my sister was on her knees, still in her beautiful emerald silk gown, retching violently into a basin on the floor.

"Chloe!"

Running to her, I knelt and held her hair back. She was nearly weeping from distress, and she couldn't seem to stop retching even after there was no food left to come up.

Finally, her body began to calm.

"Oh, Chloe," I said. "You are so ill. I'll run and get Mother."

Our mother was a healer, a skilled practitioner in herbal arts.

But Chloe grabbed my arm, clutching me fiercely. "No!"

Taken aback, I stared into her pale face.

"Please don't," she said more calmly. "I had too much wine to drink at the banquet, and if Father finds out, he'll be displeased."

She'd drunk too much wine? Her concern made sense to me, but I was still worried for her health. "Are you sure? Mother wouldn't say anything to Father, and she might be able to give you something to settle your stomach."

Chloe still gripped my arm but less tightly now. "I am sure. Just get me out of this gown and help me to clean up the mess. I'll be fine."

Nodding, I moved around to the back of her and unlaced her gown. As she slipped out of the gown, I carried the basin out into the hallway, peering right and left. No one was up, so I took the basin outside and disposed of its contents at the base of a tree.

Hurrying back to Chloe's room, I found her in bed, still pale, but looking otherwise recovered.

"Nicole," she said, "will you swear to keep this between us?"

"Yes. I swear."

Of course I would keep her secret. We were sisters, and sisters kept each other's secrets.

# About the Author

**Barb Hendee** has published twenty-one highly popular fantasy novels, including the *New York Times* bestselling Noble Dead Saga, co-authored with JC Hendee, and the newer Mist-Torn Witches series, which she penned alone. All twenty-one books are still in print. She maintains a devoted following, has had books on the extended *New York Times* list and the *USA Today* Top 150 Books, and is constantly writing and developing new ideas.

# THROUGH
## *a* DARK
## GLASS

RB
REBEL BASE

A DARK
GLASS
NOVEL

# BARB HENDEE

*NEW YORK TIMES* BESTSELLING AUTHOR

RB
REBEL BASE
A Choice of Crowns
A DARK GLASS NOVEL
BARB HENDEE
*NEW YORK TIMES* BESTSELLING AUTHOR

Printed in the United States
by Baker & Taylor Publisher Services